D0670688

HERLONG-   Herlong-Bodman, Ann.
BODMAN
            Voices over water.

                        JUN 0 4 2004

$24.95

DATE			

CHARLESTON PUBLIC LIBRARY

A20321 464870

MAIN LIBRARY   BAKER & TAYLOR

VOICES
Over Water

MAIN LIBRARY

WITHDRAWN

VOICES
Over Water

Ann Herlong-Bodman

HARBOR
HOUSE

VOICES OVER WATER
By Ann Herlong-Bodman
A Harbor House Book/2004

Copyright 2004 by Ann Herlong-Bodman

All rights reserved. No part of this book may be reproduced or transmitted in any form or by any means, electronic or mechanical, including photocopying, recording, or by any information storage and retrieval system, without permission in writing from the publisher.

For information address:
>   HARBOR HOUSE
>   3010 STRATFORD DRIVE
>   AUGUSTA, GEORGIA 30909

Jacket Design by Jane H. Carter
Painting by Bernie Horton

Cataloging-in-Publication Data

Herlong-Bodman, Ann.
Voices over water / by Ann Herlong-Bodman.
p. cm.
ISBN 1-891799-19-3
1. South Carolina--History--Civil War, 1861-1865--Fiction. 2. Plantation life--Fiction.
3. Women spies--Fiction. I. Title.
PS3608.E75V65 2004
813'.54--dc22

>   2003027509

Printed in the United States of America
10 9 8 7 6 5 4 3 2 1

For the men and women who
teach to make things right.

Acknowledgements

My grateful appreciation to

The staffs in the Carolina Room, Charleston County Library,
and South Carolina Historical Society Archives for their ready
assistance and smiling faces.

Richard Hatcher, historian, National Park Service, for sharing his
vast knowledge of Civil War history and pointing me
in the right direction when I strayed too far from reality.

Cheryl Lopanik and Cindy Senkowsky
for professional editing skills in time of need.

Susan Herlong, Maggie Bodman, and Mary Ball for astute reading
and perceptive criticism all along the way, and all the others who
have helped me see the forest beyond the trees.
You know who you are.

The true artistry of Bernie Horton and designer Jane Carter.

A community of friends for believing in me.

Robert Bodman, truest friend, for his unwavering support,
his honest criticism; especially his unconditional love
and efficiency in the kitchen while I finished this work.

CHAPTER

One

~

*S*he knew the consequences of being discovered. She'd be sent to Old Capitol Prison to wither away while Yankees charged into Charleston, flags flying, drums beating. That had happened in Beaufort. Ships moved into Port Royal in November, and a thousand Union soldiers charged into town, yelling obscenities and slapping each other on the back.

Sarah's eyes stung from peering into the darkness. She couldn't be positive she was going in the right direction, but she pressed on, clawing her way through wax myrtle, wild grape, and thick palmetto. Maybe she had made a wrong turn after leaving headquarters. She had crossed the railroad tracks, the rail line that marked the coastal defense system, and darted into woods that led to the water. Somewhere out there, across rivers, sinewy tidal creeks and narrow inlets, all velvety and black, lay Edisto Island.

She was crossing no-man's-land now. Each footstep seemed to remind her that Confederate forces encamped behind and Yankee scouts patrolled ahead. Even the sea pines swayed westward, as if to point her back to the mainland. She felt like a captive already.

She'd dropped her lantern when she heard the crash of falling branches and thought she saw something moving in the woods. Could have been deserters or runaway slaves or Union scouts. As she thought of Affey somewhere out there and Jacob waiting on Toogodoo Creek with the longboat, she barely realized her arms were stinging from scratches and bruises.

After she'd made the delivery in Adams Run, she prayed for courage; then overcome with the delirious feeling that she was doing what had to be done, she had run through the woods with limbs and brush slapping at her. All the time she was terrified she was being followed.

And where was Affey? They had separated after the delivery and agreed to meet at water's edge. Now when the moon disappeared, Sarah was more unsure than ever that her directions were correct. She waited, shivering, and was momentarily tempted to call out, but quickly realized Affey knew the plan and couldn't be far behind.

One last charge, Sarah was thinking, vaguely realizing the path was dipping down. On her final push into the blackness, she stumbled over a fallen log, floundered in a thicket of palmetto, and tumbled headlong down a slope.

She lay perfectly still, listening for the sounds she dreaded most: musket fire in the distance, mounted riflemen thundering down Jacksonboro Road, or the whinny and snorts of horses. But all was quiet except for the slapping of the water. She smelled water, fresh and clean and salty. Toogodoo Creek? Fiddler crabs scurrying about in the sand surely had nothing to fear from her.

When the darkness softened and everything turned light, there before her, outlined in ghostly white, sat the hull of a boat. It startled her so that she gasped, jumped up as if jerked by an invisible rope, and reached for Jacob's hand.

"Right here," he told her, barely whispering.

Sarah grabbed the line, took a deep breath, and climbed aboard. "Where's Affey?" She spoke with a kind of panic.

Jacob did not answer.

Sarah asked again. "Where is Affey?"

"Under canvas," Jacob said. "We thank you for bringing her with you." Even in the darkness, his teeth shone, and the whites of his eyes glistened.

"Affey's like a sister to me." Sarah sat in a tiny space between two barrels and pulled her legs under her.

"I know," Jacob said.

Sarah heard more than his words. She heard his voice saying *I know more than you think I know*, and a sudden uneasiness sliced through her heart. She remembered Jacob as her father's overseer, her father's right-hand man, a slave driver and a former slave himself, but things had changed. He was a waterman now, a river pilot transporting Rebels and Yankees alike. He would be difficult to read. Could she trust him? She desperately wanted to believe he was on her side, but he was working both sides, she had been told, transporting goods and troops and spies. Her contact at Adams Run had trusted him, so she had no choice.

As a strange sound pierced the air, Jacob stopped rowing. Sarah looked into the inky blackness around her. *Well, this is it.* After all she had gone through, it had come to this. She was being discovered two minutes after leaving the mainland. Jacob had sighted a Yankee patrol and was turning around and taking her back. Or he had changed his mind and was selling her out. *That would be the ultimate irony.* She yanked at her hood. She could not conceive of it, but Jacob had once been her father's slave.

It only took a moment before she recognized the sound of a Negro spiritual. "Nobody knows the trouble I's seen." Seconds passed. Jacob started humming the same tune, quietly at first, then raising his voice in the stillness. The song was a signal, she realized, from another waterman. The waters were safe. No Yankee patrols to stop her.

Soon the breeze picked up and whipped across the bow. The waves kept building. She clutched at her cloak and pulled it around her face to shield her. Only hours now until a warm fire, hot tea, and food. She was famished. She and Affey had been traveling the back roads for three days. Or was it four?

They'd moved steadily from the South Carolina upcountry, dodging farmers, slaves, anybody that might ask too many questions. Why would a white lady traveling with her personal servant in a carriage head for the coast? Most South Carolinians were running for the hills. Didn't she know Port Royal had been captured? Didn't she know the Yankees were crossing the islands on their way to Charleston?

She tilted her head back. The realization that she had made the trip undetected and delivered the secret package hit her, and a wave of something like seasickness overcame her. Now she was crossing to Edisto. What would she find when she got there? She and her family had left in November when the roses were still in bloom, just before the camellias and the poinsettias. Word had come that the Yankees were coming, and they'd barely had time to pick the white fields of her father's Sea Island cotton crop and store it. The corncribs had been left empty. They'd left instructions with the servants and divided the food in the smokehouse; but amid the good-byes, the sobs, and the tears, turmoil had reigned. She didn't know what she would find.

Maybe no one person could save what was left, but she would do her part. With this thought, she was overcome with a sense of duty, a sense of pride and independence, and she wondered for the thousandth time why her family had left in the first place. Why had she not stayed behind? Except the planters had asked for protection and the colonel in command of the Confederate forces had calculated the number of troops needed to hold back the Yankees, assessed the experience of the raw soldiers under his command, and sent word that he could not protect the barrier islands.

Suddenly she felt tired. The long journey, on top of the highly secret delivery she'd made in Adams Run, had strained her to the limit. The oars creaked, and a fine mist chilled her to the bone, but she was too exhausted to care. Wrapped in her cloak, she fell asleep within seconds.

It was daybreak when she woke. For a moment she couldn't remember where she was, but a familiar sucking, popping sound brought her back to reality: fiddler crabs scurrying about in the mud flat. She smelled the odor of the dark mud and marsh grass, and she knew instinctively they were in the backwater on the marsh side.

"We passed Steamboat Landing before daylight. Union guards were asleep." Jacob was poling the boat into a thicket of cassina and myrtle. He opened one of his salt sacks and inside was an array of jars. Choosing one, he gave it to Affey who was looking refreshed and excited.

Sarah smiled weakly. "There's no need for that. I won't need a disguise."

Jacob shrugged. "I'm afraid I can't be caught sneaking a white lady onto the island."

"I have a Union pass." It was fake, but her contact in Adams Run said the paper might save her.

"Keep it for another time," Jacob said, standing to look and listen, as if he knew enemy soldiers were out there on the other side of the marsh watching and waiting.

She knew it, too, and gritted her teeth, determined to show no sign of not appreciating their effort to protect her by turning her into one of them.

"Gather your hair up in a knot," Affey told her after applying the ash-color cream and pulling a bonnet from the sack. "We wouldn't want a Yankee soldier to see your red hair."

Jacob was all business. "If soldiers appear, don't smile. Keep your head down and play your part." He took up his oars, and within moments they were heading up Russell Creek.

Live oaks and black gum trees stood thick on one side; the marsh reached to the horizon on the other. The sun rose overhead; the whole place, so familiar, so inviting that Sarah felt her heart lifting as it always did when she returned home after a trip. Island life was special. She had always known that because she had traveled often to Charleston and Savannah and spent weeks in the summers with her mother's family in Newport and at Saratoga Springs. But this trip off the island had been different.

Days upstate in her sister's house had turned into weeks and weeks into months. Rumors of rape and pillage and destruction on the islands had dismayed her. Having to stay in Edgefield, never knowing the truth, but feeling the turmoil and uncertainty, had made her feel like a hostage. She'd hated every minute.

Now, gliding along the narrow winding saltwater creek, she felt the warmth of the sun, imagined the feel of the marsh grass beneath her feet, and tried to forget about the war. It seemed so far away, so unreal. She was tired and sick of the whole thing and wanted to get home.

When the boat stopped dead in the water, Sarah looked up; around the bend, two bluecoats appeared on horseback. Yankees, she was certain, looking shocked that they were encountering what looked to be three runaway slaves in a stolen plantation longboat. Their horses jerked and skittered, and the men who were afraid and nervous kicked them and swore.

Without a word, Jacob's plan went into action. In the stern, he began singing, "Nobody's seen the trouble I's seen."

In the bow, Affey sat still but could not help making a soft whining sound. She prayed, "Do Lord, help us. Do Lord."

In the center of the boat, Sarah slumped like an old woman, the part she'd been assigned, but she glanced up long enough to see the two soldiers dismount and stand, as if at attention, their fingers rubbing along their thighs, their hands moving inch by inch to their weapons.

"What 'cha doing up in here?" one asked, the short one, his sharp New England accent echoing in the woods.

Jacob answered, bowing profusely from the waist and nodding his head, playing his part so well, Sarah was impressed.

"My Gran," he said, pointing to Sarah. "She staying up a ways in the swamp. We come from taking her to the root doctor. She got some kind a strange swelling in the throat. She feeling better. She enjoyin' the weather now."

Jacob's heavy fieldhand dialect amused her. He looked at her, and for a second she thought he might grin or wink. He didn't. He pointed to Affey who was looking steadfastly at the floorboards, so terrified her hands were shaking. "That my girl up there," he explained. "She taking care of my Gran."

"Is this your boat?" The taller man's tone seemed quite civil, Sarah thought, noticing the insignia on his shoulders, the gold braid of a Union officer.

"Yassuh. . . sorta." Jacob spoke slowly, drawing out his words.

"Have you seen any Rebels? Any pickets?" the one Sarah thought was an officer asked. He seemed almost apologetic.

"Nawsuh. . . nawsuh. Don't see no Rebels."

The short stubby man with the sharp accent moved closer. "You know what happens to people that hide Rebels?"

"Yassuh . . .yassuh . . .I do." Jacob continued to bow. He was watching the current.

Then Sarah's heart sank. The boat was drifting toward land. At best they could keep their distance from the soldiers by staying in the middle of the creek. But the boat was moving toward the bank, toward the soldiers. They were drifting toward disaster.

The short man saw Affey and looked like he'd break into a gale of laughter. "Well, well, look what we got here." He ran his sleeved arm over his mouth.

Sarah read the smile, recognized the soldier's evil intent, and felt fear creep into her bones. The need to act, to do something, flashed through her, but she watched the bow of the boat nose into the bank, and Jacob stood rigid, grinning his fieldhand grin. She grinned, too, to think how stupid to get this far only to run into a deranged Union scout.

At any moment he would come to his senses. How could a soldier in the Union forces be so crude, so despicable, and so vicious? Such behavior was contemptible.

Her eyes darted to the officer. He surely would stop this.

"That's enough, Hicks," the officer said, and for a moment Sarah thought the danger had passed, but Hicks lunged, determined to pull Affey out of the boat.

Jacob stood at the stern with a look of helplessness, a stony resignation, as if he could do nothing, nothing at all except wait. Sarah's mind whirled. Do something, her mind said, and her own nails dug into her skin, forcing her body into action. What? Something, anything to stop this.

Her wail, wild and frenzied, filled the woods with a shuddering and awful sound. Her body wrenched and jerked with a gasping motion she'd seen when she visited the sick and afflicted in the slave quarters. Mad Rhoda would roll her eyes and chant and cross her arms. Sarah rose, her arms outstretched, and lunged for the soldiers, her body twitching like the root doctor she remembered. She shrieked one of Mad Rhoda's wild curses.

Hicks shrank back; he'd heard about the backwardness of these islands and the near savages who lived here. When Sarah reached into her pockets and tossed imaginary evil on him, he ducked.

His eyes flashing, the officer shouted at Hicks, and both men hurled themselves back on their horses and plunged into the woods.

When it was over, Jacob pushed the nose away from the bank, and within seconds the boat was fairly skimming the water.

Sarah put her arm around Affey and stared into the distance. Her helplessness in front of the Union men threw her into the sinking realization that this was war. She was exposed and putting everyone at risk. She hated the war so much her chest hurt.

While she was away, Christmas had come and gone with no word about what was happening here. She had worried day and night about those left behind. Looking at Affey now, she saw everything suddenly placed on a different plane, another level. This was war. Affey was not safe. No one was safe.

"We will survive this, you know. We will survive," she said, gritting her teeth.

Jacob shook his head. "Things are not the way you remember," he said gravely. "Soldiers, deserters, and runaways are everywhere. They dangerous all the same. You can't forget that."

"The quarters?"

"No place on the island is safe."

"I'll take your warning to heart." She felt him stare and wondered if he could see all the way down to where she was hiding her guilt.

"This is as far as I can take you." Jacob guided the boat into a cove surrounded by tall wax myrtle and clumps of palmetto and cassina. "I found a cart and a mare. They're both old, but it's the best I could do. I hid the cart under the bushes. I'll fetch the mare. But you need to eat a bite before you leave for the bay."

Plantation houses had been taken over by runaway slaves or desert-ers, her family's plantation house included. But the summerhouse at Edings Bay, the cottage on the Atlantic side of the island, where her family escaped the malaria-infested mosquitoes during the hot and humid months, was safe and strategically located, she'd told her contact in Adams Run. From there, she assured him, she could observe the number of Union troop ships and gunboats moving down the coast or coming into the North Edisto. Getting the information back would present a problem. She had no plan at the moment except if she were discovered, she could say she'd come to the summerhouse for family portraits or to reclaim her great-grandmother's china.

"Thank you, Jacob. Thank you for everything."

"We're just glad to have Affey back. Sully and the children will be happy to see her. They safe back up in the marsh."

It was a dark place, her father said, where slaves kept to themselves or crowded in silence against violent white masters, or ghosts, or the plague.

"In the swamp fortress?" Was Jacob hiding in that place?

"The children are safe." He sat immobile, unwilling to give away his secret.

"Here, then. I will meet you here tomorrow or the next day. If I do not return, you will know I've either been discovered or I'm being watched. Don't try to rescue me. I'll think of something."

"Don't worry about Affey," Jacob said. "We'll take good care of her."

They sat in the longboat drinking cassina tea and eating Sully's cold biscuits with fried fish the children had caught the day before. As Jacob talked about Sully and the children, Sarah tried to picture that other world–people hoeing in the garden and hanging out clothes, field hands working the crops, children laughing and playing. But the image would not stay. It faded and she saw enemy troops racing across the island and the red glow of burning cotton. Her own eyes snapped with anger. All she could see was her world turned upside down.

When it was time to leave, the women embraced like sisters. They had been through so much and here they were changed and frightened. Sarah looked at Affey, whose features she knew so well. Skin the color of light chocolate and eyes full of strength, Affey's smile was so familiar. It was true; Affey seemed like a sister to her.

A great urge came to Sarah not to go across the island to Edings Bay. She had made the daring and dangerous delivery to the coast. What more did they expect of her? Someone else could gather information for the Cause. She'd just hide out with Affey. Jacob would keep them safe until the war was over. He would think of something if the Yankees came.

She breathed deeply and forced herself to think calmly. Mentally she knew she still had promises to keep. Her contact had planned carefully. Adams Run was depending on her. Slowly she started to walk the narrow plank to land, and when her foot made marks in the sand, it seemed to her the wind rose out of the marsh to greet her.

She gazed upward, her eyes unshaded, and when she saw the shore birds gliding toward Edings Bay, all in formation, her doubts gave way. She climbed in the cart, waved at Affey, and peered ahead, as if she could see all the way across the island to the Atlantic Ocean. She set her teeth and snapped the reins, in pursuit of information that would cripple the Yankees. She must be careful. If they caught her, her delivery and all it meant to the Cause would count for nothing. She could not afford to be discovered.

Not now, not behind enemy lines.

CHAPTER

Two

~

*F*ully conscious that she could run up on another Yankee any-time, Sarah kept to the field paths that she could remember. She was rather enjoying the ride until the old mare balked at the creek, a slough really, that separated the bay from the island proper. The bridge was gone, washed away in a northeaster, she supposed; for a moment she stood, looking at where the rickety wooden span used to be. She could almost hear children running and carriages and wagons filled with servants laughing and singing. From May to September, Edings Bay was full of children and women and servants. But war had started. No one was here now.

It was so quiet it made her nervous, and she looked over her shoulder, then climbed down to unhook the cart. After hiding it behind a large clump of palmetto, she tied the animal in the shade of a black gum tree.

At the edge of the winding creek, she took off her boots, rolled up her pantalets, and waded into the stream, which flowed swiftly on the outgoing tide. Cupping her hands, she washed the dark cream from her face and arms, removed the old bonnet, and made sure her auburn curls were securely tied with a ribbon. Crossing the water carefully, she clamored up the bank, then with her skirts back in order, she stood on tiptoe, searching for a glimpse of the cottage at the bay.

When an egret burst from a cypress tree, batting its wings to protest her intrusion, she thought she'd come face to face with a bobcat or a wild boar or an alligator. Then, a quick smile flickered on her lips. Perhaps her old friend Mad Rhoda was here.

"Come along, chile," Rhoda would say, jumping from behind a bush. "Rhoda here to work her magic. She make everything safe for you."

Nothing appeared. Silence closed in around her.

The summerhouse, when she spotted it, looked smaller than she remembered, more like a Charleston single house. Once there had been a row of cottages under the cluster of sea pines that grew along this part of the South Carolina coast. Her grandmother remembered fifty families from across Edisto and some from the mainland that came to the bay to enjoy the ocean breezes and escape the torment of the dreaded mosquitoes. But hurricanes and the threat of war had wreaked havoc, and most families had abandoned their cottages.

Sarah stared ahead, recalling Fourth of July celebrations, weddings, and family reunions held under the pines, with long tables of food, music, and dancing. Once her mother surprised her with a birthday party and a poetry reading by Paul Hamilton Hayne. She could still remember his voice, his handsome face, and the feeling of being in love with the most popular literary figure in the Carolinas. She had been only thirteen and doubted now that the poet had even noticed her.

But politics and war permeated the coast like poison, and Josephine Edings, as all the other mothers, no longer felt safe here while the men stayed inland to rouse political passions and rally the troops. Then, in April when the frenzy following the firing on Fort Sumter brought the fear of invasion, her mother, too, abandoned the bay.

At the steps of the summerhouse, Sarah couldn't help touching the Derringer hidden in her petticoat pocket and looking from side to side. The shutters, which had blown open, were no longer able to hold out the rain or the pressing heat of summer or Yankees.

A shutter creaked. She spun toward the surf, her eyes darting from left to right.

Nothing. No steamer sailing toward Port Royal packed with Union soldiers. No warship. No gunboat heading for the North Edisto.

She saw only chunks of yellow paint scattered over the piazza floor. The cottage, she was sure, had been ransacked. She breathed deeply, accepting the fact that the furnishings her ancestors had brought over from Scotland generations ago had been shipped north to the home of some general. With a renewed surge of anger, she pushed the door open with her foot.

Just as she thought. The parlor was empty except for a settee so soiled she hardly recognized it. Her mother's white linen dimity curtains were gone; the marble fireplace was stained with smoke and the walls were covered with scattered drawings of steamers, Union flags, stick figures of soldiers marching. She walked around the room slowly, taking it all in.

Strangers who found their way through the summerhouse had sat in her secret places and read her books. Nothing here belonged to her anymore. How do you know when something belongs to you, she wondered, as she moved along the wall, touching the drawings, moving her fingers through the stain on the marble fireplace. Was it hers because the happiest years of her life were spent there? Because her memories were bound up in it? She shivered and wiped her hands on her skirt, as if to wipe away the past.

When she spotted a cup and saucer on the table in the next room, her heart pounded. The sudden image of Yankee soldiers digging up her great-grandmother's Blue Willow china seized her, and she ran. But in the kitchen house everything was in place. The oil lamp and candles seemed in order on the shelf. The hearth looked as clean as the day she and Affey left it. What if they had found the rifle?

Panicky, she shoved the large chopping block aside and raised the planks in the floor. Her father's smoothbore was in its place, along with cartridges. She'd hidden everything herself.

Still bent over the rifle's hiding place, she thought she heard something in the main house. Another shutter creaking? Of course, she told herself, and chided herself for imagining things. As a woman who grew up on an island, she had learned to be strong. It was an islander's way, her means of survival when the men were away. Perhaps she had learned this from her mother. But however she learned it, she could manage alone, and she was perhaps the only white woman on the barrier islands.

Quietly she replaced the planks and pulled the chopping block back. Outside at the well she tossed a bowl of old water then lowered the bucket and brought up fresh. It was sulfur smelling and acrid, but good for cooking if she could find something to cook.

The weapon under the kitchen house floor was safe, but what about the china buried in the sand? Did she suppose a Yankee had stumbled upon one cup and saucer? As though a mound of sand could stop a Yankee thief.

She grabbed a spade and dug, frantically searching for what she might or might not find. It only took a moment, and she struck the barrels she and Affey had buried when word came that the Yankees were coming.

One. Two. Three. Finally, she found all six and pried them open. The Blue Willow was there, the Chinese porcelain, even the Staffordshire soup tureen.

No harm in unpacking a few pieces to use while she was here. Later in the afternoon, she sat at the table fingering a Chinese porcelain teacup and watching the sun cast a golden shadow on the old wooden table. The surf roared in the distance. The pines hummed in a soft breeze. And she heard that sound again. Another shutter? A footstep?

Her muscles tensed. She swallowed then felt surprisingly calm as she walked into the front room. Straining to hear another sound, she looked to the right then to the left.

Nothing.

The door stood ajar, just as she had left it when she entered the house. She moved stealthily onto the porch. For a moment she thought she might call out, "Whose there?" but she didn't. She heard the sound again and whirled instinctively toward the steps.

And found herself staring down the barrel of a revolver.

Managing to stay calm, she raised her eyes and stared at the man who held the weapon and the gold braid of his officer's insignia. Could it be the same man she'd seen that morning? But he looked weaker, without the strength to shoot if she tried to take the gun away. And where was his sidekick, the short man with the evil smile?

"What, exactly, are you looking for?" Her mind whirled as she counted the hours—six since she and Jacob and Affey had faced the two soldiers on Store Creek. Plenty of time for scouts, if that's what they were, to make their way to the bay.

She waited for him to speak, or shout, or shoot, and moved her leg to feel the Derringer. She'd take her time, make him talk, distract him, then she'd defend herself.

"What are you looking for?" She repeated the question. His revolver dropped to the floor. He fell beside it.

Dear God, a dead Yankee on the piazza.

Jacob had told stories about Union troop ships caught in storms and sinking within sight of land. He said dead bodies sometimes washed up on shore. Deserters broke into houses and stole silver. Scavengers pried open caskets, stole the jewels buried with the dead, and sailed away in the night. But she had come face to face with this one on Store Creek. Why had he crossed the island and come to the bay? She caught her breath. Where was the man he called Hicks? Maybe she should let this one die.

Where would she bury a Yankee?

His chest moved. His breathing was steady, his pulse normal. No fever. A flesh wound, she decided.

Tapping his shoulder to make certain he was unconscious and not tricking her, she opened his haversack. A fresh shirt. A knife, beef jerky, a Bible, and a miniature of a girl with black hair, delicate features, and alabaster skin.

Sarah picked up the revolver he'd dropped and sat on the steps. A Colt. A new model, not the old "four-pounder." She knew her weapons. Islanders learned such things at an early age.

When the man moaned, as if waking up, she put his weapon on the floor, placed his haversack under his head, and tipped up his chin. "Drink," she told him. "You must drink water."

He drank as he was told, then whispered, "It's superficial. I stopped the bleeding. I don't usually . . .I do apologize . . ." He slumped, his head falling back, unconscious again.

Apologize for what, she wondered. For invading her island? For the war?

Suddenly the man moved and mumbled, "Line's wide open." Then speaking sharply as if he were giving a command, he shouted. "Fall back to the trees!"

A hundred or more volunteers, her young brother among them, were scattered along the rail line, the coastal defense system that ran from Charleston to Savannah. The defense of that line depended upon rapid concentration to hold it open at all cost. Did this man know their positions?

She took a chance. "Where? Where will you cut the line?"

"Upriver," he mumbled in his unconscious state. Later he opened his eyes, drank as he was told, pulled himself up, and leaned clumsily against the banisters along the porch.

"Captain Preston Wilcox from Milford, Connecticut, ma'am," he said, quite formally.

She pointed the Colt at him. "What are you doing here, across the island from Union headquarters?"

"Be careful with the weapon, ma'am. I hope you're not itching to shoot me with my own revolver."

She riveted her eyes on him. "I asked you a question. What are you

doing at Edings Bay? What are you up to? How did you get out here?"
If her hands were shaking, she hoped he did not notice.

"I could ask you the same question, ma'am. I believe you to be the
one in enemy territory."

She cringed to be reminded of that. "All I want is the truth."

"I could say I was on a troop steamer. A storm hit and I got separated from the rest and I . . ."

"Don't try." Her arms felt as heavy as the weapon she was holding.

"All right. I'll tell you the truth if you will put the revolver down. You
can keep it close by you, but place it on the steps, please. Thank you,
ma'am. You want the truth. I will give it to you. I am a Union scout.
Somewhere near the river, I slipped up on a Rebel picket and a shot
grazed my arm. I lost my direction, and when I found your cart and animal, I tied my animal up beside yours. And here I am."

"Where are the others?" *Where was Hicks,* she wanted to know.
There might be more insane ones like him.

"What others?"

"You know what others. The rest of your unit."

"My corporal was taken by the Rebels. I guess you could say we got
separated."

She felt her muscles relax. The captain might be telling the truth.
According to Jacob, a Rebel unit had set up a picket post near Point
of Pines.

"Union soldiers are garrisoned in the Seabrook House. What are you
doing out here?"

He moved suddenly, as if fighting a sudden pain, then he spoke of
reconnaissance: studying the condition of the wind and waves, observ-
ing the shifting sands.

She listened closely, piecing the information together, suspecting he
was here to assess the resources of the island and report the location of
ferries and bridges. Report specifically on the feasibility of using her
island to launch a sortie to cut the rail line on the mainland.

"For what purpose do you do all your reconnaissance, sir?"

"For the purpose of constructing a causeway, ma'am."

"Could it be for the purpose of cutting the rail line?"

He smiled, but he did not blink. "What line? Did I say anything
about a rail line?"

"You did earlier. You were delirious."

"And you believed me? You don't expect me to give a Rebel lady the truth, do you?" His voice became antagonistic, his face red.

She felt ruffled.

He stood up. "Anyway, how is it that you're out here alone? Who are you except some Southern belle looking for adventure?"

She bristled. "I have come, sir, for family belongings. We were forced to leave when your forces turned our island into wasteland. I assure you, sir, I have not come back to find adventure."

"What can you possibly know about this damned war?" he muttered angrily.

She thought of her father, whose mind was the mind of a child because of the invasion, her mother, older than her years, and a sister, who had lost a baby because she was having to manage the planting without a husband, do things she had never had to do.

"I know more . . ." Confronting a Union officer was pointless. He could have her returned to the mainland handcuffed. He could take her to Beaufort where she'd be paraded, embarrassed, and ridiculed. He could put her on a ship bound for Washington City and Old Capitol Prison.

"This is a dangerous place, ma'am. Edisto is not officially behind the lines. Not yet, but all our men won't be as friendly as I am. Besides, you've got slaves wandering around like refugees, and how do you know what they will do? Truthfully, ma'am, why did you return? What was your reason?"

She bit her lips thinking she was a fool to come back. She'd never get away with it, and for a second she was ready to tell him the truth. *I came back to gather information, damn it, and if I play my cards right, you will give me all I need.* She straightened her shoulders and smiled.

"I came back to teach the children. I'm starting a school, you see, for the children of my father's former slaves." The lie slipped out with such self-righteousness, she surprised herself. The words spilled out. She could not stop. "They are caught here, as you have seen, without knowing how to read and do numbers, caught without any preparation for. . . whatever comes."

He leaned forward and looked deep into her eyes as if to discern the soul of someone so unselfish, so devoted. "How brave," he said in a quiet whisper.

She was suddenly overcome by the ease with which she told her lie; then she felt disgusted with herself by the realization that she could speak such an untruth and feel so righteous about doing so. She wanted to change her mind, let him know she was here for another reason. Another purpose. A mission to save the island from the likes of him. Something held her back, perhaps the way he looked into her eyes.

"Oh, I don't know about brave," she said. "I am quite certain, however, that the children will need to read and be able to do numbers. Education can better their condition. Not all Southerners are heartless, sir, in spite of your preconceived notions about us."

"I did not mean . . .I apologize," he said, his tone warm, as if filled with admiration.

Uncertainty wormed its way into her stomach. What was she saying? She couldn't teach the children. Her father said they had been slaves too long. She stiffened, put her hands in her lap, and waited. He must know she was lying.

"Then you must have much work to do. I must leave and allow you to go about your business, Miss. . . ."

He hesitated, obviously wanting to know her name.

She would not give it. "Yes, I have much to do," she said, handing him his revolver, watching him closely.

He went down the steps. "I need to find my way back to headquarters."

"Yes, and you must have someone take a look at your wound," she said.

"It is best that I travel before dark." He was holding his bloodstained sleeve close to his body.

He left and turned toward Frampton Creek, where he said he'd tied up his horse, and she thought, at least she hoped, that would be the last she'd see of Captain Wilcox from Milford, Connecticut.

CHAPTER
Three

~

*S*tretched out on the settee in the front room, Sarah longed
for the luxury of linen sheets with the sweet smell of lavender water, but
she did not go upstairs. If beds were no longer there, or if the walls were
stained and the corner where she'd read her favorite books filled with
rubble, she did not want to know.

Her eyelids felt heavy. When had she slept, really slept? Not since
she'd left Edgefield, she thought, as she clasped her hands above her
head and counted the days she had been on the road. She'd nap for a
few minutes, she decided, and sighed as she heard the surf roaring on
the incoming tide and pounding the shore. Within seconds she was
asleep, tossing and turning and dreaming that more soldiers were coming in from the sea.

When she opened her eyes, she couldn't remember where she was
and lay still until she recalled the Union soldier standing on the cottage
steps, and terror set in. She leapt up, looked around frantically, and
what she saw didn't calm her.

He was back. Captain Wilcox was sitting on the steps looking across
the bay to the quiet unbroken sea. A warm wind was blowing sand up
on the porch and on his uniform.

Watching him for a moment, she could not have said exactly how she
felt, but she thought of the darkness coming on and was at a loss to
explain her sudden change of heart.

"I thought you had gone," she said, her arms folded against her chest

"I was. I came back. If I might suggest," he said trying to sit up straight, but a sudden pain caught him, and he cleared his throat. "If I could just rest here tonight. Then tomorrow you could ride with me to Seabrook Plantation, where I will introduce you to the commander. Since you have come as a teacher, you will need his permission to remain on the island. He will issue an official pass."

"An official pass. Yes, of course," she heard herself mumble, stunned by his offer. An official pass was exactly what she needed.

"To make things easy for you," the captain said, "I will say that you are my cousin."

"Your cousin?" She struggled not to look at him. Who was he? What did he want from her? Why had he come back except to play a dangerous cat and mouse game? *But if I don't play along, he will know the unsaid, which he probably suspects anyway,* she thought, allowing her lips to turn up at the edges.

His voice broke into her thoughts. "If you allow me to rest here tonight, I will owe you that much." He nodded toward his arm. "I'm sure the commander will supply your school with books. He can arrange to have them shipped on the next troop transport."

Sarah smiled the practiced genteel smile of the Southern belle the Union man thought she was.

"Of course," she said. "My students will also need tablets and slates." She stood ramrod straight trying to conjure up an image of a schoolmistress, but it was hard.

All her tutors had been male, young, and good-looking. Actually most tutors in the Edings household had been ministers or long lost cousins from the Scottish moors willing to work their way to America by teaching in god-forsaken places like the Carolina barrier islands.

But, of course, she thought, the captain could have come back because he was worried about her. A small shadow moved on the porch floor, and she imagined an insect under her bare feet. Somewhere the surf was crashing, and out on the Atlantic troops ships were charging toward Port Royal. To cover her confusion, she batted at a sand gnat buzzing around her face. The sea pines were growing dark, their trunks turning red with the setting sun. It seemed early for sunset, she thought, although it was February.

What's the harm? The captain could stay for the night. Tomorrow she would have a pass. It would be a real pass, too, not just a piece of paper signed by some Union prisoner.

"This was my family's summer home. We left suddenly, and there is little left."

"I see."

"I do, however, know where my father hid his scuppernong wine," she said, lifting her voice happily. "It might make you feel better."

"That would do nicely, ma'am." He followed her and placed his revolver on the dining room table. She raised the planks where her father had stored his wine, hoping the container was still there. It was. She poured wine into the Chinese porcelain teacups and they drank in silence.

The Colt lay on the table between them.

"My name is Sarah," she said, pulling her black crocheted shawl around her shoulders. "Sarah Edings, and this place is called Edings Bay, named for my ancestors who came to this island shortly after the English arrived in Charleston."

"You shouldn't be out here alone, Miss Edings. War is serious business. Bad things can happen. Both sides have taken to the field, even at night. Especially at night."

Her eyes fell to the china. "Some one has been here," she said, looking at the Blue Willow, the Statfordshire.

"This is a good place to hide," he said. "Or recuperate and get to know a pretty lady." When he raised his arm, he winced.

"I can fix a poultice of bark and leaves, one that will help the healing and keep down the fever until you get medical attention. Do you have any medicine in your haversack? Any laudanum?" Actually, she had rummaged in his haversack but not found any. Perhaps it was hidden.

"I'm afraid I have nothing."

"Well, I am accustomed to emergencies. I learned in my childhood out here to be prepared. There may be something in the kitchen house that will do as well as a poultice. But I'll need water. I'll draw some from the well," she said, reprimanding herself for taking on the job of nurse, but he seemed to believe her teacher story. Besides, she needed that Union pass.

Coming back with kitchen linens draped over her arm and carrying a bucket of water and a bottle of vinegar she'd found in the pantry, she said, "You are lucky."

Then looking at the wound, she wondered what she would do if she found a metal splinter buried in his arm. She knew how to dispense camphor and prescribe tonics. Rhoda had taught her how to mix roots, but at the moment, she was not sure what she'd do if she found a fragment buried in his inflamed flesh.

"Yes, I'm lucky. It was just a graze." He nodded a "thank you" and removed his shirt so she could cut the sleeve of his long undershirt.

When she sponged the wound high on his left arm, he cringed. She guessed she was binding his arm too tightly with the linen napkins. "Sorry," she said, and when she lifted her hands instinctively to push her hair away from her forehead, she saw her hand shaking. She reminded herself he was the enemy.

"You can sleep in the kitchen house," she said finally. "I placed mats beside the hearth. I will sleep on the settee."

"Of course. And you can make a pillow out of my haversack and place the revolver under your head if that will make you feel safe."

"Thank you," she said, not knowing quite what to make of him. He was a Union soldier but not what she expected. "Perhaps we both need some supper. In the pantry I spied mason jars filled with vegetable soup. Soup would go well with these." She took a tin of crackers from the basket she'd brought all the way from Edgefield. She supposed she should share what she'd brought.

"There's wood left in the fireplace," he said. "Do you mind if I start a fire?"

"Not at all," she said, deciding this was a good time to embellish the story that she had come to teach the slave children to read. She'd come to the summerhouse to gather books, paper, pen and ink for her students. Her uneasiness left her. Teaching was the answer. The perfect cover, she decided, but it was difficult to think like a teacher. What would he expect of her?

She was rescued from that concern when the fire blazed and the captain turned with a jerk to face her.

"I have never met anyone who owned slaves," he said.

"Well, now you have, Captain Wilcox. I grew up on a plantation with field hands and house people. I didn't know anything else."

"I guess I don't understand." His brows furrowed.

She bristled. "What is there that you can't understand?"

"How did you live with yourself when you knew slavery was wrong?"

His directness unnerved her. Why did his question affect her so deeply? Why couldn't she just get up and walk away from the table? Why couldn't she tell him to mind his own business? Or go to hell?

"Captain Wilcox, it's easy for me to sit here now and admit that slavery was wrong. I know what you think. You think we should have abandoned the institution long ago and given up our agrarian way of life. Well, you are on a sea island now, and you can see how much land it takes to grow cotton. Can you imagine the labor force my father needed to clear land, plant, and pick thousands of acres? It's not possible without human labor. How could we change?"

"But you knew change was inevitable."

She rose from her chair. Yes, she knew change was inevitable. During long and heated family debates around this very table, her mother warned that without change, there would be disaster. "My mother was Josephine du Pont," Sarah said. "Perhaps you know the family from Newport. My mother met my father when he was vacationing there one summer, married him, and moved south, but she reared us as she would have reared us in the North. In other words, we could not sit idly at the table without entering the conversation. In recent years we've had many heated and impassioned debates over secession and the moral question of slavery right here, over this table."

"I didn't mean to imply . . ."

"That we were uneducated and immoral and oblivious to the complexity of the problem?"

He seemed too embarrassed to speak.

"And as for my father. . . ." She paused, refusing to allow her voice to break, but allowing her mind to fill with the picture of her father astride his stallion, riding, armed, along the surf, thinking he could protect the island from Yankee invaders. She'd found him the day the family fled, fear and terror robbing him of his youth and his brilliant mind.

"As for my father, Captain Wilcox, he is only one of many Southerners backed into a corner because of outspoken and fanatical politicians."

"I am trying to understand." He leaned his head back on the chair.

She drained the last drop of wine from her cup and walked to the open window. The sky was dark, as if filling with a deep blue. She felt lightheaded, not from the wine, but from the thought that her masquerade would never work. She should stop now, she thought. Easy enough to do by just gathering the china and a few other things and telling the captain she had changed her mind and was leaving. Life would go on. She would come back after the war.

"Now, if that satisfies your curiosity about my family," Sarah said, raising her chin and breathing deeply, "I think I will go to the kitchen house and get that soup I spied in the pantry."

CHAPTER

Four

The cart creaked along, a two-wheel affair built by field hands but with so many wooden boards missing now that dust billowed up through the open floor and settled on Sarah's skirt. She looked at Captain Wilcox sitting beside her, his own horse tethered to the rear, and the image struck her as amusing, but she did not smile.

After sleeping in the kitchen house, he had appeared early that morning, clean-shaven and dressed in a clean shirt, the one she'd seen packed in his haversack. He had already washed the bloodstains from his blue coat, and when he strapped his leather belt around his waist and placed his revolver in its holster, he had caught her glancing at him. Embarrassed, she had looked away.

After he had helped her hitch the cart to the trace, they were on their way, and for the last hour she had been telling him about Affey, who would help her open the school. She explained how badly the newly freed slaves wanted their children to be ready when freedom came.

He turned with a sudden question. "Are you sure Negroes can learn?"

She thought of Affey and Affey's mother, Rebecca, the plantation housekeeper who had learned to read, and of Jacob and his Kiawah ancestors, Indians who were native to the island. Jacob's ancestors were here when the white men came and had readily mixed their blood with the Africans. Jacob and his family all read and worked with numbers.

"Of course, they can learn," she said, "It might be that most of the slaves you have seen while you have been here are woefully ignorant and unlettered, but you don't know the slaves I know."

"I don't know any slaves," he said. After a long pause, he continued. "What makes you think the children will come to your school?"

She looked him squarely in the eye. "Because freedom is coming." The truth was, she did not know if students would come to her school. She did not know if slaves could learn, but anything she'd add to her story would be another lie. Then the realization came to her that she hadn't the faintest idea why she thought she could get away with this, and she heard herself demanding, "Stop the cart."

He looked bewildered and pulled at the reins. "Whoa." The cart creaked to a standstill.

"Sh-h-h," she whispered. "Don't move."

A red ball of fur leapt across the high road, bounded over the nearest ditch, and landed soundlessly in the fern and wild violets that filled the ditch. Another ball of fur followed, then another, until five tiny kits crossed the road, all in a line.

"Foxes," she whispered, "playing like kittens. Let's watch. They roll and toss and play for hours. A vixen with her young. Their den must be nearby," she said.

She didn't know why, but she found it reassuring that life continued on her broken island in spite of violence and death and war.

The captain seemed to smile a faraway smile, as if crossing a threshold into the past, some event he was suddenly remembering. His expression seemed to indicate sadness. Or was it a yearning, a need? And for a second she felt the urge to cry out.

What's going to happen?

But she sat still, bit her lip, and after a moment, she reached out to touch his wounded arm. She pretended to make sure it was bandaged then pulled her hand back.

Here we are, she thought, thrown together, so close we can touch shoulders. Two lonely people huddled together, waiting for a storm.

When a heron swooped in to rest in a nearby tree, the foxes disappeared and the captain snapped the reins. But within seconds he pulled the animal to a stop.

"Miss Edings," he said, looking at her differently now, "we hardly met in, shall we say, an appropriate manner."

She smiled. "That's true."

"So, I thought we might start over." He cleared his throat.

Matching his grin, Sarah watched him and waited.

"How do you do?" he said politely, then without waiting for her answer, he swung from the cart. She watched while he climbed the bank beside the road and broke off a spray of wisteria.

"It would please me if you would accept a gift," he said, holding a cluster of purple flowers.

She thought of the miniature. Who was the girl with the alabaster skin, so demure, with straight, tiny perfect teeth, who seemed to be dreaming of a lover? But when the picture in her mind turned to her own aging skin turning brown as she worked in the fields, she decided the dark-haired girl was probably his wife.

"Oh, sir, I cannot accept flowers from a stranger."

"Then I will place them on the front board here. We both can enjoy them." He smiled and snapped the reins. The cart moved on toward Union headquarters. "Tell me more about your family."

"My ancestors came to the New World for a better life. They found Edisto and never left." Sarah looked across fields that were once white with cotton and into the woods that were once shaded and safe and untroubled. Then she looked up at the clear blue sky, felt the warmth of the February sun and told the Union captain her great-grandfather was a patriot, a strong and passionate patriot. Her family said he stood with General Moultrie and dared the English to cross the Coosawhatchie River.

"My father says that's why the Redcoats marched to Charleston instead. The first William Edings in the New World wasn't about to let the enemy take everything he had worked for."

Neither am I, Captain Wilcox. Neither am I.

Seabrook Plantation came into view, and she sat with her back aching against the planks behind her. She must appear calm and unaffected, she told herself, whatever she saw. She was coming for a reason, a very good reason: to gather information that could cripple Union plans. Besides, she needed an official pass.

Close enough to see troops covering the yard like ants, she felt her stomach turn and bile rise to her throat. Sentries lolled at the steps, whittling and whistling or sitting at tables playing cards, too busy at their games to challenge an old plantation cart creaking down the long driveway. Small fires sputtered and smoked in an open area that was once a vast vegetable garden. Negro women stood over kettles eyeing her and the thought occurred to her that they might recognize her and shout out. What would she do? She lowered her head.

When a sentry finally took the reins and helped her to the ground, she walked with the captain to what Northerners thought was the back of the house. She knew it as the front since all plantation houses faced the water. The most exquisite formal gardens she'd ever seen once grew here. Now sutlers sold tobacco and beef jerky, writing pads and ink—whatever soldiers would buy. Their tents stood in the middle of William Seabrook's rose garden.

"Colonel Moore," the captain said, striding toward a burly man wearing a rumpled Union uniform and looking as if he had just gotten up from a nap. His face was gray, his eyes puffy.

"Wilcox reporting, sir. I must have medical attention, but it can wait."

When the men walked aside and lowered their voices, Sarah concluded the captain was reporting his findings or telling the colonel about Hicks and the picket post affair.

When they returned, the captain introduced her. "And I have brought my cousin, a Southern lady who has come to teach the contraband. She is from Savannah but has lived in the North for some years."

"Teach slaves. Is that so?" The colonel looked dubious. "Well, well, you will have your hands full, ma'am. Another schoolmarm is expected on St. Helena Island," Colonel Moore said. "She's already shipped books and soap and clothes donated by the Ladies Aid Society of Philadelphia. You ladies are to be commended, ma'am. I hope you know what you're in for. Maybe they can learn to read. I do not know."

Too nervous to trust herself to say anything, Sarah curtsied, smiled, and felt considerable relief when the officers wasted little time with protocol and left to sit at a table in the shade. They acted more like two cotton factors than army officers, she thought, and watched as Negro servants approached them with coffeepots and mugs.

She walked along the garden path down to the river, her body tense as she looked back to the officers and surveyed the layout for a position from which she could listen to their conversation. Then she backtracked through the camellias, waited until she heard men's voices, and stayed alert for the Negro servants.

She knew the layout of the garden well. She had attended many garden receptions here. "Watch the Seabrook girls closely," her mother would say. Sarah could almost hear her mother whispering from behind her unscrolled lace fan. "Such manners," her mother would say, "such social graces," hinting that her girls, too, should at all times practice manners befitting the ladies they surely would become. Josephine Edings, always gracious and handsomely dressed in rich silk brocade with a fashionable felt riding hat to match, was known to give her daughters interminable instructions. "Hold your shoulders back, Sarah. Stand tall like Miriah. Bend your head, slightly, just slightly. That's it. Tilt your head. Smile, Sarah. That's it. Like your sister."

As long as Sarah could remember, Miriah had been matronly and dignified, but after the man from Edgefield came to visit, Miriah seemed to melt imperceptibly out of their lives . . .until the war.

Their parents had not been too pleased when Miriah met Zebulon Montgomery Pike Butler, but he was acceptable enough personally. His family was one of the most prominent in Edgefield District, but he wasn't from Beaufort or Charleston. After a season or two in the social whirl of Charleston without an engagement, Miriah had been taken to Newport in hopes of an alliance with one of the families from her mother's home territory.

But Miriah's destiny was in Carolina, and when she returned, her romance with Zeb Butler blossomed. So did Miriah. Her mother quickly warmed to the planning of a wedding and with large families on both sides, the numbers grew quickly. The wedding was the social event of the year. The most memorable event of all was a reception here in the Seabrook garden.

The Union officers sat smoking cigars; they'd chosen the best, Sarah was sure, probably Virginia tobacco and stolen from William Seabrook's silver cigar box. Smoke settled over the table. The captain was looking at his, not smoking yet, simply watching it burn. The colonel bit the end off his and spat to the ground, then said something and laughed. She supposed it was a suggestion about her or another woman or about women in general. Or they were laughing about the invasion at Port Royal, which to them was probably a game.

She stood behind a large camellia bush. Making sure the officers could not see her, she listened as they talked.

"Grant's hitting the Confederates hard in Tennessee." It was the captain's voice. "The President himself, is impressed with his campaign."

The colonel spat on the ground. "Yeah, Grant's out to make a name for hisself, awright. I knew him in the regular army. The last time I saw him he was drunk as a skunk. 'Bout time he cleaned up his reputation."

The captain sipped coffee and leaned back. "Story goes that when war broke out, he went to McClellan to look for a job. The general was not in that day, so Grant went west and wrangled his way as commander of a regiment of Illinois volunteers. Turns out he can fight."

"Before God, I hope he cleans 'em out."

"It's the river transportation network that's crucial there."

"And I'm stuck in this goddamned place with nothing to do but swat gnats and watch out for rattlesnakes." Moore put another cigar between his teeth and began to chew. "Hell, I'm sitting within thirty-five miles of the port of Charleston. If I could get reinforcements and some gunboats on standby in the North Edisto, I could be there in three days."

"I have no doubt about it, sir. Our warships have already anchored in Stono Inlet and without incident. I must tell you the James Island approach to Charleston is gaining favor down at Port Royal. If we land on the south end of the island, we can fight our way across and bring the city within easy artillery range. That seems to be the general's strategy."

"What about Fort Sumter?"

"Using the James Island approach, the army will cut off all supplies. The fort will have to be evacuated or the Confederates out there will surrender. With that impediment removed, the fleet will then enter the harbor."

"And if that don't work?" The bitterness in his voice pained Sarah. It was the sound of a man passed over too many times then sent to a scattered outpost, where there was nothing to do but drink and play cards and die the slow death of boredom.

"There's talk about using Folly Island. From there the infantry could sweep across the inlets, land troops in secret if necessary, and overrun the Confederate batteries. If we could batter Fort Sumter with heavy land artillery, the fleet could roll into the harbor."

"Yeah, well, you make it sound simple," Colonel Moore said, "but it may not work out that way."

"The railroad transportation system remains critical." The captain took out papers and began unfolding. He did not look up, but Sarah heard his words. "I brought with me the most recent map published by the U.S. Coast Survey and a drawing of the South's railroad network. Grant's next move with be toward the Memphis and Charleston Railroad."

Sarah heard "railroad" and kept her body stiff even as a trickle of perspiration touched her nose. She did not move a muscle.

Colonel Moore looked up. "The Memphis and Charleston?"

"And we're sitting across the river from a feeder line. Quite a valuable feeder line to the Confederates." The captain pointed toward the mainland, "Right there, three miles inland from Adams Run. That feeder moves goods and soldiers twenty-four hours a day."

"Yeah? How far?"

"That line connects to the Wilmington and Weldon, with lines leading north all the way to Petersburg and Richmond. Going west it connects to the Georgia Railroad and the Western and Atlantic, all the way to Memphis."

"Hell," he said. "The tracks at Adams Run are protected by swamps and mud banks and tidal streams. That stuff eats up good men. Add a bunch of damned good Rebel sharpshooters, and it didn't work when we tried to cut the line down at Coosawhatchie. You know the numbers. We got two men killed, twelve wounded and one captured." He spat.

Captain Wilcox stood and pointed up the river. Together the men went over positions, starting in an area of the North Edisto, which they both agreed was navigable, then they moved upriver on the map. "Toogodoo Creek flows into Adams Run. It's shallow," he said, "but if we assemble gunboats in the upper stretches of the North Edisto . . ."

Sarah's mind whirled. Hearing the Union men and picturing a map of the coast, she felt part of the war for the first time, part of the machine, and tensed herself, holding her muscles tight.

She must warn Adams Run.

Her contact would warn the general in command of Third District, who would warn the men hiding in the woods, all volunteers, sons of farmers and lawyers and planters whose fathers had already marched off to Virginia. Once they were warned, the men would move into position exactly as they had been trained to do.

Colonel Moore rubbed the stubble on his cheeks and neck, as if it was prickly. "I don't know. That Confederate man they got does a damned good job massing his troops."

"I hear that."

"Robert E. Lee. He's a major general in command of the Department of South Carolina, Georgia, and East Florida. In a few months' time, he's dug an inner line of defense that's hard to crack. His numbers may be small, but you got to hand it to him. He's got his young whippersnappers well organized and trained. They can concentrate what they got."

Captain Wilcox spoke thoughtfully. "How strong?"

"Rebels don't need numbers when they got cavalry and volunteers lusting for a fight."

The captain leaned forward. "They won't expect us to cut the line within range of Confederate headquarters, say a few miles south of Adams Run. Say at Jacksonboro."

Sarah moved closer.

"The navy's preparing for operations against the port of Savannah," Captain Wilcox said. "While the fleet makes its way south to Fort Pulaski and engages their forces in that offensive, we can make a move and cut the line, right here in Lee's territory." He leaned back, a look of satisfaction on his face.

She felt her eyes glistening and turned to walk down the path to the river. The wind was still, the tide low. She knelt to fill her hands with water, then she stood and looked blindly to the sky.

By the time she got back to the garden, the meeting was over and the brass buttons on Captain Wilcox' blue coat sparkled in the sunlight as he walked toward her. Apprehension and anger mingled in her throat, and she wanted to scream at him, but she held out her hand and smiled.

Stopping in front of her, so close she could smell lavender in the soap he'd used that morning, Captain Wilcox shifted in his uniform and said, "The colonel and I have discussed your plans to start a school for slave children. He has directed me to order books for your use. However, he is mindful of your safety while you are here, and to accomplish this, the colonel will need to be aware of your whereabouts at all times."

"Yes, of course. Thank you, Cousin Preston," Sarah said, playing seriously her new role and being especially careful not to stumble over his name.

Colonel Moore bowed. "Nevertheless, I am concerned about your safety, Miss . . ."

"Edings," she said quickly. Colonel Moore was obviously not as comfortable with her presence as the captain.

"Yes. Well, Miss Edings, this is not officially Union territory," he explained, "but we expect the order any day and full evacuation within a month, slaves and all. Quite naturally, I am concerned for your safety as a woman alone."

"I'm not alone, sir. I am protected by my loyal household servants who will help teach the children. I assure you that I am in no peril and in less danger than if I had remained in Savannah. I have access to weapons, and I know how to use them."

"It's true, sir. My cousin can protect herself," Preston Wilcox said with a smile. "However." It was his turn to speak as if he were truly a relative. "My family would never forgive me if anything happened to my cousin. You must take this revolver, Miss Edings, and this knife and keep them with you at all times. And of course you may keep your conveyance." He looked at the cart and the old mare, and she thought she saw a glimmer in his eye.

"The most important item for your safety is this." He handed her a piece of paper. "A pass," he said, "signed by Colonel Moore. I'm afraid I must return to Beaufort this afternoon. I'm leaving on the first steamer. Should you need anything further, my address is there. I have written it at the bottom of the pass."

Preston Wilcox helped her onto the cart, handed her the reins, and wished her success with the school. Sarah snapped the reins and held her breath. The Union officers believed her when she told them she had returned to teach the slave children. She didn't want to imagine what would have happened if they hadn't believed her, but she must be careful. She must warn Adams Run about the Union's plans to cut the line, and to do that she needed to keep her wits about her. If they found her out, if they even suspected the real reason she'd come back, the price she'd pay would be dear.

CHAPTER

Five

*A*ffey was waiting, standing on one foot and tapping the other. Jacob's children gathered around, the smallest clapping her hands, chanting, "Miss Sarah, Miss Sarah."

Of course they remembered her. Hadn't she celebrated their birthdays by taking rock candy to the quarters? Hadn't she taken blankets to be distributed at Christmas? Why could she not picture the others? And there were fifty or more children in the quarters. The thought struck her like a blow. Why hadn't she walked farther than Jacob and Sully's cabin?

"Tabitha, mind your manners," Affey scolded the youngest for running forward. "What have we practiced? How do we speak to our elders?"

The three girls stood, as if at attention, all speaking at once. "Good day, Miss Sarah."

"Good day, children." Sarah nodded then took each child's hand, but she couldn't help winking at Tabitha.

Affey beamed. "Very good." Affey turned to Jacob's oldest. "Take Miss Sarah's horse, Zack, and put the cart in a safe place."

"It ain't no horse," Zack snapped at Affey, and Sarah cleared her throat, trying to conceal her surprise.

"Don't sass me, young man," Affey shot back, her eyes wide, perfectly oval.

"It ain't a good mare at that." Zack's shoulders moved in a small, defiant shrug.

The girls giggled but grew silent after Affey grabbed Zack's arm. "And don't say 'ain't,' you hear?"

Sarah watched Zack leave and all the circumstances of teaching slave children seemed to come down on her like a flood. Whatever made her think she could teach hardened boys like this? The swamp was filled with boys his age hiding until the white man's war was over, all dreaming of freedom but remembering the past. All yearning to strike out.

Against all the injustices.

Against the world.

Against her.

Affey ushered the girls over to the cart. "Why don't you girls help Zack take care of this?" Affey sat beside a tree. "Do that for me, girls, and go find your papa. Tell him Miss Sarah's back."

The children left, and Sarah sat beside Affey in the warm sunshine trying to think of how to begin. They had grown up playing together behind the kitchen house and eating at the same table when the rest of the family was away. The days were filled with the sound of boisterous island dialect, the smell of pear preserves simmering on the stove, and the feel of wind on her face as she ran with Affey down the path to Mad Rhoda's cabin.

Now, she looked at Affey and didn't know how to tell her about her plan to begin a school. To stall for time, she waved off an insect so tiny it was invisible. Slaves had called them no-see-ums.

"It's warm for February," Sarah said, looking up at the live oak, always green with foliage. To cover the awkwardness, she waved off another no-see-um. Affey was looking at her suspiciously.

"We expected you back much earlier. We were worried."

"I have news."

"Jacob was beside himself."

"Good news," Sarah said. "I went to Union headquarters."

"Union headquarters?" Affey laughed nervously. When the children appeared, Affey shooed them off and waited for an explanation.

Sarah stood and took her time brushing pine needles from her skirt. "Affey, we are going to start a school. The first school for the children of slaves."

"Children of free men. Free here, Sarah. Free in Union territory. Go on. I'm listening."

"Yes, children of the contraband. Staying here is risky, but as long as the Yankees think I'm a teacher, we're safe."

"What do you mean 'think' you're a teacher. I'm not getting involved in any more spying, Sarah. The delivery we made at Adams Run was enough. No more. No more."

"Affey, listen to me." She heard the desperation in her own voice. "I'm not asking you to help with any more deliveries. Just help me get a school started. That's all I ask. I need you. Remember those summers when we slept under the mosquito netting at the summerhouse? I asked you once if you were free and not a slave, would you like me? Would you still be my friend? Well, you're free. You're not a slave. Not even a servant. You are a friend and I'm begging you to help me. Please."

The wind hummed in the pines and Sarah knew Affey was remembering the night they heard a rustle at the window of the summerhouse. They had looked out to see wild geese flying north. Affey had watched the geese winging their way along the coastline and called out, "I will know freedom someday. I will. I will."

Sarah, too, had felt some strange and confusing wind blowing that night through the window, that breath of air Affey called freedom.

"As teachers we will have official Union passes."

She couldn't imagine what Affey was thinking. They were quiet for a while, and then Affey scrambled up from her place. "I can visit Toby. He's working on St. Helena Island. The Northerners are keeping the plantations going over there. They pay wages."

"Yes. It will be safe to travel. You can visit Toby."

Affey's face glowed. "Let's do it. First I must find the children. It will take me a while, but Jacob knows where most families are hiding."

"The officers promised to supply books." Sarah grinned, and before Affey could ask questions, the words tumbled out about the Union officer with a wounded arm who appeared on the steps of the summerhouse. "He took me to headquarters and introduced me as his cousin." Sarah couldn't hide the smirk on her face. "He's having books shipped on the next supply ship."

She brushed back a loosened curl and tied her hair net. Of course, she could teach slave children if it meant she could travel safely. She knew the risks. The idea to masquerade as a teacher had leapt into her mind in the presence of the wounded Union officer. Now it consumed her. She was surprised that her new image had settled into her mind so comfortably, and she smiled to remember the captain who had done more to help her make the decision than he would ever know.

Affey seemed suddenly apprehensive. "Maybe the officer fell at your feet and maybe he had a hurt arm, but can you trust him? How do you know he's not a spy?"

Sarah cocked her head and raised her eyebrows. "Oh, I am certain he is a spy. I'm sure of it. That, or a special agent who came to cut the rail line."

Into the dark miasma that led into the swamp, she followed Affey and the children. White people would never brave these murky waters, but black people would. Sarah knew it as a place too mysterious for Rebels and Yankees. She forced herself to keep up with the group. When mammoth cypress trees surrounded them, hundreds of years old, rooted there since the time of the Kiawah, the Edistow, and the Creek, Sarah wanted to ask where they were headed but felt it wiser to keep quiet. She'd heard tales of prehistoric reptiles and huge alligators in these backwaters and bears and bobcats. When the British came too close to the island for comfort, her great, great grandfather armed the fortification with muskets and artillery. No one except slaves had ventured into this area of the swamp since the Revolution.

High ground appeared. Still they moved steadily and quietly. Tall pines swayed and whispered in thick woods that were inky black now, dark as pitch, when suddenly up ahead an eerie light pulsed through the trees. The woods opened up.

A cabin appeared. A lantern burned in the window.

Jacob met them at the door. The cabin was once a praise house. With the marsh and the swamps all around, it was protected so slaves used it for special times. His people used the cabin as a church for religious shouts or a hiding place when white masters turned violent.

"Why did you leave the quarters?"

"I'll tell you another time," he said.

"What happened?"

"It's not safe at the plantation from both sides fighting the war," Jacob said, and she knew from the sound in his voice that there was more bad news. Perhaps the fields were burned, perhaps the house itself.

One of the girls brought lye soap and water, another brought towels, and Sully scurried around fixing supper. Soon they were sitting at a long table eating corn cakes with a mess of fish the children had caught that morning. Later they had biscuits smothered in molasses. They ate quietly by the light of a small fire. No need to attract the attention of animals that might be roaming around at night.

After supper, Jacob's wife was full of questions. "Is it true that you and Affey came all the way by carriage?" Sully tried to keep her voice low.

For a moment Sarah did not answer. Travel by carriage had been safer since she was delivering such a precious package to headquarters. "The rail line from Augusta was too crowded."

"We had an escort once we got passed Orangeburg." Affey seemed eager to talk. "And a personal bodyguard all the way to Adams Run."

Sarah cleared her throat, indicating that Affey had said enough. The delivery was top secret.

Affey refused to take the hint. "Everything was arranged by the Governor and Mrs. Pickens."

Sarah was seething. Best to change the subject.

"Jacob was a sight for my sore eyes when I found him waiting at Toogodoo Creek."

Sully poured more coffee. "He doing right well trading salt and molasses for coffee and sugar," Sully said. "And other things," she added.

Jacob stoked up the fire. "I offer a safe trip to anybody who needs it. Both sides pay good money. I take Yankees down to Beaufort or Hilton Head, bring Rebels back, and I make money going both ways." The fire flamed and in its orange light, Jacob smiled.

For a long while they sat watching the fire burn down, and after he banked the coals for the night, Jacob turned to Affey. "Toby's making thirty dollars a month and saving up to buy land. When the fighting's over, we can buy land, you know."

The baby cried and Sully picked it up. She put it to her ample breast. When the child stopped crying, she placed it gently in Jacob's arms where he rocked in a fine mahogany and leather upholstered chair he had come by through some exchange of salt and molasses. Sarah was sure a planter had taken the chair for granted, but it belonged to Jacob now.

"Jacob, I hope to gather valuable information while I'm here. I will need to deliver that information to my contact in Adams Run. You know every inch of the rivers and creeks. You know where the patrols are likely to be located. Will you help me?"

Sully stood at the hearth, her shadow looming large. "We don't want nothing to do with spying."

"All I need is transportation."

"Miss Sarah, these are grim days for you," Sully said, "but they dangerous for us."

Jacob shook his head. "I can't bring bluecoats down on my livelihood. I got the children to protect. Transportation's my livelihood now."

Then, knowing her next thought would be earthshakingly new to Jacob and Sully, Sarah said, "Affey and I are thinking of starting a school for the children."

Sully glanced at her children already asleep in the corner on the straw palettes.

"Your children will need to know how to read and do their numbers after the war."

The baby in Jacob's arms whimpered. He rocked back and forth, saying nothing.

Sully dragged her chair close to Sarah's. "Sure enough? We hear tell 'bout Northern teachers. They already come to St. Helena. But we could sure use a teacher here. We got fifty chillun' hiding in the swamps." Sully looked at Jacob. "And I'm mighty anxious for ours to know something."

Words caught in Sarah's throat. She had no books, no training, no idea how to teach, but on Sully's face there was a look that tore at her heart. "I'm not a real teacher."

"You taught Affey how to read," Sully said without accusation. "Everybody on the place knew all those nights she was staying with you at the summerhouse, you were teaching Affey to read. If your mamma had 'a found out, you would 'a been in trouble, but we didn't tell. We were happy for Affey."

It was true. The summer her mother went to Hendersonville to recuperate in cool mountain breezes, she and Affey spent every night reading and giggling like sisters under the mosquito netting. Perhaps her mother had not known, but her father knew she was teaching Affey to read. And now Sully had just told her all the people on the plantation knew.

"Of course, I can stay only a short time. You can't assume that I will be able to stay behind enemy lines indefinitely."

Affey slid her chair near. "Sully's not assuming anything except that you care enough to teach the children."

"I care," Sarah said firmly to overcome her niggling guilt and worry. She turned to Jacob. "Affey and I will organize a school. In return you will bring me Northern newspapers, Union reports, anything you find on your trips to Beaufort and Hilton Head. Will you do that?"

"You strike a hard bargain, but I'll think on it tonight." Jacob glanced at Sully then told Sarah, "We'll talk more in the morning."

At dawn, after Jacob stoked the fire, Sarah tiptoed outside. He was sitting on an iron anvil beside the well. He saw her look at the anvil. He knew she knew that it came from her father's plantation, and she felt rising between them a wall of questions that could not even be asked.

"These are confusing times," she began as the red sun burst through the trees.

"That's for sure."

"I'll need newspapers, reports, messages, anything at all you can confiscate from the Yankees who travel on the longboat with you."

"I understand."

Jacob seemed more agreeable this morning, but should she trust him? Last night she'd seen a box of rifles stored near the mat where she slept. Probably more under the planks, too, but she didn't look. If she were wrong to suspect him of stealing guns and planning an uprising, she had to know. She sensed there was more to the matter than hoarding and bartering. "Before we go any further, I must ask you something. Why are you hoarding guns?"

Jacob did not blink. "Guns?" There was no expression at all on his reddish-brown face.

There was a time when she could have forced the truth, but her hands were tied now. Either he would willingly tell the truth or he would lie, and she would live each day watching his every gesture, every twitch. She had to know.

"I saw rifles last night, Jacob. Those boxes where Affey and I sleep. Springfields. Enfields. Cartridge boxes. Cap pouches. Why, Jacob, why?"

"You don't have to worry about the guns." He moved away, and for a moment she thought he might shout out the truth, his plans for an uprising revealed.

She sat on the stone wall of the well, still wet with the morning dew. "What if the Yankees find out you steal guns? They could come any time you know. Anybody might come."

She leaned forward, as she would to give advice or counsel to a friend in trouble.

"If you got to know, I take guns anytime I find them. I make no apologies for that. I take guns from any soldier. Yankee or Rebel. Makes no difference to me. It's your war, Miss Sarah, not mine. The fewer guns they got out there in all this confusion, the better, I say." He took water from the wooden bucket beside him, raised the dipper to his lips and drank. He poured out what was left.

Then he filled the dipper again.

He offered it to her.

She took it, surface water, brown and smelling of sulfur, but she accepted the dipper and drank. She had all but accused him of stealing. Worse than that, she had suspected he was planning the unthinkable. She was embarrassed but refused to allow her voice to hold a trace of uneasiness. She suddenly wanted to say, "Thank you." Instead she said, "I need to deliver information to Adams Run. Will you help me?"

For a moment she thought he did not understand. Or maybe he was going to refuse this part of the bargain, but he looked up, his eyes white against his face. "I hear talk. Soldiers think I'm too busy to listen and I let them think that, but all the time I'm listening," he said. "I spotted a gunboat up the North Edisto yesterday, close to Toogodoo Creek where I picked you up. Their water patrols are getting mighty tight. I'll do the traveling."

"What do you mean?"

"I'll take the messages," Jacob said. "You do the teaching. I'll do the traveling. Sully was right. The children need real schooling. They need to read and do numbers. She spoke the truth. Schooling is our only chance to get the children ready."

She had reasoned with Jacob and won. There was a light, breathless sense of relief about her, as if a burden had been lifted, and she breathed easily, more evenly. There was no going back now. No escape from doing what had to be done.

CHAPTER

Six

Children shuffled Spanish moss with their feet while Sully poured water brought over from the well. Affey joined in the fun, and Sarah couldn't help being drawn into the excitement. The praise house next to what was now Jacob's cabin was undergoing a transformation. This praise house would become a schoolhouse.

When dark faces appeared at the door, suspicious and anxious, Sully's voice soothed their nervousness. "Miss Sarah done come back to teach the children because the Lawd can't make it right now. He sent us a teacher because He needs to be a lotta different places these days. I say praise the Lawd."

School opened in March and twenty-six children enrolled. Affey began class by giving firm instructions about being punctual. They should study hard if they wanted to learn. They should behave well to allow others to learn. The children sat, meek and docile, while parents wandered in with baskets of eggs and sweet potatoes for tuition.

Suddenly Affey's voice sounded harsh. Sarah thought she had never seen Affey so worked up. "The next time . . ." Affey coughed, stopped, swallowed, and pointed across the room. "The next time you enter that door, your clothes must be clean." She pointed her finger at the children. "If we've got anything left on this island, it's water. Plenty of it. Water. And you are going to use it. Fresh water or salt water. Creek water or rain water. I don't care. And lye soap. Use it. Bathe in it. Wash your clothes in it before you enter that door again."

Sarah rushed to the front of the room. "It will be better tomorrow," she whispered, "and if they don't . . ."

Affey was not listening. "Stand. All of you. Face the door," Affey announced.

The children did as they were told.

"You are dismissed. There will be no book learning until you learn the Lord's word. 'Cleanliness is next to Godliness.' Fresh water or salt water. Creek water or rain water. Lye soap. Bathe in it. Wash your clothes in it. Remember: 'Cleanliness is next to Godliness.' And those are the Lord's words."

The next day the children's ebony skin shone like glass, their clothes smelled of lye soap, and the tatters and frayed edges had been mended. All, that is, but one older boy who stood at the door slouching. Within seconds Affey marched him out and down to the creek. When they returned, the boy smelled fresh and wore a clean shirt that Sarah thought looked surprisingly like Jacob's.

Later Jacob dropped by unannounced. He walked to the front and prayed the Lord's Prayer so loud his voice echoed outside in the live oak trees. When silence returned, he looked directly into the students' eyes. "The Lord wants you to do right by these teachers. If you don't do right, he wants your papas to lick the devil out of you. And if they don't, I will."

For weeks Affey drilled the children in cleanliness and godliness while Sarah drilled them in the ABC's. School was going better than expected.

But a month later Sarah panicked. A handwritten note from Colonel Moore arrived requesting the pleasure of a visit. Captain Wilcox would be joining him. Why the captain's appearance should excite her so she couldn't imagine. She went back over the story she had told him, turning over in her mind the details. The last thing she needed now was the fanfare the officers' visit would bring. Well, the children themselves would have to perform.

The teachers doubled their efforts. Their students would do everything but salute when Union officers walked into the school.

Neither she nor Affey asked where Jacob found the Union Jack, but they pushed back the tables to create a makeshift stage and suspended the large flag across the room. It was not exactly the symbol Sarah wanted to hang there, but it would please the school's benefactors.

When the day arrived, Sarah stood waiting at the schoolhouse door, her heart pumping, her mind whirling with reminders. Stand tall. Act like a schoolmistress. But how would a schoolmarm act? She thought of the Bronte sisters conscientiously going about their day as teachers while at night conjuring up delicious stories about the people who lived around them. If the Bronte sisters could lead a double life, so could she.

As the officers approached, she held her breath. The captain looked taller somehow, more handsome in his dress uniform, a long frock coat with two rows of brass buttons. Impeccably tailored, she thought, with velvet stripes down the legs of the trousers.

When he spoke a simple "Good day," he held one hand stiff on the black leather sheath that held his saber, highly polished and glistening. Her ears rang.

She smoothed the skirt of her day dress, washed so often its hem was threadbare. Luckily she had found velvet ribbon, and for the last several nights they had added ribbon for camouflage. That morning Sully had appeared with a gift. "You'll look extra special wearing this," Sully said, handing her an exquisitely crocheted collar.

Sarah's hand flew to the collar as Affey called out to the children. "Rise." All twenty-six came to their feet, chins up, arms clasped to their sides.

The burly older boy, the one who refused to wash his first day at school but was now scrubbed and polished and completely devoted to Affey's every whim, began reading from the Bible, making up verses as he went along. Sarah smiled. Union men did not know the difference since Northerners didn't understand anything at all spoken by Sea Island slaves. She had encouraged the boy to substitute his own words when he got nervous. The officers nodded, pretending to understand.

Jacob's youngest marched to the front, and Sarah felt her stomach tighten. Tabitha, tiny and frail, stepped forward. "The Lord is my shepherd, I shall not want," she recited exactly as practiced all week, but when she finished, she stared into nothingness. Stage fright overcame her. She could not move.

"Thank you, Tabitha." Sarah rose from her chair, wishing the production was over. Why had she put the children in a sideshow? Why must she impress the Union officers? What was she thinking? The children were not some strange curiosity. They were gentle and vulnerable, and they believed in her. They trusted her.

Before school and after school they often clustered around her, stroking her hair and holding her hand, and she patted their heads and looked down at her charges, giving them hope, telling them that life really could be different if they only had an education.

Finally, the older students marched to the stage to show off their new skill: telling time using an ornate French porcelain clock. The day the clock appeared at school, Sarah had asked, "Does anyone know where this clock came from?" No one claimed to know, but she knew the time-piece had stood for years in her home beside the metronome in the upstairs music room where her mother played the piano. Was her mother imagining she played before a grand audience in Newport?

Did her mother regret coming south? Josephine du Pont deplored slavery but learned to live with it. She wanted to speak out but listened to her husband and kept quiet. Sarah thought about her mother now in Edgefield without a home, living on the Butler farm, stoking fires to keep warm, turning the soil to keep from starving. Sarah shivered from something cold inside, something like death. Her mother had chosen a life that was doomed. Why had her mother sacrificed her ideals?

Sarah was thinking all this when she realized it was time for Zack, who had made miraculous progress in both attitude and book learning, to read from a textbook Jacob had found somewhere. She had not asked where.

When Affey nodded, Zack began. His presentation was impeccable, his recitation so precise that Sarah could not hold back her pride. She looked directly at the captain as if to say, "See what we can do?"

Up front someone giggled. Zack read on, both feet planted firmly on the floor, *Hillard's Second Reader* held at the proper viewing distance, his voice crystal clear. Suddenly, she heard her own stunned intake of breath. Affey clasped her hand over her mouth. Zack was reading from memory. He had memorized every word for his presentation. The book was upside down.

When the program ended, the Union men applauded. The children were dismissed; outside in the schoolyard, the children beamed, their brows still glistening with nervous perspiration as they served lemonade.

Sarah spoke directly to Colonel Moore. "The children will make more progress when books arrive."

"I'm sure," he said, but without the interest she wanted to hear.

"And slates. Slates for each child would help greatly," she added, not letting the moment go.

"Supplies should arrive in the next few weeks, ma'am." Colonel Moore tipped his hat. "If you will excuse us, I must converse with

Captain Wilcox about those very items. The captain is returning direct-ly to headquarters in Beaufort so if you will excuse us . . ."

The two men walked toward the back of the building.

The children huddled around, whispering, until Sarah shushed them with a finger to her lips. She motioned that they should follow Affey inside. Then keeping to the edge of the school building, she tiptoed to the back, flattened herself against the wall, and strained to hear as much as she could.

"How did headquarters take it?" Colonel Moore asked.

"The report of my reconnaissance was well accepted. The Department of the South recognizes the difficulty with the approaches to the rail line at Adams Run." The captain's voice was so low she had to move closer. "I explained that the topography and soil presents a most difficult base for such an operation."

"Did you remind them of the fiasco when we tried to get to it by cross-ing the Coosawhatchie? Hell, they'd have to dispatch a brigade up here."

"I pointed out, as well, that the tributaries of the North Edisto are mostly deep, crooked, and sluggish."

"They're damned swamps. That's what they are."

"I explained the need for naval assistance since the operation would become more tortuous as we approached the mainland."

"So, bring 'em on. That's what I've been waiting for. I'm not about to tangle with the Confederates without our warship guns to back us up." Colonel Moore waved his arms.

Sarah leaned against the building to regain her composure then walked rapidly to the front of the building in time to smile as the offi-cers walked toward her. Moore's stride was noticeably more determined. "The captain here will requisition slates, as I have requested."

"Do come anytime," she told him. The officers walked away, and where their horses were tied, the men talked briefly. The colonel clam-bered up, bid farewell, and spurred his horse in the direction of Seabrook Plantation.

The captain bowed from the waist, holding his wide-brimmed hat behind him. Apparently his arm had healed. "I, too, must take my leave," he said. "Permit me to thank you for dressing my wound. God has His wondrous ways."

"And I, in return, thank you for providing protection and safety while Affey and I do the Lord's work here." She forced a light, confident smile.

"Tell me . . .Miss Edings . . .is your work here satisfying?" He stood with a wide stance, his hands still holding his hat behind his back. Was he having second thoughts about her story? Did he suspect she was a fake? His eyes told her nothing.

"The children are responding exceptionally well," Sarah said, fidgeting with her crochet collar, condemning herself for her nervousness. She was making too much of his presence, she thought. It's just that she'd been away from male companionship for so long, and she was reluctant to admit it, but the captain was extremely handsome and very interesting.

"Then, learning is exciting for your students? You have found it possible to teach slaves to read?" He laughed and for a moment Sarah thought he might be teasing. She tossed her head and turned to go into the schoolroom, where Affey was leading the children as they sang "The Battle Hymn of the Republic." That song should impress him, she thought. He stopped to listen. But it was the tenor voice soaring above the rest that impressed him. It was Zack's voice, high and pure, echoing in the woods.

"Of course they can learn," she said. "Just as I expected." She tried to shrug, suggesting this conversation was over, but Captain Wilcox made no effort to leave. "Will you walk along the path with me, Miss Edings?"

Had he guessed that she was an informant, duty bound to gather information and deliver it to District Headquarters? For a moment she could not breathe.

He seemed too serious. "Do you know that I worry about you?"

She was conscious of his strong body and heard his words but didn't know what to make of his sudden concern.

"Oh, Captain Wilcox, why would you worry about me?"

"I told the colonel you were my cousin. I did that to protect you, and I feel responsible. You know, Miss Edings, I had never smelled wisteria until that day we rode to headquarters. Did you know that?" He paused to sniff the air, then he said, "I shall always remember wisteria and the day you rode beside me in the cart. Shall we walk?"

There was a time when something like this would happen on a cool piazza after a night of dancing and too much scuppernong wine punch, and she would flirt and act coy. And if she tingled all over, and the man was sweet and wonderful and had the right pedigree, they might disappear for an hour in a stowed-away skiff or a darkened carriage.

She was in no mood for recreation. Not now.

"Tell me, Captain Wilcox, are you proud of what you are doing?"

He seemed taken aback. She could see the shock in his face. Then he narrowed his eyes and came close, so close she imagined him taking her shoulders with both hands, shaking her body, and shouting, "Enough of this pretense. I know you're a spy, damn it. A Rebel Rose like the one in Washington. They've taken her to prison, you know. She'll be hanged for treason."

He stood very still.

"I must go," she said, reaching for her watch, indicating it was time to teach her students. "The children are forming words already."

"Then, you are satisfied," he said.

"I find working with the children extremely satisfying. The possibilities are exciting." The truth in her words surprised her. Each day brought amazement that her charges could live through turmoil and still dream of a future.

"And the rewards?"

"The rewards are endless." She stood with her hand shading her eyes.

"Please, don't go," he said, his voice filled with a need, a plea for friendship, and something in his eyes that seemed to say he had absorbed all the war he wanted and was wondering why he had joined up in the first place. "I brought you something," he said. "Do you like poetry? I brought you *Don Juan* by Lord Byron, his best, I think, an epic satire. He depicts a world filled with love and passion but a world that appears as confused as ours."

He held out a small book, leatherbound and gold leafed, and her mind shut down. She closed her eyes. Who was this man? What did he do in his other life? She'd like to see all this from his side, from his point of view. Then after the war, they'd meet in Saratoga Springs and she'd listen to what had happened to him, like a friend or maybe like a sister. She'd say she had enjoyed meeting him. She had wanted the best for him all along. But for now she had to force herself to say what had to be said.

"Captain Wilcox, it is not my intention to appear ungracious," she said, "but I live every day amid the destruction of life in a place I loved. I teach the children of slaves who may never have a future with all the confusion. My family cannot help them, as they cannot help themselves. I have lost everything. I'm not sure I believe in anything at all. I'm in no mood to read of love and passion and desire."

"Take this as a gift, please."

She accepted the book without looking at it, overcome with thoughts of the past. In that other life, love was important, but love and joy and that thing called sweet desire had disappeared with the war. Her past lay in shambles, dying around her. She couldn't bear to look at his face and stared instead at the sand at her feet.

"I want very much to see you again, Miss Edings."

"You may visit any time, Captain Wilcox."

"I am personally having readers shipped from Milford. Please accept them as a token of gratitude. Should you need anything, anything at all, I am presently attached to Expeditionary Corp Headquarters on St. Helena Island. You may find me there." He bowed low, took her hand, and kissed it.

Without answering, she turned and strode through the shadows of oak and Spanish moss, the book in her hands, her jaw clenched. Once inside the door, she leaned against the wall, not sure her legs would hold her up.

Quickly she reminded herself that her duty was to the Cause. She could not allow herself to fall for a Union officer she would never see after the war and would not care to know. She was here to keep everything she loved from sure disaster. More than that, she was here to do the honorable thing. She was here to spy for the Confederacy. She raised her head as the slow drone of the ABC's filled her head, then she stiffened her legs and walked as if in a daze into the schoolroom.

In the back corner of the cabin, Sarah sat on the straw mattress she shared with Affey. Newspapers and military reports were spread out around her. Jacob had returned from Port Royal with an armload.

The news in *The New York Tribune* was not good. General Beauregard, the hero of Fort Sumter and victor at Bull Run, had lost the Battle of Shiloh. The battle began before dawn, General Albert Sidney Johnston died about 2:30, and under Beauregard it had become a confused mess.

Her eyes blurred as she read: three massive waves. . .a mix of units. . .commanders did not know. . .command went sideways. . .exhausted army. . .final stand.

Her head swam as she read about the defeat. General U.S. Grant's counterattack slammed into the Confederates at dawn the next day. Beauregard retreated. Grant claimed victory.

Oh, what costs. Twenty-four thousand men killed or wounded. This war would not be quick and clean. She felt weak.

But it was the railroad story that caused Sarah to hold her breath. The south was also losing control of the Memphis and Charleston Railroad, the trunk line that connected the states from east to west. Her father described it as the longest connected rail line in the world, and it was falling into enemy hands. Sarah shuddered to imagine Union soldiers marching into Huntsville, wrecking the repair shops, and destroying the company books.

Her father owned stock certificates in the Memphis and Charleston. When the line opened, he had taken a barrel of salt water from the Atlantic and poured it into the Mississippi with great pomp and circumstance.

She stared at the newspaper report. Already one hundred fifty miles of the line was useless. From Chattanooga to Memphis the rails had been heated and twisted.

Long after she had gathered up the papers and blown out the candle, she slept fitfully. She woke when she heard the low, sad wail of a steam engine over on the mainland. It seemed to be a fading, desperate sound. She sat up and tried to stare through the darkness.

Across the river lay the glistening tracks of the Memphis and Charleston feeder line, and in her mind loomed a cloud of sure disaster.

CHAPTER

Seven

"Y ou sure you want to go? Bluecoats are patrolling the Dawhoo River," Jacob warned. "Skirmishes taking place on Little Edisto."

For three months now, in a businesslike manner the two of them, the daughter of a white plantation owner and his former Negro slave driver, had been conducting a courier service. Jacob was keeping his end of the bargain by confiscating northern newspapers and Union reports. When possible, he listened to conversations and dutifully repeated word for word what he heard, even adding details.

How many of her messages were important to the Confederates over on the mainland and how many were extraneous? Sarah did not know, but she had been taking care of her end of the bargain by staying behind and teaching.

It was well into May and her contact had asked her to come personally to Adams Run. "You have nothing to worry about," she assured Jacob. "Affey can take care of all students. If we leave early tomorrow morning, we'll be away only one day."

Still, Jacob seemed hesitant. "We'll make it back in one day if we don't get stopped and searched."

"Why should we be stopped? The patrols are accustomed to seeing you on the water."

"Some days they stop everything on the water. I don't want anything to happen."

"Affey will do a good job making me into an old woman."

"Sometimes, missy, you act like the bluecoats won't touch you."

But she knew Jacob would take her with him. Every time he delivered packages, she indulged in an orgy of guilt. She'd reprimand herself for being selfish and single-minded. But then she'd remind herself of the rail line that needed to be saved, and she'd feel reckless and proud.

Last week Sully had wrapped the package in food, the week before in bread, always tying everything with string.

Sarah insisted she take the risk and travel to Adams Run. Jacob made plans and today when Sully told them goodbye, she handed Sarah the package wrapped in raw fish the children had caught the day before.

"We'll be bypassing Steamboat Landing," Jacob said. "We don't need to take a chance with the Yankee soldiers lollygaging around on the docks."

Neither was he in the mood to talk, so she watched quietly as he guided the longboat through narrow unnamed creeks he knew so well. They passed dilapidated houses, neglected fields, collapsed corncribs, and burned out cotton barns, and then he wound the boat through shallow marshland where alligators, snakes, reeds, and mosquitoes thrived in thick plough mud.

Murky waters like these, she thought, should hold back Union troops who tried to advance this way, but she watched at every turn for bluecoats. Before long, she shrugged and gave up. The memory of the day the vicious Yankee tried to pull Affey out of the boat drained away the joy of this trip, and Sarah sat slumped in the center of the boat.

At midmorning, when it was time to make a quick crossing to the Toogodoo, she cleaned the dark cream from her face, packed the faded long-sleeved dress in a bag, and discarded the padding Affey had used to give her a fake hump. She removed the bonnet and prepared to meet Colonel P.F. Stevens, her contact at Military District Headquarters.

She would hear news from Edgefield, from her parents and her friend, Lucy Pickens. It was the colonel's friendship with Governor Francis Pickens that had led to the delivery of Lucy's jewels.

But another part of her was anxious as she stepped from the longboat to the wharf. Why had he asked her to come? Was there dire news from home? Some tightly held secret about the war? More bad news?

The colonel welcomed her with a kiss on the cheek and held her arm as they walked to the end of the wharf, then he placed her hand in the crook of his left arm and strode beside her across an open field. Gray smoke coiled and spiraled from behind a row of dingy white tents. Knotted together, a group of recruits cleaned equipment, spun the chambers of their weapons and sighted down them. Some were currying their horses and examining hoofs and coats.

"This group marched in two days ago," he said. "Most are from Spartanburg County. Some from Anderson and Newberry."

But they stood at attention when the colonel passed by. A brotherhood, she thought. Colonel Stevens had recruited them, brought them here to get them ready for war, and already they were bound together by fear of losing.

Sarah looked at the recruits and felt apprehensive.

From somewhere in the woods came the constant beating of a drum interrupted by the persistent rattle of musketry. Practice rounds, she told herself.

After they passed the sentries and sat alone in a large tent under the pines, she took a deep breath. A servant brought coffee and that gave her a chance to mask her growing anxiety about the news from Edgefield. But her parents were well, the colonel told her.

"Jacob keeps me informed of your whereabouts and your safety when he delivers the packages. We are much obliged. But I worry about you."

He sat erect, a Southern military man in the grand style, she thought, an officer in the Confederate States Volunteers. He was dressed in his gray wool short coat. "New uniforms, Sarah, bought with money from Mrs. Pickens' jewels. New uniforms and more importantly, new weapons. Enfield rifles arrive each day by rail."

"You were successful in selling everything?"

"Oh, yes, my dear. After your delivery, Trenholm and Company took the said package to London where European Royalty paid dearly for her rubies and the crown our First Lady wore at court."

"Lucy? Is she well?"

"Our governor's wife spends her days playing with her precious Douschka and her evenings charming her husband's political detractors. The governor has made himself so unpopular he might not get a vote if the election were held now."

Sarah sat staring at the colonel and pondering the strangeness of the life she had known upstate. It was unimaginable now, but evenings at the governor's plantation in Edgefield had been filled with gaiety and laughter, and it was during those months that she had met Lucy. Sarah could close her eyes and see Lucy standing behind a silver samovar each night, serving Russian tea to Carolina politicians, flirting with them to satisfy their egos.

The memory of Lucy Petway Holcombe Pickens struck her hard, and she thought of the night Lucy whispered, "I want you to deliver jewels to the coast. The rubies, the crown the Tsar gave me. Francis thinks the gesture will endear him to the military. His position has merit."

What else was she to do? The nearest thing to fighting for the Cause was the daring and excitement Lucy offered. So, without any effort or discussion, she agreed. Now, sitting in the military encampment with muskets firing and smoke drifting through the trees, she hoped to God her work mattered.

She had thought her work as a courier and teacher would weave itself into a pattern, and her whole being would swell with a sense of pride, a renewed conviction that the Cause was right. Instead, she felt almost numb about the war, the Cause.

Moments passed before she realized she had been looking into space. Quickly she returned to the present. "Your message said you needed to see me. You said we needed to talk."

"Do you have a Union pass?" The colonel bent his head low and furrowed his dark brows.

"Yes, from the officer in charge of the troops garrisoned at Seabrook."

"The Union colonel believes your story? He honestly believes you're teaching the slaves?"

"I *am* teaching, yes." She rolled her eyes as if not believing it herself. "Teaching is a perfect cover," she said.

She wanted to say, "I owe something to Jacob and Sully and the children." But she said nothing. The colonel would not understand, but she was teaching on principle now.

"I'll be frank," Colonel Stevens said. "We need firsthand information from Hilton Head, Department of the South, the Union calls it. Your pass as a teacher is perfect. We need someone with Union credentials who can move from island to island freely. Will you go to Hilton Head?"

"To Hilton Head Island?"

"Up to this point in time, your information has saved the rail line. But it would help us resist a future advance if we had some indication of Federal troop numbers to the south. As you know, the coastal defenses depend upon rapid concentration. We try to concentrate what we've got, but we don't have many men to put on the line. Last month when President Davis signed the Conscription Act, most of our able-bodied men enlisted for the duration, which pretty well depleted our volunteer units."

"My brother. Do you know? . ."

"He mustered into Colonel Jenkin's Palmetto Sharpshooters. They've left to join Wade Hampton. Some enlisted with Kirk's Rangers. If the Union knew the weakness of what's left with our coastal defense, they'd attack up and down the line, and we couldn't hold them back."

"The men I see today seem able," she said.

"The men you see today were plowing fields along the Tiger River a week ago. We don't know what they will do when it comes time to fight. As I said, we don't have enough men left in case of an all out attack. That's why I asked you to come today."

"What can . . .?"

"I know it's risky, but you took a risk when you brought Mrs. Pickens' jewels. The results are all around us." He patted his saber and nodded toward the recruits polishing shiny new rifles. "If Jacob agrees to take you to St. Helena Island or Hilton Head, will you go? From there you can gather specifics about ground forces and troop movement. We need numbers, sightings, and reinforcements coming into Port Royal, anything that indicates troop movement. Given numbers and time, we can concentrate our men and plan our strategy."

"Are we in immediate danger?"

"We have reason to believe they are considering a landing on Little Folly and Morris. They might be planning an artillery siege on Charleston. We do not know, but until something momentous happens, we plan to detract them. We can keep their forces busy."

"Colonel Stevens, I have to tell you I would be putting my position as a teacher in jeopardy, along with Jacob and his family who are protecting me."

"Don't think the danger has not occurred to me, Sarah, but the quicker the war is over the better. I firmly believe the Lord will be with you," he said.

She looked at the colonel, saw regret in his dark eyes, and remembered that he was superintendent of the Citadel and in command of the cadets who fired on the Star of the West. Her mother believed those were the first real shots of the war.

Now, Colonel Stevens was gathering and training a regiment of volunteers, timid and untrained farmers who were all afraid, and against them the Union would have no trouble at all if he didn't whip his men into shape in a hurry. But something in Sarah made her wonder if his belief was wearing thin and, along with it, most of his zeal. Were they both working for a cause that might be dying?

Colonel Stevens stood abruptly. "I'm afraid I brought you here under false pretenses. The men would be surprised to see a pretty young woman arrive in camp from the islands. I thought it better not to say you were there teaching. The troops think, or rather I led them to believe, that you are a Florence Nightingale, a ministering angel for the comfort of the sick."

"You told your troops I was a nurse?"

He hesitated. "I suggested that you came from Charleston with stops on the way from Wadmalaw Island where there are three hospitals. We have five here."

"Colonel Stevens, I am no Florence Nightingale," she said as they approached a row of summerhouses that looked like hers at Edings Bay. These houses, too, once echoed with the hoops and hollers of children playing hopscotch and tag and ring around the rosy.

She held her breath, dreading what she might have to face. But of course this was not the Richmond she had read about in the newspapers, where boys in soiled gray poured off rail cars by the dozens. Around here she'd seen no walking wounded with legs wrapped in bloody linens, but she had read about the casualties. There had been skirmishes up and down the coast. Eight killed and twenty-four wounded in January.

"No fresh wounds today," the colonel told her. "I promise. The scourge of the camp presently is nothing more than an outbreak of measles."

"No typhoid?"

"Typhoid has taken its toll. Fifty fatal cases in the last three months."

The rooms inside the first house were light and airy, and there was only one young man with a wound to display. His arm was bandaged. "Yes, ma'am, I'll be fit as a fiddle any day, ready to re-load my rifle and crack away at the enemy the first chance I git." Those struck with nothing more than measles laughed, and she smiled, too, and wished the soldier with the wound a speedy chance to carry out his brave resolution.

In the next house, she made a round through a room of boys with measles, trying to act as if she were accustomed to cheering the sick, and when they asked her to sing, she refused, but smiled her best smile.

The doctor who met her at the next house spoke quietly, almost apologetically. "We have in this house a Union prisoner," he said, "but we attend to him with as much care as if he were one of our own. His wound is serious, but he seems cheerful and grateful. Will you visit him?"

The word "prisoner" sent her reeling, and she thought perhaps there had been another skirmish, perhaps Captain Wilcox had run into another picket or tried to cut the line.

Perhaps . . .perhaps . . .

Her mind was gripped by the agonizing thought that the wounded man might be Captain Wilcox. What would she say? Would he look at her and laugh that today she was a nurse? Yesterday she was a teacher. How could she explain?

An orderly was busy dressing the prisoner's wound. Cloth, pins, and other paraphernalia lay on the cot.

The doctor whispered, "His name is Silas Gollither, a Pennsylvanian by birth."

She opened her fan, squared her shoulders, and slipped back into her role as a Florence Nightingale.

"I'm told our doctors are treating you well."

The prisoner smiled broadly to hear a woman's voice. "They treat me well indeed, madam," he said, blinking, choking back the tears of homesickness but keeping his jaw stiff.

Well, why had he joined and come to the South? Had he come because he really wanted to do something about slavery? Did he still believe war was the answer? Or was he beginning to question the destruction, the confusion? Seeing this Union man, she remembered Preston Wilcox the day she rode in the cart beside him, the day he introduced himself quite formally, handing her a bouquet of flowers. She had tried to read his face and had seen nothing but confusion. She saw it now in the prisoner's face. *Private Gollither, go home. Forget this war. Go home to your family, she wanted to say, looking into his eyes. Go home. Go home.*

"It's a strange time we live in, Sarah," Colonel Stevens said as he walked her back toward the wharf. "We minister to the needs of men who cause destruction. We destroy our homes to save our homes and shed our gentility and even our moral sense to preserve gentility and morality. I'm afraid the price we pay will be measured not with bodies but with our souls."

The colonel seemed to be speaking more to himself than to her. She touched his arm.

"Let's pray the end will come soon," she said.

"This is farewell, Sarah. When my ranks are filled, I will leave for Virginia. I will leave instructions with Jacob."

She stepped into the boat, and Jacob took up the oars. She could tell he was anxious, and soon the boat was skimming toward the island in the night breeze.

When a sharp Yankee voice carried over the water, Jacob whispered, "Be still. Don't move."

"Whacha doing out here?"

Jacob did not answer.

"You that nigger waterman? Okay. Go on."

For hours she pretended to be asleep, but she stayed awake, her thoughts churning about so she couldn't feel the mist that covered her face and soaked her cloak. There was a time when Colonel Stevens marched into Governor Pickens' office with crystal certainty about the Cause, a time when she was surrounded by people who acted as if the question of state's rights was easy to settle. But today the colonel seemed weary, drained, and dispirited, as if he believed the war could not be won or the Cause not worth fighting for. She wondered, too, because the conflict was not just a question of state's rights; it was more than that.

The war was about slavery and human dignity and honor. She knew this in her heart. She suspected the colonel knew it, too.

CHAPTER

Eight

"Sharecropping." Affey's voice had a lilt in it. Her eyes sparkled. "It's Toby's share of the cotton crop. His crop. His very own. Can you believe it?"

Sarah gave Affey a controlled nod then continued her work: straightening chairs, dusting tables, counting and putting away slates. How should she answer Affey? What should she say? Affey had traveled to St. Helena using the pass and now burst in after school, aglow with the news that Toby was receiving a share of Sea Island cotton.

"His very own crop." Finally out of breath, Affey stood still.

Sarah counted the slates twice then sat at the desk in front of the room and looked at her. "What are you talking about?"

"I told you. The Northern plantation owners call it 'sharecropping.' If the crop is good, Toby can sell his portion and make enough U.S. dollars to pay for next year's cottonseed outright. If he's thrifty, he can save his profit from year to year until he saves enough to buy the land."

Sarah leaned back in her chair. "I'm not sure such a thing can work."

"Why wouldn't it?" Affey took time to take a deep breath. "You know Toby. He'll make it work. He can swing an ax, cut wood, and stay behind a plow longer and better than anybody."

Actually, Sarah knew Toby only as a gentle and efficient field hand on her father's plantation, but she knew how much Affey cared for him. She looked at Affey and thought about the rumors that contraband could work for wages on St. Helena, that they could "sharecrop" as

Affey called it, and her throat ached. What was going to happen when the promises were broken? "I just don't want you to be disappointed."

"Disappointed? Why would I be disappointed if Toby bought his own land?" Affey moved around the room as if in a trance. "Think of it, Sarah. We can buy our own land." With her arms raised, Affey moved slowly, losing herself in her joy. Then she began spinning and twirling, her happiness so contagious, Sarah forgot about her misgivings and couldn't help laughing along.

On her second turn around the room Affey grabbed Sarah's hand, and before Sarah knew it, she was spinning and twirling and laughing with Affey, both of them swooping to the right, turning this way and that, raising their hands like graceful ballet dancers. Sarah felt youthful and lightheaded.

"Remember the wild geese we saw flying across the bay?"

Affey turned on a pirouette then stopped. "Oh, yes, I remember. Why?"

"That's what your life will become when all this is over. You will be free as a bird winging its way along the coast, its wings open to the night."

They stood and looked at each other, both remembering a lifetime ago. When the moment was over, Affey walked to the door. The sun was crimson as it dipped into the marsh, and there was something about the angle at which Affey bent her head, Sarah thought, something about the curve of Affey's neck and profile that reminded Sarah of herself before the war.

Lighthearted, filled with promise, and, oh, so innocent.

"I'm happy for Toby," Sarah managed after clearing her throat. "I'm sure he will do well, and you should be proud of his skill, his determination. Go tell Sully your news. She's waiting to see that you returned safely."

"Oh, I almost forgot. Toby is learning to read. I met his teacher. I visited the school. She wants to meet you." Affey reached in her pocket for a piece of paper. "Here it is. A written invitation. She says you may come anytime."

Affey left and Sarah sat at her desk stunned at the coincidence. District Headquarters needed information about Union troop movement to the south of Edisto. Here was an invitation to visit St. Helena. No need to darken her face or hide in the bottom of a longboat. She was a teacher. How interesting it would be, Sarah thought, to meet the teacher she'd read about in all the northern papers. They said Laura

Towne could not be satisfied merely sewing for the Union soldiers, not even working as a nurse.

What would Laura Towne really be like? According to the papers, Miss Towne had volunteered with the Freedmen's Aid Society of Pennsylvania and come to the South to plant Sea Island cotton in a venture the papers called the "Northern Experiment." Laura Towne was also a teacher. Newspapers described Laura Towne as part teacher, part doctor, and part plantation overseer. A Renaissance woman, Sarah decided.

Colonel Stevens needed troop numbers. She needed an excuse and here it was. She was mentally sailing to St. Helena. The invitation burned her hands.

Besides that, she wouldn't mind appearing at the captain's headquarters, surprising him, and thanking him. After all, he explicitly said Field Headquarters on St. Helena. He said he wanted to see her again. Hadn't he given her a gift? Hadn't he ordered these slates, which arrived only yesterday?

Oh, she'd be wary. Conflicting images of Preston Wilcox flitted across her mind. She saw a cunning spy who'd come to cut the rail line. But she also saw an innocent man whose heart had gone out to her by sending slates, ordering books and actually visiting her school. Which was the real picture?

She tried to summon anger. All she felt was excitement. Yes, she'd go to St. Helena, she decided, and she felt dizzy just thinking about the trip.

Human activity ended early in a swamp as dark as the heart of Africa. Frogs took over, and thousands and thousands filled the air with songs, especially after a rain. If not frogs, cicadas that sang with an ominous beat, a native cadence. Bats darted. Wild turkeys made their final clucking sound. Then darkness closed in like a mask upon the face, and silence came.

Sully said there were panthers. Only once had Sarah heard a scream. The children slept through the humanlike cry, but she sat straight up in bed. Affey gripped her arm and Jacob went to the door and hummed his song, "Nobody knows . . ." Then all was quiet.

Sarah lay on the straw mat planning her trip and listening to sounds she had never heard in her other life. At this time of night at the plantation house, there would have been music, her mother playing the piano and her father joining in with a heartfelt rendition of "Gentle Annie." As always, thoughts of her father stung Sarah with the memory that one day he was sitting at the piano singing and looking deep into her mother's eyes. The next day he had become violent and suspicious and unreasonable. Then, after he heard the Yankees had invaded Port Royal and his island could not be protected, he never sang again. He sat now in a stupor upstate. Sometimes he couldn't speak.

It was too dark to read, but she held the book the captain had given her, and now she couldn't stop picturing Captain Wilcox the moment he'd offered her the gift. Why did he give her a book of Lord Byron's poetry? And who was the girl in the miniature, the picture in his haversack?

She had used him and sometimes she felt bad about that, but across the South, women were gathering information from Union officers who were carelessly chattering. Governor Pickens admired Mrs. Greenhow. His office was abuzz with stories about informants and contacts, women delivering messages out of patriotic devotion, which meant she was one of many who were listening and passing along what they heard.

The cicadas stopped singing. The sounds of the night grew quiet. She didn't remember falling asleep, but when she awoke her heart pounded in her chest, and the swamp was exploding with wild and discordant noises she had never heard before.

"What is that?"

"Sully's chickens," Affey said, matter-of-factly.

"In the middle of the night?" Whatever was causing this disturbance was not normal, she knew that much, and was possibly dangerous.

"Someone's out there," Affey said calmly.

The lantern sent out an uncertain glow, and in the light Sarah saw Sully beside the door holding a rifle. "Where's Jacob?"

"I saw him slip out the back door. Where's your revolver?"

She gave Affey the Colt. For no reason at all Sarah remembered the look on the captain's face when he gave her the weapon and called her "his cousin."

"I have nightmares about men in blue coats." Affey was nervous. "We run and run, but we can't get away."

"It could be tack horses or wild boar on the loose," Sarah said as calmly as she could, thinking it could also be young hotheads from the mainland, white men who liked the idea of taking the law into their own hands. She knew the danger.

A shadow appeared. "You all hurry and get dressed. Stay quiet. I don't want my babies waking up and crying."

"What's going on?" Sarah yanked her day dress over her shift.

"Miss Sarah, they's lots a white folks fighting in this war that is bad people. Bad people. Sometimes they come to take what they want. Last Sunday they raided a praise house on John's Island," Sully explained. "Somebody heard 'em coming, and the men ran out and hid in the trees. All they got was horses and wagons. Nobody was hurt. So, all week Jacob and the other men been taking turns watching. He got a signal about an hour ago."

Sully returned to the door. "Come over here with me," she whispered. "Crouch low. Just watch."

Outside two white men trudged toward the cabin, their hands held high over their heads. Zack walked in front holding a lantern. Jacob marched behind holding a shotgun to their backs.

"Aw right, aw right," said one who wore regular clothes with a blue-gray Confederate cap far back on his head. The other wore a brown hunting cap with a floppy brim. Tin cups dangled from their belts, but no bowie knives or pistols. Those belonged to Jacob now.

Renegades. Dangerous men who would hate a white woman for teaching these children as much as they hated slaves. She was certain of that. Or mercenaries, raiders who would say they were looking for guns and ammunition but were really looking for buried silver, Confederate money, railroad stock certificates, anything they could sell. The war meant nothing to them but money, even if they had to steal what they sold.

"We done give up, I told ya," one white man yelled, turning, glancing backward toward Jacob.

"Keep moving," Jacob ordered, not missing a step.

"Don't we know you?" the other asked. Jacob touched the shotgun to the small of his back.

When the white men reached the steps, Jacob walked close enough to let them see his face. "Maybe you know me and maybe you don't," Jacob said. "But I know you. You from over at Rantowles. Everybody knows you."

"Maybe it's so and maybe it ain't." The prisoner's tone was ugly and dangerous.

Sarah recognized the men as mean enough to raid and plunder and terrorize Negroes, and she hated them for it. They were also mean enough to put a price on her head for teaching them how to read. One word about a white woman living in the swamp with people they considered runaway slaves would bring violence, if not from these renegades then from others on the mainland. She didn't want to imagine what they'd do if they learned she had organized a school. And if they learned she was the daughter of a planter who had fled upstate for his safety and was nowhere around to protect her, well . . .

She shivered, thinking of what could happen to Sully and the children. Before she could decide what to do, Affey shoved her into the orb of light at the top of the steps.

"What are you doing out here?" Sarah forced herself to sound calm.

Her white, cultured voice came at them, and the muscles in the white men's necks flexed. Their jaws clamped shut.

"What time is it?" one finally spoke, as if to change the subject.

"It's late," Sarah said.

Jacob backed into the darkness, still pointing the shotgun at their backs.

She took a guess. "Are you the Toller brothers?"

"What if we are?" The man who answered sounded the less insolent, she thought. The younger one perhaps.

"Your brother wants to know what time it is," she told him.

He reached in his breast pocket for his timepiece.

"If you have a box of matches, strike one."

He lit a match and held it.

"Well," she said impatiently, "tell him the time."

He read the Roman numerals, announced the time, and then cleared his throat.

"If you are the Tollers, I don't understand why you'd be out here roaming around at two in the morning." She made sure her voice sounded innocent, almost hurt by their unannounced appearance. "You came all the way from Rantowles? Is that where you're from?"

"That's right."

Just as she thought. Rantowles was a hornet's nest of small farmers, all known for their temper and cruel treatment of slaves, although few could afford to own even one, and they knew the coast like the backs of their hands. Bands of roaming outlaws like these terrified planters. She remembered the rumors, the warnings. A slave uprising had not frightened her father as much as outlaws like these.

Suddenly there were dark men, a dozen or so coming into the clearing behind Jacob, clustering about, then moving stealthily toward the renegades. She wanted to call out but her voice was frozen with the realization that the freedmen could turn their hatred and resentment into slaughter. Surely Jacob would stop this. She could only watch as the men descended upon the raiders.

"Do something." Affey nudged her forward. The dark men kept coming, revenge on their minds, the need to strike out blazing in their eyes.

"Do what?"

"Anything." Affey pushed her. "Just stop it. Whatever they have in mind."

Jacob's lantern blinded her when she stepped out into the light. Her palms felt wet.

"It's like this," she said, as if she had been in charge all along. "Jacob and his men are going to see that you get back over to Toogodoo Creek."

Jacob raised his hand. When the dark men stopped, she felt weak with relief.

"We are going to see that you get home," she said, "but we will keep your bowie knives and your firearms. We need those to protect ourselves from the Yankees. You may pass the word around that we don't have anything of value. The Yankees have already taken it."

She moved down the steps as if to imply these next words were private, just between white people. She lowered her voice. "When you get home, if you breathe one word about seeing me, I will send my men to find you. You may not understand how ruthless they can be, but they will make sure you do when they find you. And find you they will." Before the renegades could speak, Affey came into the light.

"You men hungry?"

They stood mute while Affey handed them cold biscuits and baked sweet potatoes left over from supper.

One said, "Thank ye," then spoke quickly, as if he felt the need to talk now that he was safe. "Wish old Beauregard was here. He would'a run the Yankees outta here like he did at Fort Sumter."

The other outlaw agreed. "Yeah, they'd run from Beauregard like scared rabbits."

Sarah wanted to curse at them, wanted to swear at these two white men. She thought of the thousands of bodies, dead or wounded or missing at Shiloh, all because of Beauregard and could not manage even a bare smile. She turned and walked back up the steps.

Long after the raiders left with their hands up and Jacob's shotgun at their backs, Sarah lay awake. Her work as a courier was in jeopardy, her safety compromised. Well, if the renegades spouted off about her, everyone was in danger. Gradually, she convinced herself these renegades wouldn't dare tell what they saw. They'd left looking like scared rabbits themselves.

Yankee soldiers worried her most. Once during the night, she thought she heard the sound of their sharp tongues, and she stayed awake expecting them to come marching from the Seabrook House, voices shouting, sparing no one in their search for her. They would take her to Colonel Moore who believed she was here to teach the children. What then? If they accused her of befriending the raiders and Colonel Moore dismissed her story that she was here to teach the slave children, she was doomed.

She had no one to blame except herself.

No one to blame.

CHAPTER

Nine

~

*S*arah left for St. Helena in a soft June morning shower that was more like fog than rain. The boat, a skiff that Jacob had added to his ever-growing fleet, made a swishing sound as it moved down the Ashepoo, a river Sarah had known well when she was young and flirtatious and lowering her eyes discretely to abide by the rules.

"Wind's coming out of the East," Jacob said.

She nodded. "Good day for a sail."

"Just right for crossing the sound," Jacob added.

"That it is," she sighed. "On a reach all the way."

In these waters Trent Lowndes had first wooed her, and she had tried to fall in love with him, knowing her life would be locked into a true course if she married Trentholm Pinckney Lowndes. As his wife, she would have ruled over an immense plantation on Wadmalaw Island in addition to a city house in Charleston. They would have sailed to England on their honeymoon trip. Then after a year or two, she'd have watched him struggle to take on the responsibilities of a Sea Island plantation.

Trent would have hated the land.

He'd never have fit into the mold of an island planter. There would have been turbulent years of married life. He'd finally give up trying to be content. He'd resent her, resent everything about the marriage. She would become a chain around his neck. He'd take out his rage on her and the slaves. The passionate man who pursued her on these waters would have shut her out, blamed her for what his life had become. He would have hated her.

She'd seen this story unfold among friends whose marriages turned to disaster.

"Here they come," Jacob announced.

"Who?" Sarah blinked, trying to pull out of her reverie.

"Up ahead. Here they come. A Yankee water patrol." Jacob seemed ready for combat. "You stay calm, now. Say everything just the way we practiced." Jacob seemed to like giving her directions.

She took a deep breath, rehearsed her lines, and when the Union boat rowed alongside the skiff and Jacob lowered sail, she was prepared, and gave her speech.

"Good morning, sirs. I am on my way to visit Miss Laura Towne, the teacher on St. Helena Island. She is expecting me. I am the school teacher from Edisto Island, and we are already late, so you will excuse us if we just move right along here," she said, waving her fan in Jacob's direction, indicating that he should move along, and that as her servant, he should do so immediately.

The officer recovered too quickly for that. "Not so fast, ma'am. St. Helena is Union territory."

"Don't you think I am aware of that?" She laughed with just the right note of haughtiness and ignored the stunned looks that came at her.

"Then I'm sure you have a pass," he said.

"Of course I do. I have a pass from Colonel Moore of the Forty-Seventh, which is garrisoned on the north side of Edisto. The paper is here in my reticule. If you will allow me?" She glared at him, purposely taking her time opening the drawstring on her purse, then she handed him the pass.

The officer handed it back to his aide. "Take a close look, Private Miller. It might be fake." With his other hand the officer smacked at a mosquito flying near his neck.

She fanned delicately, but in her mind there was a vision of being turned over to the general at the Department of the South who would banish her from Beaufort, St. Helena, and Edisto, indeed from the entire coast with orders that if she attempted to return, she would be hanged. Then, there was always Old Capitol Prison. According to the papers, several ladies had recently been given two hours to get ready for a carriage that would pick them up and take them to prison.

"Sir, why would I use a fake pass? You are here to give the Negroes freedom. I am here to educate. Do you not welcome those of us who come to educate them?"

The officer was speechless. He did not know what to make of her and did not dare to glance at Jacob, black and silent, and sitting behind her, so close she could hear him breathing.

Putting the fan to her lips, she whispered to the Union officer quite confidentially. "The Negroes have come straight off the plantations, you see, and they are lazy and shiftless. If we can teach them to read and do their numbers, then you will find their condition much improved when freedom comes."

She paused, half-smiling, hoping she had shocked him. If she could make him uncomfortable, perhaps he would wave her off.

"She could be a spy, sir. I hear they're everywhere, especially young, pretty ones like this lady."

"How ridiculous. Do I look like a spy?" She put her hand to her heart, fluttered her eyelids, and smiled one of her dazzling smiles that usually softened the opposition.

"I have an idea. Why don't both of you come along with me to the Pennsylvania School? You can visit the children with me. Better yet, you can meet Miss Towne, and she can give you proof that I am, indeed, the teacher from Edisto."

"Well, ma'am." The aide seemed interested in such a side trip.

The officer held up his hand. "I'll handle this," he said, mopping his brow and settling his hat. "I'm sorry, miss, but you must wait until tomorrow."

"Oh, but Miss Towne is expecting me any hour now. Please, just a short visit to the school. I insist you come with me." She sat stiff and straight and waited for their answer, knowing very well they had little enthusiasm for spending an hour or any time at all in a classroom of Negro children. She knew their kind. She'd spotted them lolling around at the Seabrook House, those who had come south for adventure and were appalled at what they found.

The officer was overly apologetic. "I'm sorry, ma'am, but duty demands that we stay in the vicinity of the Ashepoo."

"Oh? Then you must be expecting the arrival of something special. Perhaps more gunboats and troops."

The aide responded eagerly. "Oh, no, ma'am, the troops are heading to Savannah, but it's a big day on Hilton Head what with the ceremony for Major General David Hunter. He's been commander of the Department of the South for a month already. But there's a big dress parade today. Reporters from London and New York. Everything."

Sarah widened her eyes, feigning ignorance. "Is that true? I'm afraid I don't have access to the news that you have. I've been on the island since February with little chance to travel, what with the children to teach and so many runaway slaves."

The men murmured something to each other, ashamed now and anxious to make amends. "Then you must take this newspaper with you, ma'am," the officer said. "It came by boat this morning. Mr. Greeley and his gang give the new Department of the South quite a lengthy write-up."

She couldn't help smiling. She'd promised to gather information for Colonel Stevens, and this Union officer, bless his heart, had just handed her the latest edition of the *New York Tribune*. She recognized the banner. Inside this paper were troop numbers, battery sites, names and all. Everything she needed.

Quickly she turned her smile into a frown. "Oh, but it's too bad you cannot go with us. You would enjoy a day with the children." She pulled her tiny gold watch from the pocket at her waist, snapped it open, as if to check the time. "May we go now?"

The officer looked relieved. "We do apologize for delaying you, ma'am. The weather should be clearing. You can be on your way now. Have a good day and a safe voyage." His hand went to his hat, as if to salute.

Jacob lowered the boom and hoisted the sail. The wind took them across the sound so fast, the skiff whipped up a trail of foam.

Jacob beached the boat. Sarah stepped out onto St. Helena, and when she looked up, another man stood waiting, a man so black he looked purple in the hot haze of the afternoon sun. There was a look of mirth in his eyes.

"Toby." Her heart told her to throw her arms around him, but her head said she was a white woman and the daughter of his former owner. She stood battling a sea of confused emotions, not knowing what to do.

He smiled and nodded to the magnificent strawberry roan beside him. "You think you can handle this beauty, Miss Sarah? It's been a long time since you handled a mount like this."

She took the reins and stroked the horse. The men greeted each other with handshakes and warm smiles. Then Jacob left for Hilton Head, promising to visit longer when he returned. As business partners, she and Jacob had held a meeting. It was decided that she would visit Laura Towne. He would pretend to be making deliveries to the Department of the South, all the way to Hilton Head. He'd never been that far but he'd try.

Jacob left and Sarah said nothing for a moment then remembered her manners. "I'm sorry, I don't know what has come over me. Affey sends you a surprise, Toby. It's in the bag here. I promised I would not reveal her secret, but I can say that she has been sewing every night since she learned about this trip."

"And Miss Towne sends you her greetings. She's expecting you. I told her I'd get you there quick, but roads are not good like on Edisto. Here they're mostly tracks."

Toby packed away his gift; they mounted, and as he rode beside her, she noted the fields here were green with cotton and filled with people working. "Are these sharecroppers?"

"No, Miss Sarah. They work for wages. After they work this field, they'll come up my way. I sharecrop a field with the overseers. Sharecropping's a mighty good thing."

She wondered about that but decided not to press the issue. She had neither the understanding nor the temperament to discuss the northern overseers nor their ill-conceived notion called "sharecropping."

Toby stopped his mount in front of a small brick building. "School's here in the Baptist Church. But Miss Towne took the children down the road today for music," he said.

"For music?"

"Yes, ma'am. To the Chapel of Ease."

She felt a pang of resentment. Or jealousy. Life on St. Helena seemed almost normal. Perhaps it would have been better if Edisto had become an agricultural experiment. Her father's land would now be cultivated. Crops planted. Jacob and Sully would be working for wages.

Affey would be with a real teacher. Pianos and organs would not have been used for firewood.

Yanking at the reins, she turned the strawberry roan sharply, as if to leave this place, then it struck her: thoughts like this would serve no purpose. She must not let resentment get in the way. How could she think such a jumble of frantic thoughts? She had looked forward to meeting Laura Towne. This was no time for indulgence, no time for self-pity.

A horse sounded in the distance. Hoofbeats grew louder and Sarah waited, her arms dangling at her side.

And when Laura Towne appeared, she emerged out of a whirlwind, looking unimaginably fit and riding sidesaddle. All at once, the northern teacher jumped to the ground, lovingly stroked her stallion, and graciously shook Sarah's hand.

"I'm sorry I'm late. I got caught up in the music with the children, as I am prone to do. You are, of course, Miss Sarah Edings." Miss Towne's voice matched her handshake: firm, honest and indefatigable. Sarah had trouble finding her voice.

"Yes," Sarah finally managed, "thank you for the invitation."

Miss Towne handed the reins to Toby, nodded to dismiss him, then changed her mind and called him back. "Oh, Toby, I forgot my book bag." She turned to Sarah. "Affey told me so much about you. I couldn't wait to meet the teacher from Edisto. Thank you, Toby. I seem to have the habit of taking books and magazines everywhere I go."

"It's a good habit," Sarah said amid the sudden activity and her own nervousness, which she hoped did not show.

Roses, azaleas, and oleander bloomed beside the steps of the old brick building. Laura Towne took one deep breath, bent her head to smell the violets pinned on her lapel, then cast her arms to the sky.

"Oh, this air, this truly fresh air. Let's sit together on the steps and breathe it in. It's one of the charms of living here. But I don't have to tell you about living on an island, do I?"

"The weather is perfect," Sarah sputtered.

Laura laughed. "I arrived only a month ago, and already I am taken with island life."

Two workers walked by on the sandy road. Sarah thought they must be wage earners. Laura waved and they waved back in the same way.

Sarah asked suddenly, "And the children?"

"Well, they were troublesome enough at first, since they had no idea of sitting still and paying attention. I think that was typical for children who had never been schooled. Oh, they scuffled from time to time and struck each other. Why, some got up from their desks whenever they chose, made their curtsies, and walked off to the field for blackberries."

Sarah smiled. Both women laughed.

Miss Towne continued, "But they'd soon come back to their seats with a curtsy. They didn't understand me, and I couldn't understand them. I must admit, after two hours and a half of effort each day, I was thoroughly exhausted. But, I am beginning to get them manageable. Yes, I am happy to say school is running smoothly now."

A sudden sense of camaraderie came over Sarah, and she was suddenly embarrassed that she was only pretending to be a teacher. The irony of the situation hit her. She'd been discovered inside Union territory, and a sudden impulse had somehow thrown her into the classroom. She was not prepared. She'd never dreamed of teaching; in fact, it was something she was hardly suited for. The truth was she was a fake, but she didn't intend to tell this to Laura Towne, no matter how this visit went.

Sarah chose her words carefully. "Thanks to Affey, our school, too, is running smoothly."

Laura Towne bent over, snapped off an oleander blossom, and smelled it. "Please tell Affey that Toby had his first lesson in writing last week and his progress was astounding. He held his pen perfectly the first time. It is a pleasure to see him learn." She picked another blossom, then turned to Sarah. "Does it offend you that former slaves are learning to read and write?"

The question shocked Sarah, but accustomed as she was to snide remarks from her Yankee cousins in Newport, she'd learned how to handle probing questions about the South. She answered in a flash.

"No, no. I'm not offended," Sarah said, smiling and holding it until her lips hurt. "I believe in education for all people."

Laura Towne looked pleased. "I can tell we're going to be friends. Would you have some lemonade, Sarah? I made some this morning using the most delicious lemons from one of our plantations. I brought a jug for the children. I'll just go inside and get glasses. If you'll excuse me."

Bright, sharp sunlight shone down on the steps, and a feeling of relief overcame Sarah. She moved slightly to feel the sun on her face and spread her hands behind her, and when she did, Laura's book bag tipped over. Its contents spilled down the steps.

She rushed to catch Jane Austin's *Pride and Prejudice* before it landed in the sand, then a book of poetry, and a book of essays by Ralph Waldo Emerson. She caught a copy of the *Liberator*, the fiery abolitionists' magazine that her uncle mailed south to her mother, and leafed through it quickly, remembering that it denounced slavery and everything in the South and brought about heated debates around the dinner table.

"Looking for something special?" Laura returned, pushing open the screen door with her foot while holding two glasses of lemonade.

"Your book bag tipped," Sarah said, embarrassed that she was caught leafing through the magazine. "I gathered everything, but how rude of me."

"Oh, not at all. Take what you wish. Perhaps you would like to take the *Liberator?*"

"I think not. It was my mother's belief that its editor has done little to increase harmony between the North and the South," Sarah said, as casually as she could.

"He is a stubborn crusader for what is right. He stands against the evil of slavery. As I do. That's why I came here. What about you, Sarah? Where do you stand in all this? Do you suffer from pangs of guilt? What is your part in all this? Why do you teach?" Laura took a sip of lemonade. Her head moved slightly, as if she were hearing another voice, one only she could hear.

The noonday sun blazed. A red bird flew to find its mate. When she spoke, Sarah tried to keep her expression impassive. It took some effort. "I am not as oblivious to the cruelty of slavery as you may think. Many Southerners have for a very long time been torn apart by its indignities."

Laura finished her glass. "I must say what I feel, Sarah. I hope you will not be offended by it."

On guard now, Sarah felt her stomach tighten. If she admitted to being offended, what good would it do? She'd hear the sermon no matter what. The same sermon she had heard from her uncles and her cousins. "Please, go ahead." Sarah put her glass of lemonade down. She hadn't touched it.

"This war is deplorable," Laura said stubbornly. "We did not want the trouble to get to this, but the South seemed determined to take us to war."

This statement came at Sarah so matter-of-factly, it confused her, but she took her time. "I'm afraid it is not so simple, Miss Towne, no matter what the abolitionists said."

Laura shrugged. "Perhaps not. But it seemed that way to us."

Sarah flinched. "The South looked for a peaceful settlement, but could not find it."

Laura's eyes narrowed. "But did the South look in the right places? Did you use the right people?"

The mood on the steps was not the same. Laura's words had changed it, but Sarah carried on. "You have a laudable message," Sarah said, "but it's a little late to be delivered to me."

"It is never too late to make changes in the way one thinks, the way one feels," Laura said, and again she moved slightly as if she were hearing another voice.

Sarah wanted to cry but was too angry. She composed herself but her heart was pounding. "You must not assume that all slave owners were cruel and unfeeling. My family had deep and abiding feelings for everyone on the plantation, everyone. . ." Then words came tumbling out, words that surprised her but somehow she felt compelled, as if she were spitting out a vile and sickening taste. She couldn't stop. It was as if something in her had snapped.

Didn't Laura know that she had taught Affey to read, which was against the law? That her mother, Josephine Edings, had spent hours. . . . no. . . days alleviating pain and sickness in slave quarters? Her father had portioned out ample food and well-constructed housing year after year, even when cotton prices plummeted. If times were hard, he borrowed from the cotton factors in Charleston and Savannah. But he always took care of his slaves. He had given Affey's mother her manumission papers. Her father had freed all his slaves before he fled.

Why, then, did she feel so guilty?

Yes, there were early mornings when the dew was heavy and some poor runaway endured a whip wielded by her own father. Yes, her stomach turned and she couldn't eat for days. But what could she possibly have done?

She had never raised the whip. Not ever. Not ever.

Why, then, did she feel so guilty?

Sarah put her hands to her lips. Up in the live oaks across the road, the wind hardly turned over a leaf. The sun burned her skin, and her breath seemed carried away. She had not meant to say this, not to anyone, ever, and felt incredibly tired. Tears flowed down her cheeks.

Laura placed an arm on her shoulder. "We are all guilty. You do not carry the burden alone. It is a burden our country will carry for a long, long time."

Silence pounded in Sarah's ears. She drew in a breath. "I'm sorry. I don't know what came over me."

"Don't be sorry. You can help make things right. Teaching is important. I pray every day that what we do for our students will mean something. In many ways we share the same dream."

"But I . . ."

"It's a high price you pay." Laura said.

"No. . . I . . ." Sarah sat imagining each morning when hope shone brightly in her students' eyes. Then she thought of the afternoons when gratitude moved them to embrace her as she stood on the steps and told them goodbye. And thinking of the children's faith, their belief that there really was a future, bright and shining and filled with possibilities, she could agree with Laura Towne that teaching was important. But would she ever be able to catch the vision Laura had? And if she caught the vision, could she hold on?

"I believe it's a small price I pay," Sarah protested in answer to Laura's declaration.

The women stood as if they knew the meeting had ended. Laura held out her hand. "I'm quite sure we will meet again. Please take the books," Laura said plaintively.

Sarah accepted the books and walked across the yard with determination in each step.

Yes, I teach because it is important.

I teach to make things right.

CHAPTER
Ten

Riding beside Toby across St. Helena and listening to the steady gait of the strawberry roan, Sarah couldn't help remembering all the times she had ridden with her father over fields like these.

"Look to your left," William Edings would announce. "Now, look to your right. It's all Edings land, my dear, the most fertile land in the state of South Carolina. I don't have the exact acreage in my mind, but it's Edings land, Sarah. Edings land."

Then he would bring his horse beside hers, stand up in the stirrups and look at his fields with such genuine love and devotion that even now as she recalled the moment, she felt warm.

Miriah was too dignified and serious, too womanly to ride over the fields, but Sarah enjoyed riding and learning secrets usually handed down from father to son: how to preserve the finest seeds of Sea Island cotton and how to determine the best time to plant; how to deal with cotton factors whose power in the Charleston financial community could wipe out an island planter in one season.

After a moment, her father would shout, "Race you to the high road." She would ride beside him as if riding with the wind, the green fields disappearing behind them.

"You sure about this, Miss Sarah?" Toby's question shook Sarah from her daydreams.

"I'm sure."

Why not visit the captain at his field headquarters while on St. Helena? She wanted to thank him for the book of poetry. *I would like to see you again, Miss Edings.* A faint ripple swept over her just thinking about him. He'd asked her to walk down by the creek when he visited her school, hadn't he? He'd be surprised to see her here on St. Helena, but he'd be warm and welcoming, and after a while he would ask her to take another walk, nothing more.

His words had intrigued her. His accent had amused her, and the fact that he, too, was a spy contributed to the effect. If he wasn't a spy, he was certainly doing intelligence work that concerned the rail line. Of course she was beguiled. Besides, he was the sort of man who became more handsome the longer she was with him.

At school that day she had closed off the opportunity to know him. She hadn't given him a chance because she was afraid he would see her for what she was. She wished she had taken that walk down by the creek, but she had been more concerned at the time about giving her masquerade away. Wouldn't it take just one misstep? One wrong word?

The decision to come by field headquarters was not hard to make. She had been fantasizing for weeks. She would ride up to the gate with Toby and when she introduced herself as the teacher from Edisto, she'd receive an escort who would then take her to Captain Wilcox's tent where the two of them would sit and sip a wine of the local muscadine grape. She'd lived the scene in advance.

She'd even thought about the conversation and chosen a topic that would reveal something of his background. Did he enjoy dancing? Did he dance with anyone special back home?

The girl in the miniature. Who was that girl?

She'd even considered the tempo of the afternoon and planned for meaningful pauses to allow the captain time to ask her questions, hopefully of a personal nature and something she could answer openly and honestly.

If all went well, he would ask if he could come again to Edisto, and she would say, "Yes, of course." Her answer would be followed by a silent exchange, then they would talk of the days that stretched ahead. Then more silence. She'd not be in a hurry to leave, and when she did, she would not lower her eyes but stand close and lift her head in a most reserved way.

However, the reality of the afternoon proved to be a jolt, an event she could never imagine.

Union Headquarters loomed ahead. Toby dismounted at the gate, looped the reins of both horses around the nearest post, and reached for her hand. The sentry that appeared glared disapprovingly, but Sarah tossed her head, looked down at the private, and dismounted with a flare.

The Union man pursed his lips and sucked at something in his mouth, as if he'd been caught eating and something was caught between his teeth. "Well, well, well, what can I do for you?" His look was cagey, as if he recognized her kind. He knew she was a woman of the night, one of a thousand harlots following the army for money.

She forced herself not to blink. "I have come to inquire about the condition of Captain Preston Wilcox. There was a skirmish on another island. I cleaned the captain's wounded arm. Oh, nothing of any significance, but I did what I could until he could find his unit. I am the teacher on Edisto."

He looked at her, not with contempt, certainly not with recognition, just indifference; then he turned and walked toward a small shack that she recognized as a field barn for wagons and harvesting equipment. It was now a guardhouse.

"So, you're a schoolmarm."

She followed him inside where she spied a cot, a table made of a barrel, and a chair on which the sentry plopped unceremoniously. Behind him was a roll top desk.

"Yes, I am a teacher."

His lips curled up at the edges. "You think that's the best way to fight this war?"

"I do, sir, and Captain Wilcox recently contributed a number of slates to my school. He and Colonel Moore of the New York Forty-Seventh have been quite generous. I have come to personally thank him."

The sentry looked at her for a long time, as if he didn't know if he believed her. She could see doubt in his eyes. Finally he shook his head.

"You looking for Captain Wilcox. Well, I'll have to do as a substitute because Captain Wilcox ain't here."

She looked at the roll-top desk behind him, the cot, then back at him. Then she just stood there trying to breathe.

"I'm sure he said he was attached to field headquarters . . ."

"Oh, you're in the right place, ma'am. You've come to headquarters for the Expeditionary Corps, and Captain Wilcox was here all right. He's one of them field engineers that could draw maps."

At that moment a palmetto bug crawling across the roll top desk caught her attention. It flew to the corner of the room and disappeared.

She was confused. "You mean he's gone south to prepare for the siege on Savannah?"

The sentry shrugged and scratched his unshaven chin. "Well, ma'am, his unit went south. You right about that. They went on south to fight more sand and mosquitoes, but the captain you asking for went home. He went to a hell of a lot better place. He went north. Captain Wilcox was one of the lucky ones, ma'am."

Why would the captain leave without saying goodbye?

She clasped her parasol with both hands. "The captain must have felt quite well, then. The wound, I mean. His arm must have healed. Before he left."

"He seemed well when he pulled out."

"And when did that happen?"

"About a month ago." The sentry's voice softened, as if he realized he was dispensing information that was hurtful. "You see, ma'am, he'd only signed up for one tour of duty."

Through a tiny window she saw people outside working, contraband who lived in Union territory and were free to work for wages. Perhaps some had run away from plantations on the mainland when they heard the Yankees were coming. All seemed serious, grateful to be working.

There must have been a long silence, and when she looked up, Toby was at the door. "Miss Sarah, you all right?"

"I am fine. It's just that I'm sorry to miss the captain. I wanted to thank him for the slates," she said to anyone who could hear.

The truth was she had read the book of poetry Preston Wilcox had given her, imagined the world of Don Juan, and in her heart of hearts allowed herself to believe a liaison between herself and the captain was possible.

"Well, ma'am, you just too late." The sentry looked away then back at her. "His three months was up. I'm sorry."

"I'm sorry, too," she said, swallowing and tossing her head to overcome a sudden feeling of nausea. "I was simply in the area."

She walked outside, the sunlight striking her skin as harshly as the news about Preston Wilcox. She had acted too hastily, and for that reason she condemned herself. Her naivete had cost her this, but she had played her part well. She was sure he did not know she was an informant. A

Union captain would have no purpose at all in saying he would like to see her again except to tease. It was vain even to hope, worse than vain to expect, to see him again.

Toby brought up the horses, eyeing her with a curiously sad expression. She made no attempt to explain but mounted and urged the strawberry roan forward. As they rode to meet Jacob, her legs were shaking.

When she was out of sight of the encampment, she cried.

Back at the kitchen table Sarah clipped articles from the *Tribune* and jotted down all the information she and Jacob could piece together. With her notes complete and the package concealed in a loaf of Sully's cold bread, Sarah wrapped everything in salt sacks, then tied everything and sewed on weights. If a patrol came too close, Jacob could drop the bread, package and all, in the river.

With a second note written and folded until it was no larger than a thimble, she met Jacob out by the well. "The package is ready, but I have written a second. This one is for the sentry at Adams Run. It tells him to take you directly to Military District Headquarters. My contact left for Virginia. My note says you have strict orders to speak to no one except the commander, whoever he is."

Jacob stepped back and opened his lips as if to balk at the idea, but before he could speak, Sarah said, "You have nothing to worry about. Tell him the new general who has taken command seems intent on closing Savannah River before turning his attention back to Charleston. That, at least, is good news for Adams Run."

She placed the second note in Jacob's hand.

"And, Jacob, tell the commander this is my last endeavor. My heart and soul is with him, but there is little more to do over here. Ask him, please, to understand."

Jacob had the grace not to question her. "I don't know what you're thinking about doing," he said soberly, "but I do know one thing for sure. The children need you."

A lump formed in her throat. The sense was upon her that what she was doing didn't matter. She'd returned believing she was doing what was right. Her courier service had given her a purpose, a reason to feel she was part of the effort, but she didn't want that purpose any more. She had the children to think about.

Jacob continued to study her without speaking. She could tell he had questions he wanted to ask, but he said nothing.

Finally he shook his head. "You need some rest, Miss Sarah."

"It's my last endeavor. Tell the commander it's the last package. But wait. Sully's sending along a little basket of her applejacks. Tell the doctor at the hospital we thought the boys might like some applejacks."

Jacob smiled. "I remember well how Mr. Daniel liked Sully's cooking. I remember how he'd sneak into the quarters when he smelled her baking. You want me to see if they can send the basket along to Mr. Daniel?"

"My brother is in Virginia."

"That's the truth. If I know your brother, he's in the thick of it."

"Indeed. Take Sully's applejacks to the boys in the hospital. Tell the doctor to deliver them to the sick and wounded himself."

It was getting late. The sun was setting when she stood at the edge of the water waiting for Jacob to return from Adams Run. The blue sky turned to shades of mauve and lavender and the sun to crimson as it melted into the green marsh. A sudden wave of confidence swept over her.

No more deception.

No masquerade.

She was here to teach.

"I'm my own person now." She spoke the words as if it were a great awakening. The shadows deepened and spread over the marsh and she breathed deeply, allowing the feeling to sink in. The whole world seemed still and calm, with only the sound of the reeds whispering to her: you are your own person now.

She'd met a Union officer, accepted a gift from him, and taken a loathsome journey to thank him. Perhaps she would keep the book. Perhaps the day would come when the shock of his disappearance would fade. Then she would take the book out and read poetry again.

How long she'd been lost in thought she did not know, but the sound of Jacob and the longboat startled her and within seconds he appeared and stepped onto land, smiling.

"Sully's applejacks never got as far as the hospital," Jacob said. "Your Colonel Stevens met me. He won't go to Virginia until the end of the month. He says Sully will just have to bake some more."

She somehow felt safer hearing that the colonel was still at Adams Run.

"Are there many boys hospitalized?"

"Ten with typhoid."

"Any wounded?"

"None today," Jacob said, securing a bowline to a tree.

"And my message about my last endeavor?"

"He understands. But he sent a letter. It's in here somewhere," Jacob said, feeling in his pockets. "Well, I declare, I must have left it in a salt bag."

"A letter?" News from her parents, she was thinking, almost dreading to hear what it could be.

"He says you should read it quick. In it he sends a message from the Missus Governor."

"Lucy? My friend, the governor's wife?"

Jacob searched for the bag he appeared to have hidden so well. "It's right in here somewhere, unless it's in the package I threw overboard when I saw the patrol coming."

"Oh, Jacob, do stop teasing. Do you want me to come aboard and find it myself?"

"Why, here it is in my vest pocket. I suppose it was here all the time."

Jacob lit the lantern and left it hanging in a tree. "I'll run along up to the cabin and let you read in peace."

For a long time she studied the envelope, imagining the colonel traveling upstate to beg for arms again, perhaps attending a grand occasion at the governor's plantation where Lucy would have worn her Chinese silk brocade with the stand-up collar, and whispered some secret message to be delivered.

Sarah opened the letter carefully and read by the flickering light.

Headquarters Third Military District
Adams Run, Republic of South Carolina

My *dear Miss Edings,*
   I *recently had the honor of traveling once again to the Governor's plantation called Edgewood, at which time his*

honor asked me what name I was giving the legion of infantry, cavalry, and artillery I raised for the defense of the coast and now command here at Adams Run. Taken as I was with the breathless beauty of his dear wife who stood nearby, I bowed as deeply as ever I learned under the tutelage of my dear, gracious and highly cultivated mother and remembering the First Lady's full name, Lucy Petway Holcombe Pickens, I answered, "The Holcombe Legion, sir."

Whereupon the Mrs. Governor unpinned a diamond broach worn upon her bosom to add it to the jewels she so unselfishly sent for arms and ammunition three months ago.

The purpose of this letter is to tell you that in Charleston on a June day, the First Lady will do the honor of presenting a beautiful flag to the Holcombe Legion. I now reveal the message she whispered in my ear on the occasion of my visit. She extends to you a special invitation to attend the ceremony in Charleston on that day and looks forward to spending much precious time with her friend.

P.F.Stevens, Colonel,
C.S.A.

She folded the paper slowly and held it to her lips. Lucy. She would see Lucy. They would talk, perhaps share more secrets, as they had those few short months upstate. The thought of spending time in Charleston was exhilarating. She missed her friends. Living on the island and being alone was not getting any easier.

She sighed and when she looked up, Jacob had come back or maybe he had never left. He was smiling.

"The colonel said you'd be needing a ride," he said. "I told him I'd be taking you to Charleston as soon as you're ready."

CHAPTER

Eleven

~

*P*reston Wilcox stepped from the train in Milford, Connecticut, at exactly seven o'clock in the morning. The powerful engine of the New Haven and New York line creaked and groaned as it steamed away. Warm air blew in from the sound beyond the boat works, and the familiar aroma of timber and pitch almost overcame him. He was home. He stood for a long time with his eyes closed, breathing in the air.

He had sailed for days along hundreds of miles of shoreline, following the Carolinas, Virginia, Maryland, and Delaware, knowing that all was not high hopes and noble purposes in the South. There was dissension among the generals, and suspicion ran rampant in the War Department. The ten recruits drilling on the green thought they were going south to fight a holy war. Preston's lips tightened.

Oramel Williams stood at the open door to his broom shop. John Beach, red-faced and out of breath, climbed into his wagon and passed by on his way out to the country, where, Preston was sure, old John was still experimenting with new varieties of seed. Already the streets were bustling. A maze of workers scurried to the factories.

The day before, Preston had missed the early accommodation train from New York and had taken, instead, the overnight steamer to New Haven where he picked up the local train at dawn. He slept little, if at all, on that leg. His uniform looked wrinkled, and he was in a sour mood until he stepped off the train.

Rather than walk, he sat on a bench outside the new train station, his portmanteau at his feet, and looked across to the Town Hall and the cupola and bell that Wilcox money had added some twenty years before. He remembered the celebration when the entire Wilcox family had stood on the green.

The urge to go to the house on Gulf Street all but overcame him, but he shook his head, reminding himself that the house belonged to his sister now, not him. When his wife died at the birth of their child, it was his sister who had stepped in to take over the household. It was his sister who nursed the baby and helped him bear the loss. It was his sister who encouraged him to go to the South to right the wrong called slavery.

"It is the greatest service one can give in these trying times," Alisha had said more than once.

Alisha, the rock of the family since their mother died of consumption, was a leader in the anti-slavery movement and as idealistic as all the other abolitionists in the Congregational Church. Her house was a haven for the outspoken. Radicals like Mr. Whittier from Springfield came to read his poetry and Charlotte Forten came to read her articles published in the *Liberator*. Alisha often kept slaves escaping by way of the Underground Railroad.

So, he had followed Alisha's advice, gone south among the slaves and the contraband. He rubbed his arm and thought again of the woman who bandaged his wound and how he learned in a few short months that Alisha's war was not exactly a holy crusade. It was also a place where the natural human propensity for the worst spewed forth. He had left the coast of Carolina a dismantled place of ruined fields. The drunkenness of the soldiers and their rape of black women appalled him so that he had written to Stanton at the War Department and reported the vandalism and violence.

Away from the pillage and the organizational inefficiency at Port Royal, he looked across the Jefferson Bridge in his home town of Milford and decided it would be best to meet his family on neutral territory, as neutral as the offices of Wilcox Manufacturing could be. The reason for this meeting still puzzled him, but the urgency in his sister's letter left little doubt that he should come home immediately. Their brother was arriving from California, and although his sister did not know the full story, she suspected Nathan was up to something. Like drawing their father into some kind of business scheme.

Alisha's letter was followed by a telegraphed message. "Imperative that you come. Take leave immediately." Neither he nor Alisha could forget the morning Nathan left for California. Neither could they forget the fear they felt when they heard the pistol shots over the waterfront, the signal that the ship that would take their older brother around the Horn to San Francisco was leaving. Their mother had cried and held the younger ones to her side.

"Don't leave like your brother. Don't leave me," his mother pleaded. "Stay and serve the Lord, children. Promise me. Stay and serve the Lord."

All the while his father had sat at the accounting desk. "Money is to be made in the West," he kept muttering, defending his investment of $1,500 and his decision to send Nathan to the California gold fields.

At first there were a few letters from Nathan telling about prosperous diggings, which their mother read and re-read, then tied in ribbons and put in her dresser drawer. Then there was nothing.

His father, along with the other Milford investors would soon learn they had been swindled. When they called for an accounting, they learned there was nothing left. Their resources consisted of thirty picks, sixty shovels, and a share in the bark on which their sons sailed.

His mother had coughed blood that winter. Even now Preston remembered the heavy velvet drapes that covered the windows, the musty odor of camphor, smelling salts, and his mother lying wax-like in the darkened parlor. He had always connected his mother's death with Nathan's ill-fated adventure.

Only once had Nathan returned, a prodigal son to his father, but a stranger to Preston who would not have been surprised if Nathan had come stalking down the street shooting from the hips. But Nathan had come home with a firm handclasp and the sharp gaze of an envenomed evangelist who spoke with missionary zeal about "uniting the country by rail." Nathan had returned to whip up enthusiasm for passage of a Pacific Railroad Bill. He had become a disciple of Theodore Judah, and willing to milk Wilcox Manufacturing of every penny.

Nathan was back.

Preston took out his pocket watch. Nine-thirty. In a few minutes the family would gather around the conference table. He'd sent a telegraphed message saying he would be late. His delay was intentional. He wanted Nathan to understand there was another Wilcox he must reckon with, and he, Preston, was equal to the task. No more Wilcox money would be squandered in the West.

Preston stood tall amid a flurry of warm greetings and enthusiastic handshakes when he entered the offices of Wilcox Manufacturing. He walked over to the elder Wilcox who waited at the end of the long table in the dark mahogany paneled room, thinking his father seemed older but his eyes were sharp, and his accent, brought from England fifty years before, less obvious.

After five years in America, Alexander Wilcox had given up boxing and followed his hunches to serve as errand boy, secretary, and accountant to a seafarer in Milford who ran for governor and lost, but who taught the young Alexander how to fight battles outside the ring and to save his money. When the financial disaster of 1835 struck, Preston's father sank his savings in manufacturing.

At first it was straw hats, wide brimmed with fancy bands for the ladies. Even now the straw-hat factory continued to expand under Alisha's skill-ful management. The company employed as many as five hundred hands. But it was shoe manufacturing that held first place in the company these days, because Preston some years ago had insisted on using the newly patented sewing machine on a trial basis. It was a move that increased production by twenty-five percent and ensured a lucrative contract for U.S. Army shoes.

When Preston decided to join the conflict in the South, he placed the shoe factory under the management of his close friend and trusted family banker, Seth Clarke, who could not be present today.

While one of Alisha's runaways served coffee, Preston remained animated, but he was thinking of the woman he had left without telling goodbye, a teacher whose life might be in danger if he didn't return soon. Back at the station, another train whined and hissed its way into Milford then steamed away.

Already Nathan was starting in on his story of returning from California by steamer and making his point that the Central Pacific line went only as far as Sacramento.

"Lincoln allowed the Pacific Railway Bill to die in the first session of Congress. The man is proving to be quite a disappointment to us." Nathan sighed.

Alisha agreed. "I, too, am disappointed with his administration. We expected an immediate Emancipation Proclamation which has yet to come and cannot come too soon."

"Passage of the Railway Bill was part of his Republican platform,"

Nathan said, "but with the different factions pulling. . . ." Nathan furrowed his brow and jerked his head toward his sister. "Yours being one of them. Lincoln's attention is diverted. For that reason Judah had gone to Washington to push for legislation on the railroad."

Preston watched his father's face take on a reddish tinge and said quickly, "And you have come here to find investors. It's your job to keep Judah's creditors at bay."

"Why, yes, Preston. I am on my way to New York to make our case before the Vanderbilt group. When the bill is passed, as I am certain it will be, we will issue first-mortgage bonds up to the amount written into the congressional aid bill. In addition, there will be sizable land grants written into the bill and additional subsidies that I am not free to discuss. There is no doubt that with ample investment from private citizens dedicated to the Northern cause, we can realize the necessary funds."

Alisha moved her foot impatiently. "Nathan, don't be naive. Do you honestly think Northern businessmen are going to take money away from our boys and the manufacture of their military equipment, clothing, shoes, medicines to invest in a railroad for the territories?"

A smile flickered across Nathan's face. "They will if they understand that the side with the rail line over the Sierra Mountains will win the war."

The elder Wilcox kept his voice firm. "I think you should explain to all of us exactly what you mean, Nathan."

"I mean," Nathan explained, "that the side with the rail line over the Sierra and into California will be the first to claim Nevada's silver and gold. And it is with silver and gold that the war will be financed."

"I suppose you are speaking of the Nevada territory?" His father's look concerned Preston, but it would be useless to speak out now.

Nathan seemed to smother a smile. "Why else would there be such a rush to add all the territories to the Union? The Comstock Lode has the richest silver deposit on the continent," he said. "It produces millions. That's why we propose immediate statehood. Old Abe likes the idea because he will need plenty more votes if he plans to pass the Thirteenth Amendment."

Case made. Nathan sat back, arms folded.

"So, what are you proposing?" Alisha spoke sharply.

"I propose that we sell our shoe manufacturing division. It is at high risk now that the center of leather goods is moving to Massachusetts. We sell and invest the capital where it will do the most good for us—in the Central Pacific. With the shoe factory out of his hair, Preston will be free to save all the black men, women, and children in the South. It won't take long."

As Preston thought of Jacob and Affey and the school children singing the ABC song, their faces shining, he spoke out. He could not hide his agitation. "Don't count on it, Nathan. The war may last longer than you think; and when it ends, our mission in the South may not be complete. There will be much to be done after the war."

"I think it is wonderful and noble that you have a mission," Nathan said, condescendingly, "but I do not believe you understand the situation. When you come back from saving the darkies, it will be too late. While you sit gathered with them around the campfire, other Northerners will have already made their fortunes."

Alisha appeared visibly upset. "I believe the greatest service Preston can make in these trying times is to give of himself. It is our duty to help free the people who have been exploited and abused for two hundred years."

"Come, come, Alisha, can a piece of paper that declares the darkies free really make any difference?" Nathan's question cut through the air.

Alisha squirmed in her seat, looking repulsed and shocked. "Preston was called to do his duty. Like our dear mother, he is the champion of those who groan beneath the hand of oppression and cannot speak for themselves. Thank God he is not like you."

Their father seemed agitated. "The war is not about slavery. It's about the sovereignty of a section of the country. They feel we in the North are infringing on their rights."

Preston decided if he pushed too hard, his father would side with Nathan. He and Alisha would vote against liquidation and reinvesting any capital in a questionable railroad deal and the vote would tie, two against two. Again he wondered why Seth Clarke was not present.

Within seconds he had worked out in his mind that the only way to save his division of Wilcox Manufacturing would be to stall for time. And yet, time was precious.

"I have only just arrived and I long to see my child," he said as he looked around the room. "Let's stop bickering about war and slavery and enjoy being a family for the time we have together."

Alisha looked relieved. "Oh, yes, let's do visit the little one. We can meet again after our lunch. Don't you agree, Father?"

At the house where Preston and Emily had lived happily as man and wife for a year—their first and only year—Preston stood, letting his mind go back all the way to the day his world crumbled. After Emily died, he drove himself by day, then hurried from the factory at night to this house and to his child. Throughout the summer he kept it up, the work, the silence, the grief, and only when Alisha came to see the baby did he talk. Even then Alisha did most of the talking.

"Preston, you haven't slept for weeks. You avoid your friends and family. Look at yourself. You can't sit down even when I come to talk. Why are you doing this to yourself?"

"Emily counted on me to take care of our child. I promised."

"You will not be a good father if you keep this pace. You are tormenting yourself. Let me take care of the child."

"What?" He thought he'd misunderstood.

"Let me take care of little Emily for you. Just for a while. My Hettie can nurse her better than your nurse. Little Emily can grow up amid the laughter and singing and shenanigans that go on in my modest house. I know how you and Father feel about John because he is German and a simple carpenter, but he is a good husband and a devoted father. He would welcome the child."

At his wit's end, he desperately needed advice.

"Do you think it would be best?"

"God wills a thing and it's hard, but we must go on," Alisha had said. "Your grief is eating at you and me. Do something different with your life."

At the end of summer, after he moved Alisha and her husband, John, into this house, a larger, tighter brick structure on Gulf Street, he worked with his friend Seth Clarke day and night to teach him manufacturing. No need to worry about the financial end. Seth was a banker.

Then he wrote to his old classmate at West Point and learned that the War Department needed engineers to follow the first troops to the Southern coast, topographic engineers, responsible for reconnaissance, for mapping, and for assessing the resources. In November Preston was sent to Port Royal to discover the weaknesses along the Charleston and Savannah rail line. He reported directly to the Secretary of War.

Standing now outside the room where his daughter was playing, Preston stopped to collect his thoughts. He felt apprehensive, so fearful he forgot to hang his frock coat on the hall tree downstairs. Smiling sheepishly toward Alisha, he tossed it on the wooden bench outside the bedroom door, squared his shoulders, and trusted his daughter would love him.

The child was small-boned and delicate like her mother. She seemed healthy and plainly delighted to be part of Alisha's brood of three others--another girl and two boys, all older. The nurse, Hettie, placed the little girl in a chair and when Preston bent over, she showed a marked interest in him, as if she somehow knew he was her father. Hettie said she had taken two steps on her own today and pointed toward the primrose bush on the porch outside the nursery.

"Isn't she beautiful?" Alisha asked softly and a sad, sad wave of grief rolled over Preston, a loss he thought he'd conquered but was still so great, the emptiness wracked his chest and weakened his knees.

"She looks like her mother." His voice was husky, his mind flooded with memories. He had met Emily at a party, a distant cousin, fragile and demure. She was immediately devoted to him, and when he returned after graduating from West Point, he gave up his commission and his dreams. They married and within a month she was expecting. He had felt trapped. Now he felt guilty.

Alisha hugged her brood of three and gave instructions to Hettie. "Would you like to have lunch outside?" She turned to Preston. "I have something to show you."

She held his hand as they wandered through her newly planted herb garden. "Do you like it?" She pointed to her lavender and calendula, her rosemary and lemon verbena, all labeled with pride.

"Of course, I like your herb garden. Your lemon verbena is my favorite."

Alisha sighed. "Now, let me look at you. Really look at you. How are you?"

Knowing she did not need a response, he sat on the nearest iron bench, leaned back, and looked up at the clear blue sky, the sweet smell of herbs filling the air.

"War is taking its toll on you. It surely is, but we must believe in something else, something beyond grief and self-pity. God has His ways. It was God's will."

Preston rose and looked down at his sister. "I don't accept that. I don't accept what God did to me. I've learned not to give in. It's best to fight back in times of trouble. I despise slavery, Alisha, but I have learned to accept many things I despise."

"Oh, surely not the evils of slavery." Alisha looked visibly disturbed. "Surely you have not gone to the South and learned to accept their evil philosophy."

"I have met people in the South, yes. I've learned to accept the people as individuals, Alisha, while I detest the institution of slavery." Then seeing that his words upset her, he sat again and patted her arms as if to assure her. "I have met slaveholders, Alisha, and I tell you I cannot dislike them as individuals. They are our countrymen. We must remember the contribution they have made. We must respect their heritage."

Alisha moved away and spoke in a steady voice. "I cannot believe you said that."

"War changes a man, Alisha. I think now about my dreams. My dreams, not Father's, not Emily's. I hated manufacturing. You know that. I dreamed I'd follow the railroad. Oh, not like Nathan, not as a promoter, but as an engineer and a planner. We both know the promise I made to Mother. I saw the fear in her eyes when Nathan left, and I promised I'd not leave. Emily was here when I came back from West Point. She was waiting for me and . . ."

"What are your plans when the war is over?"

The silence was deafening. He sat on the edge of the bench wishing he could share his feelings fully, tell her about a summerhouse and a woman, but he knew Alisha could not understand. "I'm not sure. One thing is certain. I'd like to stay in the South."

"You can't mean that. Our wounded that come back say the coast of Carolina is wet and hot and mosquito-ridden. The danger of typhoid and malaria is ever present."

"A man loves it or hates it. When I think of the coast, I see wide-open spaces, a shoreline that slopes gently, not like ours. I see white chalky sand, soft to the touch and tall green pines standing along the shore humming in the wind. It is there that planters build houses safe from . . ." He stopped, realizing he was describing Edings Bay and the summerhouse and remembering Sarah waking up from her nap on the soiled settee in a highwaisted dress of blue, the color of her eyes.

"Is there something you need to tell me?" Alisha bowed her head, waiting for his answer.

"I'd rather bite off my tongue than hurt you, but I cannot go along

with Nathan's request.   I will need the profits from Wilcox
Manufacturing for investing in the South after the war. The need will be
great."

Alisha leaned toward him. "Do you have something in mind? Have you
met someone?"

He was aware of his own breathing. "She is a teacher on an island that
is devastated. The future there seems hopeless, but I can envision a
change."

Alisha breathed deeply before she spoke. "All our futures seem to be
changing in these uncertain times," she said.

"I will not give in to Nathan's schemes. I am deadly earnest. You must
believe me."

She looked into her brother's eyes. "I do. I believe you."

When the meeting resumed after the lunch hour, Preston and Alisha
felt prepared. An unnatural silence descended when Seth Clarke entered
the room. Preston had sent an urgent message, and Seth appeared only
seconds after the others were seated. When Nathan saw Seth, he looked
as if a boulder had struck him. The elder Wilcox rose from his chair,
shook Seth's hand, and stood leaning against the mantle under his portrait.

Alisha spoke so suddenly their father stared at her, as if she were speaking out of turn. "I have decided that I will have no part of Nathan's railroad
deal," she said.

Nathan's eyes darted from person to person.

"When the line reaches the summit of the Sierra, it will be the engi-
neering marvel of the century. You will have invested in the future."

Seth shook his head. "The project is unthinkable, absolutely impossible, and you are doing nothing more than promoting stock issues which
I predict will be worthless within the year. Theodore Judah is a madman.
He'll be lucky if he's bought out by those partners out there." Seth
Clarke's recent investments outside manufacturing were doubling in
value. When he sold, he sold his interest for cash. No one in Milford
questioned his judgment.

Unwilling to let Seth Clarke squelch his plans, Nathan went on the
defensive. "You are wrong. His partners include the likes of Stanford and

Huntington. Hopkins is treasurer."

Seth kept his voice even. "Can't you see what's happening? Theodore Judah is using you and your good family name to sweeten the government deals back here in the East."

Nathan banged on the table with his fists. "Opportunities abound for investors. Opportunities like land rights and government subsidies for the asking."

"You are wrong," Seth argued. "It is corruption that abounds."

Alisha's worry was the war, the crusade to free the slaves. "The time is not right to ask the government for subsidies."

Nathan's face turned beet red. "What do you mean?"

Preston stood across the table from Nathan. "She means you are expounding self-interest at the expense of the national interest. While you promote questionable deals in the territories, we are locked in a bloody war to save the Union. Our family will have no part in questionable deals in the territories."

As Preston sat he heard Nathan draw in a deep breath. "You are blowing the damned war out of proportion. It's nothing more that a nasty confrontation between fanatical rich planters in the South and equally fanatical do-gooders in the North, like our dear sister here."

"You go too far, Nathan." Alexander Wilcox spoke angrily and Preston tried to stifle a feeling of victory.

"Too far," Alexander Wilcox blurted. "I came to this country with nothing but the clothes on my back. I could have chosen the Crown, but I chose to become an American, and I believe that citizenship carries with it a responsibility. I do not believe the war is between fanatics as you say. It is about the sovereign rights of those who stood against the Crown. We must fight to keep our country together or our independence will surely be taken away from us all. No, son. We will have nothing to do with the rail deal out West."

The door vibrated. When Preston looked up, Nathan was gone.

Rolled in a thick blanket on the deck of a commercial steamer heading south, Preston knew he would not sleep. It was his third night out, and he lay looking up at the cloudless sky. In spite of the warmth of the blanket, he felt a chill. He reckoned it was only hours from daybreak and the ship was somewhere outside the bar at Charleston, perhaps closing in on Port Royal. The damp mist of the Gulf Stream moved over the ship like fog.

In a jumble of thoughts, he realized he was thinking of Sarah and anxious about her safety. He imagined the danger from the drunken soldiers garrisoned at Seabrook or from raiders or bands of lawless Negroes and gave up trying to sleep. He pulled himself up, his back resting against the bulkhead, and looked into the darkness that by his calculations would be the barrier islands south of Charleston.

He had left Wilcox Manufacturing safely in the hands of his friend Seth Clarke. Alisha would keep controlling interest while Preston was at war. The danger of losing the family business to Nathan's wild dreams was over for now.

The night before he left Milford, he had bounced his daughter on his knee and basked in her winning smile, looking into eyes that seemed to accept him as her father. Alisha played the piano for the children and "Big John" sang in his clear and lusty voice as the children clapped their hands. Little Emily had joined in. Back there the war seemed far away and unreal, and he had let himself believe there was hope.

But now, peering into the darkness, he knew the war was real, and the woman he cared for more than he wanted to admit was alone and in danger.

CHAPTER

Twelve

*L*ucy Petway Holcombe Pickens alighted from the open carriage with the elegance of a queen, a demeanor so regal the crowd on Meeting Street pressed forward, elbowing their way to satisfy their curiosity about the governor's wife. She had come directly from reviewing the troops on Sullivan's Island and was still dressed in her riding costume. It was made of black velvet, and she wore a large black hat turned up on one side with a long white plume as its only ornament.

"Three cheers for Mrs. Governor and the Republic of South Carolina."

"Hip, Hip, Hooray."

"Hip. Hip. Hooray."

"Hip. Hip. Hooray."

The entourage moved quickly inside Hibernian Hall. Sarah squeezed in among them. She had arrived early that morning and rushed to an inexpensive boarding house on Rutledge Street to change into her best visiting dress. Yesterday, before leaving with Jacob on the longboat, she had washed and starched the green striped skirt while Affey re-stitched the green military jacket and removed two torn gold tassels. Actually, Sarah felt rather resplendent as she stood inside the great hall where she had attended many a function with her Charleston cousins.

The crowd stood transfixed by Lucy's charm and her extraordinary beauty as she presented the flag to the Holcombe Legion:

> "I can find no words with which to thank your gallant colonel for the compliment he has paid me, in giving to his noble command the name I once bore. I feel assured that the noble motto inscribed on this banner, 'It is for the brave to die, but not to surrender' is but the expression of the spirit which animates the breast of every soldier in your midst. Patriotism ranks with us, as with the ancients first among virtues, and life is only worth keeping that we may perform the duties belonging to it.
>
> > Death comes but one to all,
> > Then how can man die better,
> > Than facing fearful odds
> > For the ashes of his fathers,
> > And the temple of his gods."

Lord Macaulay's poem, "Horatio at the Bridge." Sarah recognized it. The applause seemed to last forever. The flag Lucy presented was huge. Eight by five feet, one soldier whispered.

One Charleston lady standing next to Sarah said the flag was made from one of Mrs. Pickens' ball gowns. "The blue silk, I heard, the one she wore to court. Chinese silk. Nothing was too good for our 'Empress.'"

"The palmetto tree painted in the middle is perfect," another lady said, "and look, there's a 'Lone Star' for her home state of Texas."

Colonel Stevens accepted the flag and spoke eloquently. He was followed by an array of local politicians; then the sweet white-haired ladies from Charleston served dainty sandwiches.

Lucy went around the room speaking to the soldiers, smiling, and asking about their food, their families. When she left, and Sarah joined her in an anteroom, where, after warm greetings and a few awkward moments, they sat in handsomely carved chairs. Lucy smiled, happy to see her.

"Were it not for my duties as First Lady of the sovereign state of South Carolina, I would have come days ago to see you."

"You bring news of my family?"

Things were no easier for those living on the Butler Plantation. When Zeb Butler enlisted and followed Wade Hampton to Virginia, most of his slaves had deserted. There had been very little planting. Miriah herself had planted necessities such as vegetables and corn.

"And Father?"

Lucy's silence was so long and frightening that Sarah felt weak. "You must tell me. How is my father?"

Still, Lucy said nothing but rose and stood by the small window that looked out into a garden, as unkempt and war-weary as the rest of the city. Lucy sighed. "He thinks he is here in Charleston. He thinks he is visiting his brother."

"Our uncle left long ago for Mississippi."

"Neither Miriah nor your mother make any attempt to keep your father from believing that he is here in Charleston. It is better that way, Sarah. Believe me. He sits in the drawing room at Miriah's house waiting for time to pass, asking for nothing, just waiting."

Sarah could see her father as clearly as the day she left him upstate, a man who had tried to save his corner of the world, the only place he had ever known, and failed.

"And Mother?" Sarah stiffened. The war hovered over her family like a cloud of destruction.

Lucy's beautiful eyes lost all expression. "We are all doing what we have to do. Francis is governor in name only and that fills him with despair. The cocky Colonel James Chestnut and his council have successfully usurped the power of the governor's office. And Mary, his wife, whom I ignore at parties, continues to make snide remarks about me. I hate her for it."

"You don't mean that, Lucy."

"Don't I? It's their intent to strip Francis of his constitutional power. They contend that he is incompetent, and it is true that Mr. Pickens in despondent. But the problem is our state, which has a paucity of resources. Nevertheless, at the moment, I seem to be the only hope Francis has. Therefore, I must bow to the powers that be to keep my husband's political enemies at bay. I flirt openly with the weak little men who crowd around me and call me the *Fleur de Luce.*"

Lucy paused, took a deep breath and seemed to hold it. Then she added, "I do what duty and honor demand. I despise doing it, but Francis is too depressed, too self-absorbed with his dwindling power to help himself."

It was true; the governor was a surly and unfriendly man. Everyone whispered at parties: why would Lucy marry a bewigged man half her age? Some said it was because of his land, one plantation in Edgefield, three others in Mississippi. Others said she married Francis Pickens because he offered her a titillating social life, first in Washington, then at the court of Alexander II, where Pickens was ambassador.

Now she was wife of a governor. The Palmetto State had become the Palmetto Republic and Francis Pickens had become its leader, but his political fortunes were dwindling. Lucy was right. *The Charleston Courier* no longer supported him and, in fact, accused him of producing nothing but confusion.

Last night during dinner at the boarding house on Rutledge, Sarah had heard her share of jokes about him.

Lucy seemed so downcast that Sarah said only, "I'm sorry."

"The only comfort in all this mess is a little good talk now and then." Lucy's eyes brightened. "Once I led an enchanted life in St. Petersburg. Did I tell you?"

"Some things."

"Did I tell you that my darling baby girl was born in the Winter Palace?"

"Yes."

"That I danced the night away with the Tsar?"

"Yes, and that you had an audience with Queen Victoria."

"Oh, but fate plays cruel tricks when you are not looking, my young friend."

Instantly, Sarah was pulled into the secret Lucy once shared with her. Ah, Lucy had known love. Tragedy struck when her lover, Lieutenant Crittenden was executed while participating with General Narciso Lopez in an expedition to free Cuba. Heartbroken and withdrawn, Lucy had published a romantic account, a love story, and given a copy to Sarah.

"We must move on," Sarah said, thinking it best to reassure her friend. Lucy's bravado seemed to be faltering. But war had changed them both, Sarah supposed, in ways neither of them understood.

Lucy gazed out the window. "When my little Douschka is two, I will take her and go to a safe place in East Texas. I have family there."

"Douschka is happy?"

"Yes, and precocious, if I say so myself. I must consider her safety. Carolina will not be safe for us when. . .if the South loses this war."

"I would miss you if you moved away," Sarah blurted. "Please stay."

"Oh, but I refuse to grow thin and pine away in Edgefield." Lucy's voice was firm.

Sarah blinked and cleared her throat. "I apologize. I had no right to say that. You are still the First Lady. It's just that I detest all the separation between friends and family."

"Then promise me you will come live with us when Douschka is older. Or join me tomorrow when I take my leave. If the truth be known, there is little more you can do in Charleston."

Sarah smiled a weak smile. "I have other responsibilities here."

"Other responsibilities?"

"I have started a school on Edisto Island. Affey is helping. We are teaching the slave children, They will need to read and count their wages after the war. Children need to be prepared."

Lucy visibly drew back. "You are teaching the children of slaves? You and your personal slave? That is hardly what one would expect of a plantation mistress."

"Ah, but I am no longer mistress of anything, Lucy. My father's plantation lies in ruins. And Affey is no longer a slave. She is free." Sarah said this, rising from her chair slowly, almost stiffly, and taking a deep breath, knowing what she was about to admit could end their friendship but hoping that Lucy would accept the meaning and purpose of her new life. She decided to speak her mind and added, "I have come to believe that no human being should ever hold another in bondage."

Lucy's lips opened, but she continued her polite attention; then she placed her hands in her lap and spoke quietly. "The War of Secession is separating some of us from our good senses. It is also separating some of us from our principles and our Southern traditions."

Sarah waited for Lucy to finish. "Perhaps," Sarah said, collecting her thoughts, "the South has been wrong. Have you thought of that? Perhaps we were wrong. Perhaps we need to question our traditions. Principles crumble when built on unquestioned traditions. Perhaps we need to . . ."

"Stop."

"I hoped you would understand. I have strong feelings."

Lucy looked earnestly into Sarah's face. "This news costs me tears, but I do not think less kindly of you for it. I did not come all the way to Charleston for another lecture on doing what is right for the South. Of course, I, too, know slavery was wrong. Of course I feel the guilt. I pay heed to the old culture," Lucy said in an irritated voice, "because I'm trapped in it." She walked to the window, then swung around. "Tell me,

Sarah, do you have a lover?"

The shock of Lucy's question made Sarah blush. "A lover?" An unbidden and very graphic picture of Preston Wilcox filled Sarah's mind, his blue frock coat professionally tailored, his wide-brimmed hat he held in his hand. His smile.

"Why do you ask me a question like that?"

"Because the future is uncertain, Sarah. I wish I had more time to spend here, but I must leave Charleston in the morning. The present alone is what matters. Therefore, we must make the most of what we have. We must amuse our soldiers, comfort them, and give them strength for the fray. The Holcombe Legion must dance tonight. You must come with me. Dancing will be good for you. You look surprised. Are you well?"

Suddenly, Sarah felt a twinge of anger. "Of course, I am well." She wanted to say, *I am tired. Don't you see? I'm tired of worrying about my family. I'm tired of staying awake at night listening for renegades and outlaws who come to steal and plunder and rape.* But she said nothing.

Lucy shrugged. "You need a night of gaiety."

Sarah looked down, hating her worn visiting dress, but it was the best she had. "What would I wear? I brought no ball gown to Charleston with me. What am I saying? I have no ball gowns."

Lucy smiled. "The *Fleur de Luce* brought gowns. You may choose one of mine. Perhaps you would like to wear my Chinese silk," Lucy suggested, her smile widening. "The scarlet one. Oh, Sarah, you would look ravishing in scarlet."

In a magnificent house on East Bay Street, soft music played in the drawing room. There was a fire, lounge chairs covered in velvet, and fresh flowers in antique vases. Officers from the Holcombe Legion, standing stiff and solid in their new uniforms, spoke about the heroic defense in the Battle of Secessionville.

"Valiantly defended," said one.

"There'll be no more southern approach to Charleston," said another.

All were sure General P. G. T. Beauregard would accept a reassignment if it were offered. He was the man to defend Charleston.

An orchestra played on the second floor balcony while below, in a garden surrounded by hedges, dancing began under an arbor of fragrant jasmine and tea olive. Coiffured women wearing puffs of tulle danced and swirled in a myriad of dazzling colors. Lucy, laughing her deep and lusty laugh, nodded to acquaintances as if she were royalty, then moved among her male admirers.

No wonder the papers called Lucy the "Empress." Within seconds Lucy was swept into the arms of a dark and handsome nobleman.

"An Italian count," a young woman standing beside Sarah said. "A cousin of the Middletons who has come to aid our cause."

Sarah took a glass of Madeira when the butler passed by and crossed the garden to look at the river. She hoped Lucy understood her determination to speak out. Josephine du Pont, who believed all women should contribute to the intellectual as well as the social world, had taught her to do that.

Lucy, too, believed that women should exert their independence. Lucy had strong opinions about politics and government and had written for *New Harper's Monthly Magazine* and signed her articles with her initials, L.P.H. She told Sarah she studied the style and delivery of political speakers. Once Lucy visited the statehouse in Jackson, Mississippi, to listen to the political debates.

Sarah tasted her Madeira. She, too, had a dream of what she could become.

Across the way flowed the Ashley River, its gray waters moving swiftly out into the harbor. All was quiet at Fort Sumter. Sarah wondered how much longer it would stay that way.

"May I have this dance?" The voice shot though her head like a streak of light.

She whirled to face Trent Lowndes, looking taller than she remembered and wearing the latest style in city clothes She stared, first at his face, which was lightly bearded and beamed with new dignity, then at his buff nankeen trousers that fit tightly.

Embarrassed, she blinked. "Trent."

"I wrote you. I looked anxiously for an answer." He kissed her forehead and pulled her onto the dance floor.

She was so nervous she thought she might trip, but she glided onto the floor, just like old times.

After the dance, they sat in the garden. "I've worried about you, about all the planters' families," he said. "Are you safe?"

"I serve the sick at Adams Run and do what I can for the military."

Better not to reveal the truth.

They spoke briefly of families and mutual friends.

A smile flickered on Trent's face. "And you've come back to spy on those of us who dared to stay behind."

She knew he was joking, but her brow shot up as if she were offended. "I came into the city to meet our First Lady who came to perform her duties for the Republic. Miriah's plantation adjoins Governor Pickens' in the upcountry district called Edgefield. She and I have become good friends."

"In times like these it's safest to suspect everybody. I didn't realize that you and the Empress were friends."

"For that reason, will you take me to the dance floor again? I should stay within Lucy's call."

After supper there was more wine and more dancing. "I never made it to New Orleans," Trent told her during intermission. "Too many opportunities here. I'm part owner of a steamer that runs the blockade in Wilmington. I've outfitted another, this one to run the blockade here in Charleston. It will be the fastest in the fleet. I would have named it the *Sarah* if we had married," he said, taking her hand. "Do you think you could love me if I named it Sarah?"

"Trent." She didn't want to go through another awkward proposal, which would, of course, spoil the evening.

"I apologize." Trent whirled around. "If I cannot name my steamer the *Sarah*, what name should I give it?"

"The *Caroline*."

"Then the *Caroline* it is. If you will come to the docks at noon tomorrow, we will christen the fastest steamer in Charleston Harbor. Nothing but your gracious appearance will bring the *Caroline* its fortune. I will walk the docks waiting. Will you come?"

She felt an old warmth in Trent's presence and hoped she would not regret it.

"Yes," she said, "I will come."

It was midday when her rented carriage came to a halt at the end of Market overlooking the docks. Wagons packed with sails, rigging, anchors, and chains filled the street and blocked the way. Boxes of muskets, sabers, revolvers, and rifles lay stacked on the docks. Gun carriages, water casks, mattresses, and lanterns were being loaded onto ships. Slaves flung goods to each other over their heads, shouting with every toss. Crewmen shouted orders so loudly her ears rang with the noise. The smell of pitch stung her nostrils.

She leaned forward to tell the driver to pull away. Why did she agree to christen Trent's blockade runner? Wasn't that something like piracy? Something like the renegades and scavengers who stole goods and war supplies then sold them for profit?

Her doubts scattered, however. Coming down the dock was Trent.

Stepping from her carriage, she all but stumbled into a dozen seamen, obviously drunk, wearing sailor pants and nothing on the upper part of their bodies but undershirts.

Trent steadied her. "You will have to excuse my crewmen who are already celebrating," Trent said, handing her a bottle of champagne and guiding her down the dock to the bow of the steamer.

"The *Caroline* it will be." He gripped the bottle, his hand over hers. She raised her arm. Twice more she tried and when the bottle burst, they laughed together and blotted the spray from their faces.

Back on Market Street, he helped her inside her carriage and clambered in himself before it lurched and jumped into the pack. He slid open the coachman's window and gave the order. "Down Bay and east to White Point Gardens. Drive slowly."

He rested a shoulder against the red velvet cushions and looked across the harbor where bright sunlight sparkled on the crest of the waves. She leaned back, too, and watched a flock of pelicans dipping in the air and swooping over the cupola of the Exchange Building at the foot of Broad Street. Black women who had earned their freedom through good works stood on the corner selling baskets they made from sweet marsh grass. An old black man carried a tray of fresh vegetables.

She saw the satisfaction written on Trent's face. "So, you like being a privateer?"

"Blockade running is hardly privateering. But yes, I'm doing what I want to do," Trent said, smiling wryly. "Why do you ask?"

"Isn't it a bit like piracy?"

"Privateers confiscate ships and turn them over to the Confederacy. We take goods out of port and return with other goods. We keep trade going. That in turn, cripples the enemy."

"I loathe anything that could prolong the conflict. Isn't that what you are doing?"

He leaned forward. "Muscovado sugar in hogsheads will bring seven and three quarters on the market when the *Caroline* returns. Molasses is already selling at forty-two and a half a gallon. Honey brings seventy cents. Mahogany and cedar from Cuba will bring a fortune. Within months I will be independently wealthy. You will find the prospect of living without wealth a dreadful thought after the war."

The carriage struck a curbstone and rocked. Without warning Trent fell against her, then he leaned in and pressed his lips against the back of her neck. He was breathing heavily. "Love me, Sarah. I will show you scenes abroad that will astound you. I will make you wealthy."

"Stop the coach," she told the driver. "The gentleman is leaving."

Trent opened the carriage door. "You will need me after the war, my love. Mark my words. I will be walking on marble floors with the rich and powerful. You will need me."

He stepped from the carriage, smiled, and bowed low.

She reached for the handle and slammed the door so hard the carriage bounced. The horse jolted as the coach pulled away. Her throat ached.

"Should I drive on?"

She didn't know how many times the driver had asked for directions, but she nodded, gave him an address and the carriage swayed to a halt. She was halfway inside the entrance to the shop before she looked up to make certain the driver had brought her to Russell's Bookshop and ran back to dismiss him.

"I'll walk from here," she told the driver and poured into his hands the last of the coins she'd saved for the trip. Inside the sun cast shadows across a room of priceless leather-bound books, and within seconds a familiar voice came from behind the shelves.

"Ah, *Mon Cheri*." The owner recognized her immediately. "I have missed you," he said, clasping her to his barrel-like chest. "I miss all the *literati* of our city. No one reads now. Everyone talks war talk. I hear nothing but bluster and threats and manifestos and resolutions. It leaves little time for reading."

The owner of the bookshop finished with an audible sigh. Men who spent hours there called him "Lord John." His shop had become an institution in the city. For half a century doctors and ministers, students and politicians, had met to smoke pipes and discuss politics in the back room.

As Sarah gave him news of her family, he shook his head sadly.

"I never thought it would come to this," he whispered, glancing at the door. "I stand with the South, but no amount of fire in the belly will make up for our lack of money, our lack of industry, men, and ammunition. I am sick of it all. We should not have fired on Fort Sumter."

"I never thought I would say it, but I, too, believe it was a mistake," Sarah said. "Do you think the enemy is planning to overtake the city with a siege?" She glanced at his collection of handsome leatherbound books and thought of the history stored between the covers. Would his books be safe?

"We are preparing for heavy fire power." He shook his head from side to side, his eyes sad and his lips tight. He reached out to touch her arm but pulled back when the bell over the front door rang.

"Excuse me, *Mon Cheri*. A customer."

While Lord John and his customer chatted, Sarah walked up and down the aisles reverently touching this book, then another.

She must be careful.

"Nothing dangerous," Lucy had promised before her carriage pulled out. It was still dark. "Just a farewell note written in Italian to a gentleman friend. . .thanking him for last night . . .for the pleasure of his company."

One more mission, not for the cause but for her friend.

Lucy had slipped the note in Sarah's hand and told her to place it in a copy of Miss Bronte's *Jane Eyre*.

Lucy had bent her head. "Submissiveness is not my role," she whispered, "but certain platitudes on certain occasions are among the innocent deceits of the sex."

Lord John's customer left and when Sarah came to the counter, he thrust a package toward her.

"I want you to have this. It's a special edition printed in Richmond and I dare say it will be the last. It's a copy of *Les Miserable*. Victor Hugo is the best since Scott. I only have old newspapers for wrapping paper. Supplies are short. We give our orders to the blockade runners, but the ships don't always come back."

Sarah said good-bye, her voice so soft Lord John had to bend down to hear. Their heads almost touched.

Out on King Street in the afternoon sun, she opened her parasol and strolled. At Wentworth, she turned south for no reason except it seemed quiet and isolated. Only the clatter of carriage wheels echoed from King Street. She turned east on St. Philips and suddenly heard a familiar sound. Could it be? She thought she heard the hum of children reciting multiplication tables, stumbling with numbers, sounding out letters.

Instinctively, Sarah moved toward the sound that seemed to come from a small single house with peeling yellow paint and dark green shutters. Without thinking, she pushed against the heavy wooden door that opened directly onto the street.

The door creaked and a woman appeared down the piazza, a woman with light chocolate skin and gray hair.

Embarrassment held Sarah glued to the spot. This was a school for free blacks.

Standing in front of her was the teacher, the woman who started the school, and the same woman who lived with Trent's father after Trent's mother left to go back north. Although the woman of color and Trent's father were never seen together in public, their liaison had been much discussed in Sarah's social circles.

It was no secret that Trent's mother had hated Carolina and refused to live out on Wadmalaw Island. She refused to be left alone with Negro slaves while her husband was in Charleston or Savannah taking care of business.

Trent's father had tried to make his bride happy and had taken her on an extended trip to Europe, where they had discovered Italian architecture. They had returned to build The Grove, a city house built on land near the old city gate and patterned after an Italian villa.

But attempts to make his northern wife happy proved futile. Planters' wives clucked their tongues, shook their heads, and passed along the rumor that the marriage was less than felicitous. The girl from the Hudson River Valley was miserable in the South. Only one son came from the union.

Trent.

Word was that while his mother lived at The Grove, she locked the bedroom door, but by then Trent's father was hardly aware he had a wife. By that time he had met a gracious and engaging free woman of color and established her in a small house on St. Philip's Street where she ran a school for the children of free persons of color.

"May I help you?" When the mulatto woman spoke, Sarah felt her mouth fly open. Was this the woman? Sarah forced her lips to close and took time to swallow before she finally said, "Perhaps I am in the wrong building."

"Perhaps you are, my dear. This is a school for children of color, our Negro population," the woman said. "Memminger Normal is across the street."

"Yes. Memminger. I know. . . ." Memminger was the experimental school for girls of the white working poor, a "public school," planters called it condescendingly. Sarah moved uncomfortably in her travel dress. Suddenly she hated the green striped dress with its military epaulets. She wished she had worn something plain, a blue gingham, perhaps, or an ordinary brown calico.

"Memminger Normal is across the street. Perhaps you turned into the wrong building. It's easy to do," the woman explained, her dark eyes suddenly gleaming with an idea. "But since you are already here, please come down the veranda. I'd like you to look in on our classes. Most students are already in the second reader, and, of course, I am proud of them. They are eager to learn when they arrive. They've missed so much, you know. I'm always happy to show off my students."

Girls packed the room, some the brown-skinned elite; others the dark-skinned children of slaves who had bought freedom with good deeds or money they saved. Most were so young their feet could hardly touch the floor and all were reading aloud, their eyes gleaming, their faces shining.

"The older girls are helping the younger ones with their lessons," the woman explained. "We don't have enough teachers because many of our free people have emigrated to Canada. Our city has suddenly become so paranoid they have cracked down on freedom of movement and in some cases, caused such harassment that our people have abandoned their businesses and fled. The ruffians make threats, you know, and it's easy to become frightened in all the upheaval."

"Ruffians don't understand," Sarah attempted to explain. She knew the teacher meant the people from upstate who didn't know there were hundreds of Negroes in Charleston who were not slaves at all, but sea captains from far-away places or merchants from Barbados who owned slaves themselves.

"You could help, you know," the teacher said. Behind the brown-skinned woman's smile and gentle eyes, Sarah was sure she saw a long line of Egyptian nobility, and she stood immobile, mesmerized by the long gray braids wound around the teacher's head and held in place by delicate mother of pearl combs.

"If you could find the time," the woman was saying, "you could read or recite poetry. I read aloud from Mr. Stevens' travels to the East. They find his account of his journey through the wilderness exciting, especially his visit to Petra, the city of rock." The woman's refined voice came to Sarah evenly modulated. "Of course, only a few hours in the mornings. We need teachers so badly that I feel desperate, as you can see."

Sarah wanted to say she knew how the teacher felt; she, too, felt desperate most of the time.

"I teach also," she blurted. "I teach children on Edisto."

"Out on the islands?" The woman looked at her, cocking her elegant head and blinking.

Gaining confidence, Sarah said, "Yes, I teach the children of the freed slaves. It's hard. I'm not a teacher, you see."

The woman smiled. "Most of us are not. Why do you teach?"

Sarah had tried to explain this to herself, and she'd been thinking about it night after night.

"Because something in me wants to change the way things are."

The woman's smile turned wise and comforting.

"There is so much to be done," the woman said, "and we can do so little. We simply do the best we can."

Yes, the best we can, Sarah thought, *but what if the best is not enough?*

CHAPTER

Thirteen

On the way back to Edisto, Sarah sat in the bow, her head held high as if daring a Union patrol to stop the boat. But her pass was ready just in case.

"Yankee soldiers moving on, I hear," Jacob said.

"Not far enough." She meant to joke.

Jacob did not see the humor. "They moving on up the coast," he said solemnly. "I guess they think they can blast their way into Charleston."

She didn't answer, but she had heard General Beauregard was coming back to build earthworks. Charlestonians planned to hunker down for a long siege.

"Runaway slaves from the mainland keep coming over to the islands. What do you think will happen?"

"Hunger makes people dangerous."

"They've been told everything is plentiful and free. I heard rumors. They say unscrupulous white men are selling stakes for two Federal dollars and telling runaways all they have to do is drive it in the ground and land on the island is theirs."

Jacob nodded. "They'll have to live out in the woods and eat whatever they can find. They can hunt for rabbits and deer, but that's about all this time of year. Course there's always fish in the streams."

She hesitated, but she had to ask one burning question. "When the refugees come, how will they feel about me?"

"You the teacher." Jacob smiled and that was that.

"After the war, where will you go, Jacob?"

His head lifted. "Why, right here." Jacob shielded his eyes and peered at her as if she had asked if he would move to the moon.

"Here? On Edisto?"

"Why, yes, Miss Sarah. This is home."

The prospect of freed slaves loving the islands as much as the white planters startled her. "But you will be free. Why would you stay?"

Jacob looked at her as if this line of questioning was absurd. "I don't plan to run from nobody. I got my family. I want to stay here and work at something that binds us together, makes our lives easier. I've had enough of tearing families apart, tearing down lives. I don't want any more of the old days."

She swallowed, determined to be honest with Jacob. The words came hard, but she wanted to say this. "I guess the old days were not as good as I wanted to believe. It's taken me a long time to realize that. It's hard for me to say, but I'm not proud of those days."

Jacob didn't take umbrage. "No, ma'am. I'm not proud of those days either. The things I did when I was your papa's overseer makes me sick to my stomach when I think about it. Toward the end I came to hate it."

Sullen, she watched Jacob stop rowing long enough to pour coffee and hand her a cup. "Thank you," she said. "I don't think we had to have all this confusion. No need for a war. There should be another way to settle this, but men smarter than I am couldn't find a way. So, here we are."

"Yes, Miss Sarah, here we are."

She turned to look into the fog, gray and hanging heavy over the water, and was pulled back to that November day when her family packed up in the rain and left the plantation house. She could hear the wagons rolling and Jacob shouting orders. In her inner eye she could see her father out by the bay when she found him, riding along the surf as if in a trance. Impotent. Exhausted. It was then that she took control. She held him by the hand, led him back to the plantation, and boarded him on the last boat to leave Edisto.

Jacob rowed along as if giving her time to remember. Suddenly he turned up Pierre Creek. "I thought we might take a side trip."

Of course she knew where they were going. She recognized the creek that flowed in front of the plantation house.

Jacob put his hand to his lips. "Sh-sh-sh," he warned. "Voices carry over water. We can't get too close, but we can maneuver up a ways. Soldiers left and some right queer people living in the house, I hear."

"What kind of queer people?"

"They black. They from across the water, and they strange. The man, they say, came here from London, and Sully hear tells he robbed a bank."

"Pshaw," Sarah said, not quite believing Sully's story. "Where did she hear that?"

"From white people." Jacob shrugged, then he asked, "Do black people live in London?"

Sarah wished she had books to give Jacob. The thought of Jacob as a literate and informed man pleased her. "Black people live all over the world, Jacob."

"Are they free?"

"Some are as free as you will be after the war."

"But not free to rob a bank." It was Jacob's turn to make a joke.

He stopped rowing. "Look hard through the trees."

For a long time she could say nothing, just stare at the house where she was born, her sense of time lost. Her father had built the house for the sensitive, beautiful girl he met in Newport, wooed all summer and brought to Edisto as his bride in 1837. To guests who had come to visit from far and near, he boasted that the house was built of eight hundred oaks and four hundred acres of loblolly pines, all grown on Edings' land then felled, sawed, and planed into lumber by the hands of three hundred Edings' slaves.

Sarah peered through the mist and imagined her mother standing in an upstairs window as a bride, young and dreamy in her white nightgown, throwing the shutters back and leaning over the windowsill, her eyes reflecting the sunrise of a new day. But today mist coiled around the house and lifted up into the sky, and Sarah felt whatever gave the house its meaning was gone. The spirit that was her mother's house had slipped away.

Seconds passed before she realized the boat was not moving. Why was Jacob not rowing? They needed to leave this place. She turned to glare into the face of a muscular dark man who was holding a rifle at Jacob's head.

"What you doin' here?"

Sarah shook her head, struck dumb with fear.

"I ast you what you doin' here? The man who lives here don't 'llow no white folks round here."

Thankfully, she found her voice. "We hear a man from London lives here. Is it true?"

"I don't answer no questions about my boss."

Jacob decided to be friendly. "We just riding by looking."

The muscular man rammed the rifle at Jacob's shoulder.

She drew a deep breath and watched wide-eyed as Jacob tore the rifle out of the man's hand, raised the stock over his head and then in a virulent and involuntary motion flung the man's rifle into the water.

The man did not make a sound. He smiled effusively, pivoted at the waist, and drew a knife. In the fading sun, the flint of steel glittered, and she heard a strange cry coming from her own mouth. The woods grew quiet. The man licked his lips and stared, choosing his moment.

A flock of ducks squawked and flew away.

And another dark man appeared. He stood almost motionless, holding a rifle at his side. "Let them pass, King. We're not looking for trouble."

But home was gone, she thought. *The house and everything it ever meant was gone, gone, gone.*

Thunder rumbled. Lightning flashed and Jacob's face turned solemn. It had been a long trip. He had taken her to Charleston and waited for three days to bring her back. Of course, she was an extra burden.

The trip had been a needed distraction for her, but now her thoughts were returning to Affey and the school children who were loving and warm and the only thing real in her life.

Jacob poled the longboat between a skiff and a raft, but by now the rain was falling in sheets and Jacob motioned that they should make a run for the cabin. She scrambled out, the damp cold of the rain seeping through her hood and running down her face. Once when she slipped on the path slick with wet pine needles, she caught a tree limb and willed herself to keep up with Jacob.

"Sully." Jacob stood in the open doorway reaching for his knife.

Something snapped inside her head. "Where is everybody?"

It was like a nightmare she sometimes had in which the Yankee soldiers came storming in to arrest her, and when they entered the door, they were faced with Jacob's dark and muscular freedmen. When the fight ended, all those who were trying to protect her from the Yankees were left sitting or slumping or lying around the room in a tangle of bodies and rifles.

Jacob ran to the kitchen, and she took it all in: the children's clothes strewn on the floor, their small toys smashed, their marbles crushed. The long kitchen table stood on end, chairs broken and scattered. Kitchen utensils lay tossed about.

A streak of lightning blinded her for a moment, and when she opened her eyes, Jacob was yanking at the floorboards where he stashed his rifles. He surveyed everything with a look of dread and anger.

Whoever did this had not come to steal the rifles. And Sully knew the plans. She would have taken the children to the fortification.

The thunder sounded distant. The rain stopped. Jacob pointed to the corner.

"They came for that."

Newspapers littered the floor around her bed. The clippings. The Union war reports. Her bed covers had been tossed aside and her straw mattress hacked to pieces with a bowie knife.

Whoever did this had come for her.

She leaned against the back door to steady herself. She didn't see the blood, didn't hear the moan, but she heard the sound of water rushing under the back door steps.

At the bottom of the steps lay Affey, crumpled and motionless on the ground.

"Here, Jacob. Under the steps. Oh, my God."

She had no idea how long she'd been holding Affey or what song she'd been humming to give comfort when Sarah realized they were inside the cabin and Jacob was wrapping Affey in blankets.

"Where is Sully?" Jacob's voice was tight. "The children. Where are the children?"

When Affey did not answer, Sarah whispered, "Squeeze my hand if Sully and the children are safe."

She felt Affey's hand contract, weak and faint.

"Are they are hiding in the swamp?"

Affey opened her eyes and blinked.

Jacob raced out to find his family. Sarah knelt to wipe the blood from Affey's face, too ashamed to be angry. It was all her fault, she was thinking. Pain and hurt was upon Affey and the people protecting her, and she wanted to scream, but there would be time enough later for that, time to place the blame, time enough to ask who did this.

Affey was sleeping when a shadow fell across the bed.

"Rhoda." Sarah stared at her root doctor friend. "I've kept her warm."

"You done good," Rhoda said.

Sarah thought she heard the bittersweet sound of reproach. "I couldn't think of any roots."

Rhoda patted her bag. "Rhoda brought merkle and life everlasting. Rhoda got amy root. She got everything she need right here."

"How did you know?"

"Rhoda know everything. We talk later. Now, I need lots a hot water."

As Sarah stoked the fire, Rhoda soothed Affey's tears with old familiar songs and gentle brown hands. "You jus git all the cryin' past, chile, then we wipe the memry from your mind. We wipe all the bad memry out while we wipe away the tears."

Sarah took the wash bowl and towels to Rhoda. "I knew you were alive. I saw Mother's china teacups on the table at the summerhouse. I looked for you, but you disappeared. Where were you hiding?"

"Rhoda don' like nobody pokin' round," Rhoda said, speaking the African's deep dialect, her heavy voice echoing in the room.

"Is it true? Were you living at the bay?" Sarah whispered, as if to remind Rhoda this was a sick room now.

"Rhoda part Edistow. She like it out there all by herself, but she come quick to see 'bout Affey. You leave us be," Rhoda said firmly. "Leave us be."

The air in the woods was cool after the rain. Sarah walked until shame overcame her, then she sank to her knees. She'd been fighting a war she didn't believe in, and now she was bringing pain and hurt to the people she had come to love. What was she going to do?

A heron burst out of a cypress tree, batted and flashed its wings, then swooped into the air. She watched it fly away as she lay in the wet pine needles, motionless, too exhausted to get up.

Her head was pounding when she heard the palmetto fronds rattle. She looked up to see Rhoda.

"Come on back inside, chile. You bearing too much pain in your heart."

"What do you mean?"

"You tell me, chile. You the only one who knows why you needing to cry."

"All this is my fault, Rhoda. I said I came to teach the children, but the truth is I came back for another reason. I didn't come back to teach. It was all a lie."

"You came back. That's what matters."

"The children matter now."

"You right. They matter."

"If I leave, they're in danger. If I stay, they're in danger."

"They in danger. You in danger. Danger everywhere, chile."

"I know that. You see what happened to Affey. White people filled with hatred came to punish me for teaching black children. They came to find me and retaliate, but they found Affey instead. I can't protect her."

Through a long silence, Sarah thought Rhoda might begin to wail and chant, but she didn't. Rhoda touched her hair and said. "You got pain you not telling Rhoda 'bout. Don' you understand? Rhoda know how you feeling 'bout that Yankee soldier. You feeling mighty low."

Sarah felt a shock go through her. Were her feelings so evident? Her mother had trained her to smile, say thank you, and move on when people disappointed her.

She raised her chin and looked at Rhoda. "How do you know about the Yankee soldier?"

"I just know. Rhoda feels the hurt in her heart, too."

"He's gone," Sarah said, surprising herself with her honesty. "He left. Did you know he left? Without as much as saying goodbye?"

Rhoda stroked Sarah's forehead as a mother would soothe her brokenhearted child. "He left," Rhoda said. "That is so, but he might make it his business to come back."

"No, I think not," Sarah said, but she would learn to live with it, the grief over her lost world, the places and the people who lived in her no matter how hard she tried to forget. Even the loneliness.

"You think 'no' tonight, but tomorrow comes." Rhoda looked through the pines and began to chant.

Sarah accepted Rhoda's madness as intuition or wisdom, something beyond understanding, and it came to her that she had always felt safe with Mad Rhoda by her side. People who believed in magic, truly believed, had been made well when Rhoda mixed her potions or waved her hand. She had seen it happen time after time. Could Rhoda's prediction about Preston Wilcox come true?

For a moment she imagined walking with the captain beside the surf, her hair whipped by the ocean breeze. It would be sunset and the captain would be striding along with her, clutching his wide-brimmed hat in his hand.

"Hum. . .hum. . .hum. . ." Rhoda ended her chant. "Tomorrow comes," Rhoda whispered. "Tomorrow comes."

Sarah nodded. She wished she could believe. Rhoda wanted her to believe, so she said, "Maybe it will work, Rhoda. Maybe your magic will work."

"You'll see, chile. You'll see. You not like Rhoda. You different. Some people not meant to be alone."

CHAPTER
Fourteen

*S*mallpox.

When Jacob spoke the word, the very sound chilled Sarah. Long seconds passed before she could ask the question that had to be asked. "How bad?"

"Mild," Jacob said, but his face had turned ashen. "Five people on the Pope plantation."

"Surely the Popes vaccinated their people." Sarah stepped away, thinking how the vaccine had stopped the plague on Edisto years ago, but on other islands the fever had been known to wipe away whole populations. Survivors told tales that conjured up the horrors of sickness and death.

"I believe the Popes vaccinated their slaves, but I'm not sure," Jacob said, shaking his head.

"Where is Rhoda?" Sarah didn't know who else could help.

"Rhoda refuses."

"What?"

Affey joined in, calmly, almost businesslike. "Rhoda believes someone has put a hex on the place."

"Surely she will go teach cleanliness," Sarah insisted, resenting Rhoda's disappearance but knowing that with Affey well now, Rhoda had gone back to the bay because she'd had enough of people.

"You go, Sarah. The people will listen to you. I can handle school," Affey declared. "I can manage for both of us."

In a flash, Sarah went over the roots and herbs she'd need for tonics. She knew which worked. Rhoda had taught her long ago.

"What will you need?" Affey glanced around the cabin for medicines.

Jacob grabbed his hat and coat. "I'll barter for anything you need. If the Confederates won't have the medicines you need at Adams Run, I'll trade with the Yankees."

"That will not be necessary." Sarah could mix the potions, what Rhoda called part of the "seven-day creation," medicines that came before time, roots like snake root, black root, and devil's walking stick.

"Black root can only be found in swampy areas," Affey reminded her. "Do you remember how to identify it?"

"Yes." Sarah grabbed her portmanteau. Not that she would need travel clothes, she thought, but at least she should take an extra morning dress and a wrapper.

"And watch the moon," Affey warned, helping her pack. "Collect garlic on a new moon and make sure it has seeded."

"I will. And place the sickest people in cool water soaked with pine tops and life everlasting."

"Horehound works for sore throats." Affey closed the bag and stood, questioning Sarah as one doctor would question another. "Do you remember how to draw the roots?"

"Steep the root until it's bitter. That's the way Mad Rhoda taught us."

Affey nodded. "The more bitter the better."

"Are you sure you feel well enough to manage school without me?" Sarah held Affey by the shoulders. "Listen to me. Tabitha needs more work in subtraction. Zack may lead you to believe he is ready for the fourth reader, but I'm not so sure. Don't forget to give him extra work. He needs the challenge."

"Everything will be fine." Affey seemed confident.

Sarah looked at Affey and felt a deep admiration. Affey was more like a sister than Miriah. The emotional bond was strong, like an invisible tie holding them together. Their friendship was firm and everlasting. She could never doubt Affey's devotion. "Take care of yourself," Sarah said, smiling meekly.

The smell of sickness nauseated Sarah, the steamy smell of urine-wet cloth on the beds, the stench of sores and infection.

"Open the windows," she demanded. "Prop open the doors."

When friends and family members of the sick refused to budge but continued to stand outside, wailing and moaning, Sarah shouted, "You, there, come inside and help me. Get these people outside."

The mourners looked astounded but followed her orders.

With that done, she announced, "This cabin and all the people in it are now under quarantine. Leave us. Go to work. Go back to the fields."

She stood in the center of the group. They were quiet except for a little mumbling, afraid enough as it was, she guessed. And undernourished and hungry.

"I will do what needs to be done for the sick. Those who are well, go to the fields. We need to put food into everyone. If this is the disease I think it is, we all need to strengthen our bodies."

She boiled water, washed clothes, and changed beds daily. In the afternoons, she gathered roots, then mixed, concocted, and dispensed tonics. At night she called the people together to explain the importance of sanitation.

Still the people refused to go back to the fields. How could she do more? One thing was certain. She could no longer threaten to disown them. General Hunter had issued a proclamation when he arrived in Hilton Head. Lincoln had rescinded it immediately, but it was only a matter of time before the President proclaimed an all-out emancipation. They must learn to fend for themselves.

Before dawn one morning, Sarah felt a hand on her shoulder, shaking her into consciousness. "If you want the people to go back to the fields, come with me, and be quick about it. It's time they planted sweet potato slips."

Moving groggily, her head pounding, Sarah sat up, thinking she needed help and here it was. "Thank you. They need food. And, yes, I need help."

Outside, while it was still dark, the woman handed her a hoe. "My name is Martha. I was housekeeper for the Popes, but I still remember how to work the fields. Do you know how to plant sweet potato slips?"

"I've watched," Sarah admitted. "I learn quickly."

The two women hitched up their skirts with string and set off, aware that the people were watching from their cabins, some standing along the edge of the fields, huddled in small groups, and speaking a mix of dialects Sarah did not understand.

"They talking 'bout you," Martha said. "They sayin' . . . 'well, now, this ain't just any buckra.' They saying. . .'this here the lady who teaching the chillun. She a lady and a teacher and she trying to show us how to make our lives better. Let's see what she can do,' they saying."

Martha raked the furrows. Sarah dug the holes and together they started planting the tender slips of sweet potato. Soon the two women's faces were glazed with sweat, their hands sore, their muscles aching, but neither slowed down.

By midmorning, a half dozen women came to help, but the others stood in groups of two or three or alone at the edge of the field. By noon women flooded the fields, laughing and talking and working in teams.

And at the end of the day when the sun went behind the live oaks and the great blue herons swooped in to nest for the night, the field had been planted.

Sarah forced herself to leave the field without stumbling. She blinked and tried to focus. "Help me," she whispered to Martha. "Walk beside me." Martha held her arm.

"I know you doing this because somebody's got to do it," Martha said, "but it's too much of a sacrifice, Miss Sarah, even for a teacher."

"I just need rest," she insisted, but she felt hot and weak.

"It's too much of a sacrifice, too much." Martha made a noise with her teeth as she helped Sarah into her cabin.

Sarah shivered. "It's the fever, but I don't want the people to be frightened. You will have to take over. And find someone to take me to Edings Bay. Surely there is someone you can trust. I will recuperate there."

When it was dark, someone halted a horse outside.

"Take her to the bay, Lijah," Martha told the field hand who came with horses. "And be quiet about it. No one should know, but the teacher is weary and needs a rest."

During the ride she struggled to stay astride, fever burning her skin, perspiration filling her eyes. Once when her bonnet fell back, she reached to push her hair away at her forehead, and she touched nothing. She reached again and found that her hair was tangled and knotted with dirt. Well, it wouldn't do to look like that at the bay. She'd bathe in the surf when she got there. The field hand leading her horse came close. "Heah's the way, ma'am," he said. "I kin see the water from over here."

Lijah helped her into the summerhouse, but she barely knew where she was, barely knew which tonic she was swallowing, and hours passed before the herbs worked their magic. When she slept, she dreamed.

She and Affey were burying great-grandmother Edings' Chinese porcelain teacups behind the kitchen house.

"Look at me," Affey said, brushing sand from her dress. In Sarah's dream, Affey's skin had turned dusky with the white chalk-like powder.

Sarah teased, "Someone would think you were an ordinary field hand."

"We need turpentine." Affey was out of breath after doing all the digging.

"Turpentine? Why do we need turpentine?" Sarah wiped her face with the hem of her petticoat. "What's wrong with using water from the cistern?"

"That's how we store rugs every year before we leave for the winter. We roll all the rugs up in old newspapers dipped in turpentine."

In her dream they rolled up the rugs. The summerhouse smelled of pine resin, and she was sitting on the bare wooden floor thinking of the long trip upstate, and feeling as if she were heading on some great Biblical migration. The portrait of her mother still hung over the mantel. She knew if the Yankees came, it would be ripped off the wall and she would never see it again.

Affey kept saying, "We've got to go now." Her voice was flat. "We've got to cross the creek before the tide turns."

Sarah knew she was dreaming and when she bolted up and looked around, she knew she was upstairs in the summerhouse. She felt the bed wet, soaked from her own perspiration, knew she was sick with the fever, and lay down to dream again.

Back in her dream, she heard Affey. "If we don't leave now," Affey said, "it will be dark before we get back to the plantation house and Jacob will be on his way to see about us. We'll have everybody worried."

Sarah knew she had to leave and why. She closed the front door and locked it, then she walked outside along the piazza, smelling the salt air, feeling the cleansing effect of the pines that surrounded the place where her ancestors had spent summers for over two centuries.

She could hear Affey making a clicking sound with her tongue and see her tapping the mules on their hindquarters. "You know how high the creek gets," Affey said impatiently.

Over the causeway on the other side of Frampton Creek, Sarah turned to look back at the bay. "Does it work?" she asked Affey.

"Does what work?" Affey looked tired. Sarah knew she was dreaming and wondered why Affey looked tired. It was only a dream.

"Mad Rhoda's magic," Sarah said, and she knew in the dream she was speaking aloud. "Does it keep evil away? Does it work?"

Affey did not look at her. She did not look down. She just looked ahead. "Sometimes nothing we do can stop it. Nothing." Affey took the reins and tapped the mules so hard, the leather popped in the air like a gunshot.

Sarah raised up, half awake, half in the dream, still hearing the loud popping noise, her body shaking, her heart still pounding. She saw Affey and knew she had been sick, very sick.

"How long . . .?"

"A week." Affey took a step forward, her face lined with worry.

Sarah inhaled and lay back on pillows, on linens and coverlets that Affey had brought for the sick bed. "So long?"

"That long. And your fever was so high I thought I'd have to draw off bad blood."

"Oh, God," Sarah gasped. "I would have had you whipped."

Affey's smile was forgiving. "I found Peruvian bark. It worked."

"How did you know I was sick? I made Martha promise."

"Rhoda makes everything and everyone her business. She came to tell me."

"Where is Rhoda now?"

"On the beach sweeping away the evil spirits."

"I see." Sarah leaned back. She did not resist when Affey bundled her up and helped her downstairs. At the dining room table, she glanced at Affey and wondered if she, too, was thinking of their childhood in the summerhouse. She wished she could find the right words, say something that would wipe away all Affey's bad memories and perhaps make up for the past.

No words would come.

But when their eyes met, she knew Affey had something more to tell. Affey's eyes teared.

"What is it? Tell me."

Affey sat wearily at the table. "While you were under the fever a message came from upstate," Affey said slowly. "From Miriah. It's your mother."

"My mother?"

"She. . .it was sudden. . .they couldn't get to her."

"Mother? What is it?"

"A chill. Exposure. She's gone."

Word had come from Lucy Pickens to Adams Run, the message relayed to Jacob, who came to tell Affey. Josephine Edings was dead. A late spring tornado upstate had caught her mother far from the house gathering firewood for Miriah's kitchen. Miriah had found her and tried to help her feverish and chilled mother back to the house, but they had been forced to endure a wet night without shelter. Her mother had become delirious with fever, and although the old house servant—the only one still on the plantation—had searched all night, he did not find them until the next morning. By noon, Josephine Edings had slipped away.

After Sarah heard the story, she sat all day and into the night, unable to cry.

Affey watched her closely. "Will you come back with me?" Affey asked, but she seemed to know the answer. "There's food here. I made tonics. Will you be all right alone?"

"Yes."

"I will come back for you in a few days, but I must return to school. For the children. . ."

"Yes, the children."

"The children need me," Affey said, gathering her things, and looking directly at her. "They need you, too."

Reluctantly, Affey left, and Sarah walked from room to room. No need to close the windows. All the glass was shattered. Standing on the piazza, she listened to the surf and forced herself to remain silent, hoping the sound of the water would soothe her. She knew if she cried now, she might not stop. A cool sea breeze brushed her skin. Pine scents, pungent and fresh, filled the air, and she remembered a ritual of mourning she'd seen performed out under these pines. It was an Edistow Indian tradition. Slaves thought it was African.

She'd seen the slaves, overcome by grief, slash their wrists, mix their blood with the golden pitch, and smear the sticky mixture across their foreheads and down their cheeks to form a trail of tears. Would the ritual wipe away her grief and give her the strength she needed? Her mother's death had changed everything. She was alone now. Utterly alone. She opened the knife she kept in her pocket, rubbed the sparkling steel, and walked down the steps.

"Sarah," a voice called out.

She turned, the knife clenched in her fist, and shouted, "Leave me alone."

"I brought supplies." The voice blended with the surf.

She went closer and peered into the moving shadow. "Preston?"

"I brought more books. Laura Towne sent all the books she could spare. I'm having more shipped from Milford."

Why was Preston Wilcox here? Was she dreaming again?

"The children need more books," the shadow said. "I saw the need myself. I came to help."

She stood as steady as she could, still weak from the fever. "Who are you?"

"Give me the knife, Sarah. I told you the truth."

"No," she said, holding the knife high. "Who are you, really?" They stood in the dark under the pines, the only light, a lamp he held casting shadows on the blade of the knife.

"Please give me the knife. I'm Captain Preston Wilcox, ma'am, from Milford, Connecticut."

She made a weak sound. " . . . who came on a holy mission to preserve the dignity of mankind." When she reached both hands to the sky in a gesture of disbelief, the knife fell to the ground.

He picked up the knife, stood looking at her then at the knife with the dazed eyes of a foreigner.

"I did not come on a mission, Sarah. And I don't believe this is a holy war. I'm not sure what I believe."

"Then what are you doing here? You were furloughed home. Why return?"

"I'm an engineer. I know how to build railroads."

"Which means you came to destroy railroads."

He seemed not to hear that. "There are many reasons men fight in a war, Sarah. Some join for adventure, some for misplaced loyalties. I joined to escape bad memories. I was suffocating. I contacted a friend."

"You came to spy," she said more sharply than she intended.

His head jerked. "I know railroads. I know bridges. People in high places offered me duty in Special Services. I accepted for reasons I didn't understand myself. That's why I'm here. But not tonight. I came because I delivered supplies to the school, and Jacob told me of your mother's death."

She studied him. "I went to St. Helena," Sarah said quickly. "I visited Laura Towne. I tried to find you at field headquarters. I wanted to thank you for the readers you sent. You were not there." She waited for an explanation.

He looked embarrassed. "I. . ." He paused as if to choose his words carefully. "It was imperative that I go home. It was an emergency."

She remembered the picture of the dark-haired girl in the miniature. "To see the girl you left behind?" She had to ask.

"Yes . . .her name is . . . Emily," he told her haltingly. "She is demure and tiny and not yet one year old."

"One year?"

"My daughter." He seemed to wait for her reaction and when there was none, he told her about his wife who had died in childbirth. His wife, too, was demure and tiny and innocent. "My wife believed the Union flag was unspoiled. She believed this war was a holy war. I was lonely. When my wife died, I was lost. I thought joining the war would make me feel noble and brave," he said.

"And do you?"

"Do I?"

"Do you feel noble and brave, Captain Wilcox?" She tried to stand and look into his face.

He looked at her closely, as if trying to read something in her face. She tried to project understanding and compassion, perhaps forgiveness--but not her real feelings. She would not reveal how much she had missed him, how much she could care.

"No. I don't feel noble and brave," the captain said without moving. "I feel humble. You are the brave one. I see you alone on an island teaching slave children, and I think you have more courage than any general in this war."

He told her that his mother, too, had died on a cold winter's night. He could still see her wax-like figure. He told her the story of a brother, Nathan, who went west to find California gold. Afraid to say anything, she watched as white puffy clouds drifted across the dark sky. A full moon appeared with a large circle of vapor surrounding it like a halo. A natural phenomenon, she thought, staring at the moon on the horizon as she

tried to give her emotions some kind of focus. Her heart ached, and feeling lonely and small, she walked toward the moon with its rays lighting
up the night, thinking she'd like to touch it.

She took a step toward the sea, her hair flowing free, waiting for the
next wave. She felt naked, in another body, above the world, immortal.
Perhaps, she thought, I feel nothing. But she heard the wind. The pines
began to hum. The surf beckoned, and with the sounds all blending
together she swayed, not falling but bending just the same and watching
each wave upon wave upon wave and not opposing...

The captain caught her as she fell. "You should not be out in this
night air."

"I'm tired."

"I know you are."

"It's the fever."

"Come," he said, guiding her back into the summerhouse, holding her
steady. "You will feel better tomorrow. Perhaps we will ride across the bay.
Jacob told me where I could find a boat."

"Perhaps." But the memory of his disappearance, the weeks of hurt,
made her curious.

She wanted an answer. Why did he leave her?

When Sarah opened her eyes, the sun was high, and the tide was high.
Downstairs, Preston Wilcox welcomed her with bread for breakfast and
tea. Later, she walked beside him to find the boat. Though still bleary-eyed
and weak, she stepped aboard with as much grace as she could muster.

He adjusted the oars and they were off. What did a Union railroad
engineer know about the sea? Could she manage if his talent as a seaman
turned out to be an illusion? So be it. She leaned back in her seat. She'd
slept all night in her bed. She'd not dreamed about Rebel raiders or
Yankee deserters. She'd awakened without reaching for her Derringer.
And now she was deciding that life was worth living again.

At Jeremy Cay they picked wild flowers. In the afternoon she felt well
enough to gather shells and look for sea turtle eggs. Preston dodged the
crests crashing along the shore, and she longed to join him, throw herself
into the waves, but she did not move.

That night as the moon made the water burn in a blaze of light across the bay and they sat on the steps watching, he leaned close and kissed the back of her neck lightly. When she tipped up her face, his lips came down on hers, so tender, so soft, so filled with need, it took her breath away. When he unbuttoned her bodice, her body trembled.

"I want to make love to you, Sarah. I have since the first day I saw you."

She wanted him, needed him, and feeling that sweet sense of desire, she moved into his arms like a child drowning. They made love on the cool piazza with the sound of the surf in her ears. When she was rocked by spasms of pleasure, it was easy to imagine they were far away from hostility, far beyond the reach of war. Conflict between North and South, between brothers, even lovers, did not seem important anymore.

She awoke later but did not speak. It was odd to think she felt this way about someone she hardly knew. She watched him sleep. She felt young and safe again.

Enchanted. In love.

CHAPTER
Fifteen

"*G*o," Affey whispered from behind Sarah. "Your heart's bleeding. Go with the captain."

"The captain has a duty. I have mine." Sarah pressed her lips until she could pull herself together. Then she turned and walked up the schoolhouse steps.

"Duty?" Affey followed, raising her voice. "What does 'duty' mean? Does anyone know? Does anyone care anymore?"

Sarah looked back. "I can't leave the children. It's my duty."

"Ha." Affey grabbed her arm. "That word changes meaning depending on where you are. Who you are. You can cross any river around here and 'duty' changes meaning. You can turn your back and it changes. One man's 'duty' today is another man's 'duty' tomorrow. It has no meaning anymore. I'll stay with the children. Go with the captain. You belong with him."

This morning when Preston appeared in uniform, Sarah knew they were going their separate ways. After sleeping like man and wife, comforting each other, and laying open their hopes and dreams amid the wreckage of war and waste, this morning it ended. Her throat ached. Her heart hurt, but she would lose her pain here. The children needed her.

Affey stepped forward so that her body blocked the doorway. "We have new students."

"New students? Where are they from?"

"Everywhere. Refugees. That general announced an early emancipation. It was a mistake, but the refugees think it's true and keep coming. I couldn't turn them away. I didn't know what to do. I did the best I could." Affey looked tired.

The schoolroom was bedlam, children running, jumping over desks, playing tag. Older boys in the back leaned back in chairs and rested their feet on tables. Sarah glared. One glared back, his body stiffening, refusing to pay attention, certainly not to a white teacher, ever again.

Sarah took a deep breath, marched over, lifted his feet from the table, and placed them on the floor. "What's the matter with you?" She didn't wait for an answer. "Where did you learn your manners? If you want to come to school, you must follow rules."

Before she could finish reprimanding the first boy, the one beside him pounced on another beside him. Reaction was instantaneous. Five more surrounded the first two, egging the fight on with guttural sounds and phrases. "Hit 'em up side the haid," one said. "At him, gator," another said. Within seconds the group on the back row was circling warily, the look of animal hatred in their faces.

Sarah looked at Affey, who did not move to separate them but stood as if watching a weird nightmare. Young students screamed and ducked under tables. Older ones swarmed up aisles and stood on tables for a better view. Soon, Sarah thought, they will be upon us. The room was becoming a battleground when suddenly a uniform appeared at the door. A black man dressed in the uniform of a Yankee soldier stormed into the fray.

"That's enough," he commanded. "You want to fight? Fight me. Here I am." The older boys froze in their places. She froze, too.

Jacob was dressed in a uniform. What was Jacob doing wearing a Yankee uniform? *What kind of game is all this, and I'm standing here like a goose taking it seriously,* she thought, watching Jacob as he raised his rifle and commanded the boys to stop.

"Halt these doings, or I will shoot," Jacob said, looking very serious.

The boys who started the fracas backed away, their fists held tight, arms dangling at their sides, mouths open as if unable to move. Jacob walked over, turned both boys to face the door, and commanded, "March." They did.

When boys nearby slapped their knees and laughed at those who were marching out, Jacob shouted, "You," and Sarah heard in his voice a new sound--the sharp sound of the military. Her mouth flew open.

"Step up here and march," Jacob commanded. "March right out of here with these others. And none of you, don't none of you say a word 'til I say you can."

The cluttered schoolroom was heavy with the July heat. Sarah had insisted they begin classes immediately after the brawl. Now, at the end of the school day, she felt the effect of the emotional turmoil of the morning.

"Jacob dressed in a uniform like a soldier," she said, chuckling. "Jacob, pretending to be a Yankee soldier."

Affey placed the chairs upright and moved tables back into place. "He is one," she announced in an uncustomarily blunt way.

"One what?" Sarah asked, looking up and blinking.

"A Union soldier. They recruited him into the first Carolina colored unit. They call it the First South Carolina Volunteer Infantry. Toby joined, too. The way things are going around here, it looks like they may have to shoot somebody."

Sarah didn't know if Affey meant the volunteer colored unit would have to shoot Rebels or refugees or what. She didn't ask.

"We can't last like this, what with the refugees coming, bringing hungry women and children. We don't have the food. There's anger everywhere. You saw the boys today. They're desperate. They've been traveling for months. Refugees are not the only hungry ones. More soldiers are coming."

"More soldiers? What do you mean?"

"Didn't the captain tell you? Union troops are on the move. They plan to take Charleston. They're marching across the islands. Jacobs says they will take Edisto first."

Sarah could hardly breathe. This was coming too fast. When did all this happen? She had forced herself to believe Edisto could avoid the conflict, and now she was faced with the news that the Yankees were coming.

Soldiers. Horses. Cannons.

The island would be trodden. The horror of being caught amid the troops hit her hard. She felt hollow with an indistinct fear that something dreadful would happen to the children.

"What do you mean you will not take me to Adams Run?" Her face felt stiff. She had run down to the cove where Jacob kept his boats. She was out of breath, and when he looked at her coldly and steadily and shook his head, she heard herself screaming at him.

He stopped sanding the skiff, gritted his teeth, and stood up. "I'm telling you I'm not having any more to do with spying."

"Because you're Union now." Her words exploded in the trees. "Is that right?"

There was a long chilled silence. "You're not the one to question which side I'm on."

"Then why did you join a colored Union unit?"

"Because I was told they rounded up all the colored men on St. Helena and forced 'em to join. They hunted 'em down like dogs, Miss Sarah. Like dogs. I'm not about to let them take me like that. I'd rather play the part. Besides, with more blue uniforms than gray uniforms on the islands these days, it's good for business."

In another long silence she had the sense of sinking. Her legs felt weak. She had returned to the island and stayed on to teach his children. And now she was left powerless, a victim, and Jacob stood there mocking her.

"So, you're afraid a patrol will recognize me as the white teacher. I understand how you feel. I'll dress up in slave clothes."

"I cannot take you. The bluecoats are on guard for anyone suspicious. They're stopping trains and boarding boats. If they saw us today, there'd be no mistake about it. They'd know we were delivering a message. I will not take the risk."

Sarah blinked and felt warm tears against her lashes. Behind Jacob, across the vast marshland, the mainland seemed to rise in a purple haze, and she thought, I must warn Adams Run. Anger and frustration rushed through her, and in a fraction of a second she decided she'd find a way. As she darted back up the path, she could hear Jacob calling after her.

Surely it was an apparition. She closed her eyes and when she opened them, Preston, dressed in his field uniform, stood on the schoolhouse steps. Affey stood beside him. The men in blue looked grim.

Preston looked at her with hardly a glimmer of recognition in his eyes, and she almost chuckled. He seemed to be posing, his buttons glinting in the light. How could he act as if they had not shared a bed, laughed, and loved? Her throat tightened.

She tried to swallow. What had he come to say? She was not to be made a fool of. She knew so little about him, yet she had wondered if there would come a time when he would look at her as if he'd never needed her, never touched her, never made love to her. They had promised each other nothing.

She saw his lips move but heard nothing until he spoke the second time. "You do understand, don't you, Miss Edings? You need to escape the danger."

Affey was nodding, tears welling up in her large brown eyes.

"The island is under orders," he said, his tone strange and different. "All the people will be evacuated. All animals. All farm equipment. Food stored in barns and storehouses. Everything goes to St. Helena."

Sarah rushed toward him. "We will not go." After one long and pathetic moment, she realized she was shouting at him and flailing wildly, her fist beating against his chest.

He stood with his arms at his side, as if he could not move. His eyes pleaded for understanding. "Everything will be removed to St. Helena."

"Leave us alone." She gained control and stepped back. Her tone, too, became indifferent, almost businesslike. She had known all along that he'd come to say good-bye, come to say he was leaving for another post. She'd never see him again.

He straightened his sack coat. "I carry orders, Miss Edings. Every animal, every piece of farm equipment will be moved. All contraband moved to other islands. You will not be allowed to accompany the contraband."

She clenched her fist. "Then I will stay out of the way at the summerhouse."

"The bay will not be safe. Nothing along the coast will be safe. After an unsuccessful battle at Secessionville, our forces fell back to regroup. But as we speak, General Hunter is reorganizing. You cannot remain. It will be too dangerous."

For a moment she was quiet, then she spoke so softly she thought he might not hear. "What will happen to Jacob?"

"Jacob and his family will go with all the others. They will be safe. I promise you that."

"Affey?"

"I have spoken to Miss Towne. Affey will have a teaching position at the Pennsylvania School."

Soldiers stood so close she could see their chests move as they breathed. She spoke, but her voice was small and pained. "Can't you tell your men that I have no place to go? Don't I count for something? I can't. . ."

She was choking under the sense of helplessness.

"You must leave." He moved toward her, then as if thinking better of it with his men watching, he stood firm and placed his hand on his saber.

She turned and walked away from the glaring eyes of his men. Preston followed, and when she whirled to say something, to protest, to plea, she felt him so close she could smell him.

His mouth twitched. "Can't you see? I cannot protect you any longer."

"I do not ask for protection. I choose not to leave." She looked from side to side trying to grasp the enormity of the situation.

"You have no choice. You cannot remain in the center of a war. I have made arrangements for Jacob to accompany you to the outskirts of Charleston. There you will be met and put on the train to Edgefield. If my information is correct, upstate may be the only place where you will be safe."

She had no words. She could only look at him, unable to separate her hurt from fear. It all blended together in a pain that was almost intolerable, and she lashed out in cold-eyed anger.

"Adams Run knows all about your plans to cut the rail line. I was a spy, didn't you know? A courier. I gathered information and sent it back to the mainland. I used you." She spoke flatly, thinking of the miniature oval and his wife with the porcelain skin.

What did it matter that she'd be taken into custody, shipped down to Port Royal, and turned over to General Hunter? What did she care that she'd be returned under a truce flag at some agreed, out-of-the-way location? What did anything matter? She glared at the captain and waited for his response.

He dropped his arms from her shoulders but did not drop his gaze. "I know, Sarah. I knew all along."

Somewhere there were the sounds of horses and hooves and a sharp command to attention. He seemed not to hear the noise and asked, "Do you think that changes the way I feel about you? It's just that we have duties of our own."

He took her hands in his.

She did not move. His hands were warm.

"Sarah, there's nothing more you can do to help your cause. I know you don't believe it now, but I care about you, and you must leave. Nothing here is safe."

"Then don't let this happen. Let me stay." She glanced instinctively toward his men.

He did not look their way. "It's too dangerous. I care too much to let you stay."

Their eyes met. "Will I ever see you again?"

"I don't know." He paused. "When this madness settles and the time is right. When I can, I will come. But for now, it is important that you move to safety."

His kiss was tender. She moved away to look into his face. A soft wind rushed through the pines.

She was not strong enough to fight this. "I understand."

Preston cleared his throat. This time his voice came out in a whisper. "I must go."

She could not breathe as he put on his wide-brimmed hat and walked away.

CHAPTER

Sixteen

Captain Wilcox watched the crest of a moon turn the tall pines to silver and signaled his men to stop. A breeze moaned through the branches, and he thought it sounded like people. Could be refugees. Could be deserters. He held his breath and forced a mental picture of his position. Three miles south of Adams Run. Ahead lay the shimmering tracks of the Charleston and Savannah Rail Line.

"Might be them sharpshooters," the man beside him whispered. "I heard of 'em all the way out in the territories." Cox was a wiry Ohioan who had learned about setting explosives out West. Cox knew his business but needed no distractions to get this job done.

"Mounted riflemen," guessed the man crouching on the other side of the captain, a man whose name was Dorn. Wilcox guessed if the riflemen were around, he'd hear them soon enough thundering down Jacksonboro Road. He did not flinch.

"God help us if it's them. They shoot at anything that moves." Dorn was a grungy thick figure with a straggly beard who talked too much, but Wilcox took his word when he said he had experience with the Union telegraph system. Wilcox hadn't realized how hard it would be to find men for this mission.

"Lower your voice," Wilcox said.

"They riding from Savannah to Charleston harassing our men," Dorn muttered. "I hear tell they barely twelve years old."

Wilcox took out his watch but couldn't see. He guessed it was quarter past midnight, but the time didn't matter. They had come up Toogodoo Creek on the ebb tide and timed the mission to leave on the outgoing tide. Jacob would be waiting in the reeds, his dark face anxious in the night, his eyes piercing through the darkness. Jacob was Preston Wilcox' only source of comfort this night.

He gave his men their last instructions with words that were terse, spoken in monosyllables. Dorn would move out first to cut the telegraph line. After that, Cox would move out to set the charge. When the moon hid behind the clouds, they would separate. "I'm covering," Wilcox said. "We'll meet back at the boat."

This was his final duty in this war. He'd agreed to the assignment because he could not forget the pain in Sarah's eyes when he told her she had to leave the island. He could still see her standing alone and helpless as he turned to his men and rode off. He could hear her small voice asking, "Don't I count for something?"

The misery this war was causing sickened him. He should have stayed home and left the South alone. He'd come to believe that: the North should have left the South alone. We didn't have to go to war. He had looked at it like an adventure, an expedition, but now he realized it was a hideous nightmare befalling innocent people. The slaves were free, but they were wandering around in the woods, displaced and hungry. The more quickly this war was over, the better, whatever the cost.

He had tried to forget Sarah, but some things could not be forgotten. It was impossible. A man didn't automatically stop thinking about a woman like Sarah. Weeks had passed since he volunteered for this sortie. Last night he'd stayed awake for hours planning this attack, but most of the time he thought about Sarah. About midnight he had dropped off to sleep and dreamed he heard the train coming down the track. He dreamed he heard the explosion and saw smoke billowing everywhere, pines blazing, sparks raining down enough fire to cover the woods for miles.

In his dream, people stood on the other side of the tracks—school children singing their ABC's. He saw Sarah standing there and heard her calling to him. He couldn't believe she was there.

Even now, just remembering the dream, he wiped the sweat from his eyes with the arm of his shirt.

In the dream, he warned her, told her she was risking death from the explosion, but she refused to move. Instead she pulled the children to her, sheltering them with her arms, her hair wet with perspiration, her eyes reflecting the hot glare of the burning woods. The children kept singing, unaware of the destruction around them while Sarah asked him from across the rail line, "Why, Preston? Why?"

"Sarah," he shouted in the dream, thinking any moment she would be hit. "Take the children. Run. Leave this place."

Everything was flaming, snapping, roaring, and the fire racing up the line. She didn't hear. Her eyes searched for him, her voice pleaded with him. She held out her hands to him.

The breeze picked up, the pines moaned, and Captain Wilcox blinked to clear his mind. He smelled smoke, decided it was drifting from the direction of the tracks, and knew Cox had laid the powder charge and lit the fuse. Time to fall back.

He waited. Where were his men? In his hand he held the Adams he'd bought from an arms importer in New Haven, his other revolver he'd given to Sarah. He smiled to think of Sarah when she'd told him she was a teacher.

Where the hell was Cox? Time to fall back. Fire lit up the trees on the other side of Jacksonboro Road, and what he spotted was a silhouette that popped up and fired when the moon crept from behind a cloud.

He fired back.

The sharpshooter fell but a split second too late. Wilcox smelled burned flesh, knew the flesh was his, felt nothing but a sting in his leg, then nothing, nothing at all. He stumbled and kept moving until he crossed the shallow waters of Adams Run, a trickle really, then made his way along the route of snakes and vines that led back to the Toogodoo.

Once he took a wrong turn. He stopped to listen for the sound of water and, for one horrible moment suspended in the darkness, he heard nothing. He peered ahead desperate to spot Jacob and the longboat. He'd memorized every fork. Jacob was waiting.

But where?

Pain shot up his leg and into his spine. Blood drained down into his shoe. He heard the squishing sound and wondered if this was all the South he would ever see. He wanted to laugh, but the pain pulled him down, down, down into the water, into the darkness, and he felt far, far away.

When he woke, he thought everything was snapping and roaring and the fire was racing up the line and Sarah was standing, holding her hands out to him.

"Run back, Sarah. Run back. I'm sorry. I'm sorry. Please understand."

He saw a dark shadow standing over him and felt someone shaking him. He tried to sit up and made a gasping noise when he spoke. "What is it?"

"Nothing, cap'n. You're just having a nightmare. A sharpshooter got you on the leg. The bleeding's stopped, but you need to keep calm and quiet. Voices carry over water. We can't afford to have more Rebels jump up on us. A lot of outlaws roaming around out here now."

"Where are we?"

"Back on the island. In the cove where I used to hide my boats."

Wilcox looked around and realized he was lying in the longboat pulled up under cassina bushes and wax myrtle. "Cox and Dorn?"

"They doubling back to find that sharpshooter. They took my skiff and we gonna meet 'em around the bend at nightfall. Meanwhile we gonna stay right here where we are and let your leg mend. It's not bad, but you'll need to be rested when we get you to the doctor."

He slept and when he woke, he thought about the question he'd begun to ask himself so many times. What had happened to the war his sister thought so holy? That noble and honorable war that abolitionists ranted and raved about, that "sense of purpose?"

Part of the answer lay in his own forces. The behavior he had witnessed in Beaufort, the shameless, animal-like rape and pillage, the humiliation, had nauseated him. They'd made a mockery of the war.

"I'm mustering out of service, Jacob. I'm going home."

Jacob looked determined not to say anything, not to ask questions.

"Home. Milford. I have a daughter there, a little girl. She's alone. My wife died, you see." He hesitated, thinking Jacob might have questions. "Or I might decide to go out West. There's gold and silver to be mined out there. And railroads to build. They need good railroad men. They're building railroads over mountains as tall as the sky."

Jacob was looking down the river. Wilcox raised his voice enough to get Jacob's attention. "After the war I'll come back and you'll have yourself another boat, maybe three. Maybe you will own a whole fleet of boats."

"Just might, sir. Just might do that." Jacob grinned.

"I've been writing a letter to Miss Edings. I want to tell her my plans. I didn't know how to post the letter, but I brought it with me. I thought if I gave it to you, you might . . ."

"Yes, sir, I'll see that the letter gets to the right place." Jacob said. There was no need to say more. Jacob had contacts.

Wilcox had spent hours composing the letter. He remembered every word.

Headquarters Expeditionary Corps
Hilton Head, South Carolina

Miss Edings,
I know not when I will be able to post another letter, but you must believe that I think of you always. You must believe that I did what was best for you and that our separation has a meaning beyond our understanding.
Affey continues teaching with Miss Laura Towne. With high hopes

they are adding a building to the school across the road from the Baptist Church. Affey is blissfully content living in a modest cabin on a plantation with Toby, who is plainly proud to be trusted with his parcel of land.

The colored unit has been disbanded; thus Jacob could not be more dedicated to his family nor more dependable as a waterman. Due to the uncertain state in the city of Charleston, he limits his trips there, but I understand from him that his business in these parts is far ahead. He and Sully have moved from a small cabin and this week will move to larger quarters on the Fripp Plantation where he, too, will become a sharecropper.

It has been quiet here so far, but there is much danger on the islands and in the city itself. You would not be safe, yet I yearn to see you and feel heavy at heart to know the end of the war is slow in coming. I wish I were well out of it.

Yours faithfully,

Preston Wilcox
Captain, U.S.V.

He looked at Jacob out of the corner of his eye, and wondered what the future held for the freed man. What did it hold for himself? They were both entering a period neither of them could imagine. Nor did they see what lurked in the palmetto bushes beside them. They failed to sense any danger at all until a dark hand reached out and grabbed the line that secured the longboat.

For a second Wilcox thought of Mad Rhoda and how she played her tricks. Sarah believed the old woman lived at the bay.

"Well, well, well. Who do we have here?" The voice was not Rhoda's. It belonged to a large black man with a pinkish welt across his face, who stood on the creek bank, holding a knife, his legs spread wide apart. "What you doin' heah?"

"What business is it of yours?" Wilcox spoke like the officer he was, but as soon as he spoke, he regretted it and looked at Jacob as if looking for help. Jacob cleared his throat.

The black man stepped forward. "We do the askin', white man. We do the whippin'." He turned the knife blade so that it glistened in the sun. "We do the cuttin'."

Wilcox heard deep laughter from behind the palmetto bushes. His eyes darted in the direction of the laugh where another man appeared. An unseen outlaw lurking in the bushes.

Jacob yelled into the bushes. "Call your man off, King. This white man works against the secesh, not with them. He's a good white man."

"They ain't no such thing as a good white man. Anyhow, you a nigger. What you doing out here wid a white man? You wid us or you wid them?"

"You know who I am, King." Jacob seemed to know the man he was dealing with behind the bushes.

"Yeah, I know you; your territory out there on the water. This here's my island now. What business you got here? You got to explain where you going just like any other nigger."

"I'm not just any nigger, King. Call your man off. We just stopping by to rest. We plan to be gone by nightfall."

"See to it you are. We got guns."

"I'm sure you do," Jacob replied coldly.

Within seconds the outlaws were leaving, their laughter echoing deep in the woods.

Wilcox swallowed, trying hard to sit up, and shivering with the realization that law and order would pull out with his troops. He had allowed himself to believe the war would end quickly and within months he would come back to find Sarah polishing silver and serving tea, her old plantation house rebuilt, the summerhouse rented out to rich Northerners. He'd been wrong. Somehow, no matter how formidable the odds, he'd return. He'd rebuild Sarah's island. Her life.

At dusk Jacob cast off, and they floated away to meet Dorn and Cox around the bend. Preston Wilcox sat, silent and thoughtful. The wind freshened. His vision blurred by the wind. He blinked and turned to look behind him. He wanted to take one last look at the island.

One last look, he thought. *One last look.*

CHAPTER

Seventeen

April 1865 - Three Years Later

"*S*arah Caroline Edings."

The name pierced the air so harsh and sharply, Sarah hardly recognized it as her own. She glared in the direction of the voice. Then she raised her shoulders, approached the table, and thrust the Edings family Bible under the government processor's nose.

"I will use my own, sir." She pulled a veil over her face and tucked it tightly under her chin. A black veil. She hoped he noticed she was in mourning for the South.

The agent's face turned pink. He took his time. When he looked into her eyes, his expression was blank.

She'd been waiting for two days, during which time she and her father had been sleeping on the floor in Trinity Episcopal. Taking the oath of allegiance to the Union was her ticket, the only way she could stay on the island. In January, after Savannah surrendered, General William T. Sherman set aside all the Sea Islands for the exclusive settlement of freed slaves, the thousands who followed his army through Georgia. Sherman had no way to feed the throngs. His own men survived by stealing from corncribs and smokehouses, devastating the fields and breaking into houses. Killing anyone in the way if they had to.

Sarah and her father had started for the coast some weeks after word came about the surrender at Appomatox. She had followed the back roads William Edings could point out when his mind was clear. When it was safe to do so, they stayed with cousins. Sometimes they slept in churches, but most nights they had made camp on ground that was cold and hard on April nights. Along the way they had passed through charred fields that should have been green and thick with knee-high cotton this late but were now lying fallow. The smoldering ruins of plantation houses and the silence was frightening. Where were the people? Scattered like her own family, she supposed, living with cousins or friends.

Dispossessed.

Dead.

The government processor seemed to smirk. "You the lady come to teach the niggers?"

That last word made her head jerk. With difficulty, she focused on the man sitting at the table.

"That's what I've come back to do. I teach children. I am employed by the Rev. Joseph Walker who has connections with your Freedmen's Bureau."

"The Rev. Walker from Philadelphia? Yeah, I heard of him."

"Yes, well, he was a well-known minister at the Episcopal chapel on St. Helena Island until your forces ruined everything."

"How do I know who you are?"

"I have with me a letter of introduction." She shoved papers toward him. "I believe you will find my things in order."

He looked at the list and squinted. "You have with you a planter by the name of William Evans Edings? Planters are not allowed on the island, miss."

"I know your regulations. I am aware that planters are not allowed to claim their land. Not yet. However, my father is not returning to his plantation. He will be living on church grounds with me. He is not well." Sarah nodded toward an old man sitting on a bench in the ballroom at the Seabrook House, staring into space.

"Number four." The agent bellowed and pointed to another table, above which hung a picture of Andrew Johnson. Of course she knew

Abraham Lincoln had been shot, but she was surprised they already had the new President's portrait hanging on the wall. She almost smiled. Johnson was a Southerner. "His Accidency, the President," one paper called him. During last year's presidential campaign, he'd called the South traitors. He had said, "traitors must be punished and impoverished." Well, government policies could change. But she would not wait for that.

She'd live day by day. Feel nothing. Believe in nothing. Her conviction that right would win had evaporated the day Preston Wilcox appeared, giving orders to evacuate. She had waited for a letter, which never came, and then Sherman marched across Carolina and burned Columbia to the ground. War could reach out and take everything. She'd learned that the hard way.

She took the oath of allegiance to the Union, not listening to the words, only looking around the ballroom, stripped now of its priceless European paintings, replaced with pictures of the new President. The glittering French chandelier was gone. The walls had been scratched and marked by men she'd come to loathe.

With the piece of paper in her hand, she joined her father then headed for the stairs and fresh air. A colored sentry blocked her way. "Ma'am, you have to wait. You must have an escort."

"But I have taken the oath," she said, waving the paper in his face. "See. I have a form to prove it."

"Yes, ma'am, I see the paper. That don't matter. Nobody is allowed to move around the island without an escort."

A white corporal came to her rescue, a talkative sort she liked immediately who took her father by the arm, led him down the stairs and out to the wagon.

"That's it, sir. You just come along and we'll get you in this conveyance and on your way now that they done give you a fresh horse."

Sarah corrected him. "They have loaned me a horse and only because Reverend Walker insisted."

"That preacher friend of yours must have powerful connections inside the Freedmen's Bureau if they lending you a horse and wagon. Yes, ma'am, powerful connections. This here's a good horse. What name you giving him?"

"Coosaw," she said, recalling a favorite strawberry roan she'd had as a child and feeling unduly satisfied. She would savor not only the horse but also the comforting feeling of being home again. Well, she was on the island, at least.

"You say you gonna' live in a church?"

"Actually in a cabin behind the church."

"All the churches belong to slaves, you know. The whole island belong to 'em." The corporal's voice implied his displeasure.

She shrugged. She knew Field Order Number 15 had given the islands to the freedmen. Sherman even promised that each family would receive forty acres of land and an army mule to work the land, but she had come to reclaim the Edings land. She had taken the oath. She tucked the paper in her pocket.

"Where're the crates, ma'am? You said you come to teach the freed slaves. I couldn't hep but notice you got no crates."

She didn't understand the reason for his question, so she only nodded while he looked at her as if what he was saying was perfectly obvious.

"Yes, ma'am. You brought a trunk. I see your trunk. But I'm asking about them wooden crates filled with them city clothes. Dresses and boots and them silly hats."

"Dresses and silly hats? What do you mean?"

"Like them teachers from Massachusetts bring with 'em. The young ladies who come down from the North to teach for the Freedmen's Bureau. They bring crates of fancy clothes with 'em. It's a sight for sore eyes, the way they dress up them darkies. The Northern teachers say if you want darkies to come to school, you'll have to give 'em clothes."

Sarah sighed. While she was upstate, she'd taught white children during the day then slipped quietly down to the Episcopal Church at night and helped Reverend Walker teach black children.

She knew how to teach slave children because she had taught more than her share. She knew how to handle restless, angry children. She knew how, and she liked it. Maybe teaching on the mainland would have been a better idea, but this is where she belonged.

"I'll need no fancy clothes to entice the children to learn, corporal. I will, however, keep those fancy clothes in mind," she said, stepping into the wagon with all the schoolmarm poise she could muster.

Sitting stiffly beside her father, she forced herself to look ahead. She took a deep breath and urged Coosaw to move on down the road.

I can do this, she kept telling herself.

I can. I can do this.

She had returned once before, back when she was young and hopeful and thought she could save the island from destruction. But those dreams had died. When Captain Preston Wilcox demanded she evacuate, she left Edisto, bewildered and heartbroken. Jacob had packed her belongings and put her on board his longboat. In a rage, she had caught the train to Augusta.

All this time she'd secretly wondered if the captain remained on the island. Day and night, all the time she was in Edgefield, she taught children to escape her thoughts of Preston Wilcox.

She had found no escape.

After federal troops burned Columbia and she helped Miriah with the planting, she knew it was time to leave the upcountry. By that time Lucy had fled to Texas with her precious daughter, and Sarah was grateful Lucy had been spared the terror of Sherman's troops, Federal forces that marched across the state and cut a path thirty miles wide. Somehow Sherman missed Francis Pickens' plantation.

Lucy and Douschka had arrived unharmed in Texas. Lucy had taken what was left of her jewels and bought safety along her route, but once at home Lucy found her mother was taking in boarders to pay taxes. The Holcombe homestead was in disrepair. Her sister's husband had come home from the war, determined to pack his wife and four children off to Mexico.

In her last letter, Lucy sounded resigned.

"As you well know I do not always agree with Mr. Pickens. But in this, I do. He writes: 'We have to accept our condition for the present.' Alas, I try. I try. I shall return shortly and insist that my sister return to Edgefield with me. It breaks my heart that I cannot give my mother financial aid, but we are far too poor for that. I tell her, as I tell you, my dear friend, Sarah, you will always have a home with us."

After Appomattox, Sarah's desire to leave for the coast overcame her. Lucy and Douschka were gone. Miriah was lonely and melancholy. Sarah was sick of all the gloom and tragic apprehension in Edgefield District. Everyday a freed slave was being whipped or abused or shot. Bushwhacking and murder was going on all around. Miriah's old slave woman was afraid to go into town. The shock of losing the war had turned Edgefield into mayhem, its citizens lashing out, retaliating.

Freedmen became their scapegoat.

Sarah was sick at heart at the racial divide. She needed a change. She wanted to believe she could do something worthwhile.

So she was back on Edisto, the memories of Preston Wilcox returning.

When she stopped the wagon at Trinity Episcopal, smoke coiled from a cabin behind the church, and Sarah thought she smelled bread. She was certain she heard a chant.

And there, standing in the doorway of the cabin, smiling and waving, was her old friend, Rhoda.

CHAPTER

Eighteen

It was July when she received a note asking her to meet secretly with a group of planters. At night. In an abandoned plantation house.

They could be flagging her, setting her up. For what Sarah could not imagine, but for their own purposes, she was certain of that. Here she was, the only planter living on the island, but she had no way to pay her taxes. She was teaching freed slaves. Frankly, most days she felt she was swimming against the tide.

She must act first and foremost as a teacher. She must not forget. Otherwise, they might assume she was the chosen one with the new government, which was certainly not the case, but they did not know that. She had to be careful.

She arrived at the Brick House Plantation early and found her way to a room she recognized as the library. Within seconds she was brushing dust from empty shelves. Where were the books? Ripped apart and used to kindle fires, she guessed. Priceless figurines lay broken and scattered on the floor. The stained glass window at the end of the long room had been shattered.

The men would arrive by rowboat, the note said, but they would wait until the government processors were drunk and falling asleep. It would be dark by then. That's good, she thought. The Westcoat boys didn't need to see the sad condition of their grandfather's house, the only house on Edisto made of brick. Her father had always explained to visitors that the Brick House was a notable structure of Georgian architecture. Tonight William Edings couldn't remember anything about the Brick House. She had tried to explain where she was going, but Rhoda waved her off saying, "You leave him be, chile. He don't need to recall the past."

The men entered, their hats pulled low, looking furtively behind them, as if they expected the government processors to be on their heels.

"Lee Westcoat," the first man inside said. He lifted his lantern and studied the destruction of his family home place. As he placed the light on the mantle above the marble fireplace, he noted the missing portrait of his grandfather.

"It's probably hanging in a drawing room on the Hudson, among some Yankee general's collection of trophies." He spoke this to no one in particular, then buttoned his jacket securely and stood, straddle-legged, in front of a make-believe fire.

"Miss Edings, the teacher, I believe." He smiled the smile of a man who wanted power and knew how to go after it. Also the smile of a white man who hated her for teaching slaves to read.

"Sarah Edings, of the Edings Plantation on Pierre Creek."

"Of the former Edings Plantation," he corrected sharply then added, "And a summer place at Edings Bay." His lips grew thin, as if he wanted to make a disparaging remark about William Edings' daughter who was now a teacher, but he was trying hard to control his tongue.

"Our fathers were friends," Sarah said, standing directly in front of him, willing herself to maintain her composure.

"I hear reports that your plantation house was burned."

"Only a portion. Much of the main house remains. However, a foreigner claims it as his own. I live in a cabin behind Trinity Episcopal. I am an employee of the church."

"Miss Edings," Lee Westcoat said, continuing his smooth smile and starting in on a diatribe he was obviously prepared for. "You are in a very unusual position, and the truth is, we need your cooperation. You see, on some of the barrier islands, the treasury agents are dividing the land into forty-acre tracts and selling it to the slaves outright. Now, God forbid they do that to us, but the nigras are armed and between them and government agents, we have little hope of regaining the rights to our land. Word is the new government plans to drive the white population off the islands entirely."

"I'm not convinced the government can do that," she said flatly.

Westcoat fired back. "The government can do that because there is no one in Washington who can stop it. We don't have anyone in place to stop it because we don't have representation."

Sarah scowled. "What do you mean?"

"We now have a provisional government, as you well know, but even after we have duly elected officials, word is that Congress will refuse to seat any elected representatives from the Southern states. The Radicals declare that we are not a state, that we are not entitled to the formation of a state government. There's a group up there that wants us to remain under military rule. The kind you now live under each day."

Men in the back of the room mumbled. If she could see their faces, she would recognize them, for they had lived here on the island most of their lives and attended social gatherings. Surely they understood that Lincoln's policy was now Johnson's policy.

"But it was Lincoln's view that the southern states never left the Union," Sarah said. "South Carolina is a state and a state we will remain. How can a few Radicals refuse to admit a state government its representatives to Congress?"

"Maybe I have not made myself clear. I had hoped it would not necessary to ask this straight out. But I must. Miss Edings, where do you stand?"

Her hands and feet tingled. She had known in the back of her mind that the old life was over, but she had refused to face it. She was beginning to believe that for the past three months she had been living a dream. Lee Westcoat was waking her up.

"Radicals rule Washington, Miss Edings. We don't have representation."

"But Johnson is following Lincoln's plan, the same plan Lincoln would have put into place. It seems simple to me."

"Believe me, Miss Edings, there's a definite move afoot to keep the South under a long and ruthless military rule. Senators like Thad Stevens are vindictive. If they have their way, the South will be treated like a conquered foreign country indefinitely."

"But Lincoln made his position clear in his inauguration speech." She closed her eyes and quoted. She knew it by heart. "*With malice toward none, with charity toward all . . . to bind up the nation's wounds."*

Harsh words came from another planter. "Lincoln's dead and Andrew Johnson is a drunkard. A backwoods lout."

Lee nodded. "The new president is no match for the likes of Thad Stevens, that's for sure."

Other men agreed. "Nothing but a bunch of opportunists up there."

"Promoting nigger freedom."

"They don't give a damn who owns our land."

"It's imperative that we find some way to speak out." Lee seemed firm. He was obviously in charge of the group.

Another voice came from the dark, and in it Sarah heard a desperation that sent a shiver up her spine.

"We already spoke out. We spoke loud and clear, and then went up and signed the papers to secede. You see what secession cost us? Look at us. A group of white men so defeated, so afraid the niggers might run tell the government men we planning to take our own land, we afraid to meet in the daylight."

The man's eyes were watery and bulging, his mouth twitching, moving nervously. She hardly recognized him but he was the other Westcoat boy. She was sure. Tally was the age of her brother.

She turned her head to look Tally in the eye. "We can begin again."

"It's too late," Tally snapped.

Lee Westcoat's face turned red. "It won't be if we get organized, if we get representation and start packing committee meetings."

Tally moved to the front, dragging one leg across the floor. "Well, it's too late for me. They burned everything. Land. Houses, corn cribs. The smokehouses, the quarters. If they allowed it, there's nothing to come back to. Nothing. I got no money. I don't give a damn about the land. I'm leaving."

Sarah stared incredulously, remembering that Tally had followed Beauregard to Virginia then fought in a battle the papers called the Wilderness. Now, his mind seemed confused and war-weary, his emotions paralyzed. She moved toward him.

"Tally, this is our land. We must find a way to hold on to what is legally ours."

"There's land in Brazil." He stood in the light now. She could see his crutches in the corner.

"Brazil?" She closed her eyes, trying to visualize a globe.

"Brazil," Tally said, matter-of-factly. "We can begin a colony there." He pulled an advertisement from his shirt pocket. "A ship is sailing next week. 'A commodious ship of ample tonnage with comfortable accommodations for at least five hundred passengers. Anyone desiring to become members of this colony can do so by applying.' Who will go with me?"

She felt a sudden anxiety. What if Tally sailed to Brazil and all the other planters followed? What would that mean? She'd be the only white left on the island, and she'd be alone and penniless and rendered helpless in the face of rising taxes.

All at once she felt hostile, threatened by Tally's announcement.

"This is my home. I am not abandoning Edisto again," she said.

Tally's eyes grew larger. "We can make another home. Think about it. A colony of our own. A life like the one we had before the war."

She had seen the advertisement and didn't believe a word of it. "It's a travel scheme dreamed up by Langston Hastings. Don't be taken in by the likes of his kind. Look where the Donner Party ended. Lost in the Sierra Nevada during the worst winter on record. Dead. Or worse. Hastings is not to be trusted. It's one of his get-rich-quick schemes, and you need to think long and hard before you fall for it."

Tally took a book from his pocket and held it up. "It's a land of milk and honey. The soil is superb. The climate is tropical and water is plentiful." He grinned. "You can scratch in a few grains and the crop never needs to be worked."

Lee Westcoat lifted both hands to gain control of the situation and looked at Tally coldly and steadily. "There's no need for any man here to run to South America. With enough pressure in Washington, we can reclaim the land. There's no reason to think we can't double our acreage."

"Double our acreage?" Tally's laugh echoed in the empty room. "You got ten thousand freed slaves running loose on these islands claiming all the land belongs to them. Demanding contracts for wages. If you agree to wages, you ruin all prospects of any profit. You got no say in the government. You got nothing. Nothing. I'm joining the Southern Colonization Society."

Tally moved toward the door, his crippled leg trailing behind him. When he reached the corner and grabbed his crutches, the other men stood aside to let him through. Sarah turned to Lee Westcoat and glared.

"It seems to me that the first thing we need to do is work out terms with the freed slaves."

"Work out terms?" Lee Westcoat sounded thunderstruck.

Sarah did not blink. "Yes, by validating contracts and paying the rate they pay in other states." There was a pause. She heard the silence pounding in her ears. "I, for one, am willing to employ our people at a reasonable rate. Indeed, I wish to."

There. She'd said it.

"Miss Edings, that is not what the nigras want. They don't want your magnanimity. They want your land. They want to own the houses they were born in. They claim the land for their own and are making plans to take over. One group making plans calls themselves the Worthy Sons of America, and they've got some very outspoken leaders. Like your Jacob."

Her head snapped back as if someone had slapped her. "Jacob?" She hoped Lee could not see the shock in her eyes.

He looked at her warily. "Your man, Jacob, is buying up land right and left. He made all kinds of Yankee friends during the war. He worked both sides as a courier. Didn't you know?"

To her horror all she knew was that she was about to cry. Her eyes filled and she thought, no, not now. She spoke quickly. "Jacob traveled the waters freely. He saved his earnings. That doesn't mean he was a friend to the enemy."

Lee Westcoat seemed to gloat. "He worked both sides, Miss Edings. He made friends with the Yankees. They are now repaying him by selling him our land."

She wondered what else Lee Westcoat knew. Did he know that Jacob delivered messages to Adams Run? That he had risked everything to transport her on his longboat, to gather the information she needed? Yes, he joined the Union Army unit on St. Helena but only because it was the safest thing to do. If he worked for the Yankees after that, then he was doing so to provide for his family. It could be wishful thinking, she supposed, but she could understand why he would do that.

Then she remembered the guns, the rifles Jacob hoarded during the war. She had seen them with her own eyes. But he had explained. He would not deceive her. Surely not.

She shook her head, unable to speak, only looking at the door.

Oh, God let me out of here before I cry.

Lee Westcoat turned his attention elsewhere. "We need to form alliances. They think all Democrats are schemers. Well, we'll show them how good we are. We start by packing their committee meetings. Everything will be fine as long as we do it on the sly. We need to join forces with every Rebel we can contact, every man who saw his brother die, every planter's son or daughter who lost a home and wants to rise up to take back what is rightfully theirs. Can I count on you, Miss Edings?"

She didn't bother to answer. She didn't even say goodnight but marched out to her mount and headed Coosaw straight ahead. She didn't slow him down until the turnoff from the main road. Moonlight struck the giant trunks of the dark oaks. Silvery moss hung from the limbs. Wild grape and muscadine vines wrapped themselves up and over the path to the cabin, as if to form a canopy, and when a night heron rustled its wings and flew from its perch, she thought it was a sign.

She would have nothing to do with schemes and alliances.

Sitting astride Coosaw, motionless, she felt melancholy, not unlike the sense of sadness she'd felt when she saw Tally's broken body at the Brick House. The wind hummed in the pines, and she had an odd notion that the past, the innocence she knew as a child when she perched in the window with Affey to watch the wild geese fly north, was moving farther and farther out to sea.

Or wherever ghosts go when they realize nothing can stop the unstoppable.

CHAPTER
Nineteen

*S*he'd be the only woman in the church. The only white person except for two Federal agents coming to explain the unexplainable to a thousand freed slaves who were angry, frustrated, and resentful because the new government was not keeping its promises. Squatters spilled out across the cemetery and stood on grave markers, openly irreverent, noisily preparing for a showdown.

She tried to smile and was grateful when they stood back to make way. One held up a stake with a number painted on it. He grinned proudly. "Good evening, Teacher. This be my number. When they call it out, forty acres and a mule be mine."

They'd been waiting for months, living in scattered tents and shanties, the ten thousand who followed General William Tecumseh Sherman across Georgia. When the general announced that the Sea Islands between Savannah and Charleston belonged to freed slaves, the squatters praised the Lord, Mr. Lincoln, and the new Federal government. Now, eight months later, they and their families were sick and weak and angry.

And they were hungry.

Their women lined up at the Freedmen's Bureau store carrying a sack or a box or a tub on their backs and waited for handouts of government rations of corn and molasses. No one was taking to the fields. Babies were dying. At school the children were getting harder and harder to manage.

Promises and false hope had changed her school children, changed everybody, Sarah thought, entering the sanctuary. Trinity Episcopal was a shell of a church now, the silver chalice stolen, linens used to wrap wounds, the chancel furniture used for firewood. It saddened her. She walked down the aisle looking straight ahead.

It was a hundred and two degrees inside. Children were fanning with palm fronds to keep the air stirring. The two Union men were already seated in the pulpit. Wedging herself into the front pew, she wondered what they could possibly say. At the best of times, it would be difficult to deal with men who were desperate and hungry. Squatters in a rage might well be impossible.

The agent in charge, now starting the meeting, was short and bald, and when she saw the top of his head shining with nervous perspiration, she wished she could feel sorry for him, but she didn't.

"It is the President's desire," he began slowly, enunciating clearly, as if he were talking to children or foreigners, "that the land owners be allowed to return to their plantations."

A thousand variations of anger sounded, voices shouting in unison: "Mr. Lincoln promised."

"Mr. Lincoln is dead," the Union man responded. "We have a new president and Andrew Johnson desires that you enter into government contracts with the land owners."

"Never," the squatters shouted. "We can't do it."

Loud guffaws. Shuffling of feet. Down the row, the gleam of a knife blade. Until this moment Sarah had felt safe, but an angry crowd could turn. There were all those stories she'd heard as a child. Stories about slave uprisings, rumors of rape and kitchen house murders. The tales about violence against white women were the worst. But she was a teacher, the only teacher on the island, she reminded herself. This crowd wouldn't turn on her. She squirmed, crossed her arms, and covered her breast.

"Sir." From somewhere in the back a voice boomed, but it sounded calm and forthright. "You are asking us to do something we cannot do."

The tone of the voice was so conciliatory that she felt more secure, and she turned to look at the man walking toward her. He wore a dark frock coat and a bow tie with a stand up collar stiff with starch. His bow tie was neatly tied. His hair, peppered with gray, stood out against his reddish brown face and sharp cheeks. Indeed, there was something about his gait, something from her past that seemed so familiar, so agonizingly real that she felt faint and held to the edge of the pew to keep her balance.

It had been three years since the evacuation, since Jacob took her to Charleston on the longboat and put her on the train for Augusta. Three years at her sister's house plowing fields and planting crops, canning vegetables and scrubbing floors. Three years teaching in Edgefield, wondering, worrying what was happening on the coast, not daring to think the worst, trying to hold up her father and her sister, trying not to sink.

What had it been for Jacob? Was it true that he worked for the other side after she left? Had he spilled her secrets?

He passed by so close she could touch him, but he gave no notice that he recognized her.

He stepped into the pulpit. "I speak for the Worthy Sons of America, sir. We cannot sign government contracts without equal footing. We are free people now. We must conduct our own affairs." When he spoke, he seemed taller than she remembered, more alive, more animated.

Squatters around her clapped, stomped their feet, and whistled. Jacob raised his hand, and when the crowd was quiet again, he said, "You see, sirs, your government says one thing one day and another on another day. The President needs to wipe the slate clean with us."

The officials looked shaken, so uneasy they could hardly speak. "I beg you to lay aside your bitterness," the second agent said, "and sign these contracts with the planters." He got his handkerchief out and wiped his face, his head, and his neck.

"No, sir," Jacob said. "The day has come when we've got to stand up and say 'no' in the name of liberty. We demand fair and equal treatment before the world and Washington." On Jacob's face there was the look of salvation, the same look she'd seen in Baptist churches upstate. "If the white planters want to cooperate with us, let them stand here with us, side by side, cheek by jowl and work out something. The people here are aroused, sir, and rightly so. The government says they want the best for the free men. They tell us it's the law. Then they step in and tell us another law."

"The law is what's best for all people," the agent said, angry now and frustrated but trying to recover.

"*All* people? *What* people?" Jacob asked, his skin glistening, his voice

deep and rolling. "I'm worrying about the truth. We invite the landowners to come among us and look us in the eye."

Jacob glanced into the audience and when he saw her, it seemed an
eternity before he smiled. Sarah didn't know how long they looked at
each other before he spoke again.

"I hope you will forgive us," he said. Was he speaking to her?

She felt flushed. It came to her that Jacob's face was handsome in an
exotic way, and she trembled to think he was stepping across two hundred
years of slavery, standing before his own people and gazing at her, the
daughter of his old master. He smiled, and something leapt up in her,
something she pushed out of her mind, but it was there for one clear,
clean second while she held his gaze. It rose up and settled in her chest
like something tangible.

"Jacob, please forgive me," she wanted to say. "You saved my life. I
could have been discovered, captured as a spy but you saved me. I am
sorry that I did not stop the floggings. I was a child. What could I do?
That was then. Now, I'm trying to stand for something. Everyday I
remember and feel guilty. For slavery. For war. For humiliation. None of
it should ever have happened."

She said nothing.

An old man walking up the aisle on crutches brought reality crashing
back. "We been living all our lives with a basket over our head," he said.
"That basket done been taken off."

"Hallelujah," the squatters shouted.

"We smell air."

"We can see sunlight."

"Amen."

Excitement grew around her and something moved her spirit. Before
she thought about what she was doing, she responded. She clamored out
of the pew, strode into the pulpit, and stood beside Jacob. The church
and the people outside became so quiet she heard an owl, the one she
heard every night out in the woods, and for a moment she felt light, as
though lifted on the wings of a new day. She felt like a savior, sure that
she could mend this madness. Someone had to stave off another disaster.
She opened her lips to speak, but nothing came out. What could she say?
The crowd waited.

"Your interest and ours began in the cradle together," she told the con-
gregation, her mouth trembling. "Your interest is our interest. We all love
this island. We all want to preserve our homes, our land, something of

what we had before. Surely the chasm is not so wide it can't be breached. Surely there is a way for us to live together." She paused and looked from face to face across the room. "Free men need to live in peace. Now that the fighting is over, we must find a way." She was so frightened she thought the crowd could see her heart pumping.

There was a loud "plop" and something hit the wall behind her. Rotten eggs. She knew by the smell and stared ahead, seeing no one in particular, just holding her lips tight, steeling herself, thinking, I will not let them see that I am afraid.

The next second she was moving, weaving, feeling the shoving. How long it took her to get to the back of the church she did not know, but Jacob was beside her, hovering over her, shielding her from the confusion.

Outside they ran, turned off the path beside the cemetery, and pushed through a palmetto thicket to a clearing in front of the cabin. They stood panting, breathing deeply.

"I thank you for speaking out," Jacob said rather sadly.

She reached out to touch his hand. Was it really Jacob? She wanted him to be real. Please be real. How long ago was it when we lived here pretending all was right with the world? If the war hadn't happened, we might be pretending still. But what would our lives be?

What was it like after the evacuation? Where did you go? She had so many questions. About Affey. About Sully and the children.

"St. Helena," Jacob explained before she had the chance to ask. "Things are better there."

"Better?"

Jacob nodded. He coughed and ran his fingers around the collar of his stiffly starched shirt. The fabric was frayed.

"You sharecrop with the Northerners?" she asked, remembering the fields on St. Helena were white with cotton during the war.

"I own my land, yes. And what you did here tonight won't make white landowners happy."

"Happy?" she said in surprise. They both laughed. Jacob had not laughed often during those months when she lived in the cabin with his family, but when he did, it had warmed her heart. She remembered how he played with his children, surprising them coming around the corner of the praise house and making them laugh; and once when he was bringing her back from Adams Run on the longboat, she had made him laugh with her impersonation of a Yankee patrol officer.

She wanted to ask, "When were we happy?" But she thought better of it.

Jacob looked back at the church. "Better times are coming," he said with a reverence in his voice and an intensity in his eyes that alarmed her. But what would they have to go through to get to that point? War had been dangerous enough. She wasn't sure either of them would survive this kind of turmoil.

"Maybe better times are coming. Will it be soon enough?" She knew she was shivering.

"You best go inside," Jacob said, letting go of her hand. He stepped away. "The master?"

"Papa's here with me, but he doesn't know anyone. He doesn't remember." Her throat felt tight.

"No need for you to be afraid."

"What happened tonight is not what frightens me, Jacob. It's what we're heading for. And I'm not sure I'm strong enough."

Jacob pulled at his frock coat and straightened his tie. "I thought when the war was over we wouldn't have this mess. I thought it was all going to be a jubilee. But it seems like the tumult's just starting over again. " He stood so close she could feel heat from his body.

The owl in the pine tree stirred but did not fly away. The silence around them was like a distant tornado. Feelings she was determined to deny stiffened, expanded, and burst in the air, in the trees, and all around. Her face felt numb, but she did not move away. She looked straight at him, waiting. What she saw was sadness and regret. It was over in a second. She was the first to move away. She swallowed. She must regain her pride before it, too, exploded in the night.

"How did things get so split in two?" Jacob's question was not directed toward her, and he did not wait for an answer. He turned quickly and walked toward the church.

She sat on the cabin steps watching him leave, his question ringing in her head.

How did things get so split in two?

The wind picked up in the trees and muffled the shouting and the hoopla back in the church. She buried her face in her arms until she could hear nothing, only picture Jacob standing before his people like a man resurrected, raised up within himself. She had hardly recognized him.

She hardly recognized herself.

She could write a handbook on memory: how to blot it out, sometimes for weeks, for months. Oh, from time to time she remembered what once was, and it gnawed at her and caused her to take a detour, like crossing Store Creek instead of heading straight down the main road. She'd stop Coosaw in his tracks, dismount, and take a walk in the woods, then she'd sit under a tree and cry until there were no tears left.

Upstate they told her it would "go away;" it would "get better in time." She had to "move on." But here, where troops had trampled the fields and burned the barns, destruction filled the air with the warm, greasy odor of poverty, and she could see nothing to move on to.

Then, tonight when she saw Jacob, she realized she didn't want the memory to go away. As long as the memory was there, the pain was real. Jacob was real. Whatever she had when she was living with Jacob and Sully and Affey and teaching the children was real and filled with purpose. Why, then, had she returned after the war? She had come back to make a place for herself in the center of it all. But the center was melting away, and there was no going back.

Nothing was the same.

She looked up through the sea pines, but could not see the moon, not even the stars. It was dark.

What have we done, she wondered.

Oh, Jacob, who are we now?

CHAPTER
Twenty

*S*itting in the saloon bar at the Mills House Hotel, Preston Wilcox looked around and admired its air of dignity. He liked the old building. He liked Charleston. He took note of the dark mahogany paneling, the polished brass and marble floors and mentally compared it to hotels out West. His favorite had been built on a hill someone had called Gold Hill. The name turned out to be a mistake, he recalled, almost chuckling aloud, for they had found more silver than gold in the Comstock Lode.

He smiled as he remembered Virginia City, but when he looked at the men around him making business deals and smoking cigars, his smile turned to a frown. Half the men in here were from Massachusetts and Connecticut. He'd seen them on the train with their clothes packed in newfangled cloth bags. He'd heard them bragging that they were coming to the South to make a fortune. Carpetbaggers made him uncomfortable. He felt ill at ease now because didn't want anyone to think he was a sharp-talking pretentious Yankee coming to take advantage of the defeated. He was here for another reason.

The rain on Meeting was turning the street to clay and when a black man appeared at the saloon entrance, Wilcox looked hard to see if the man was who he thought he was. Then he rose from the barstool and walked briskly toward the door, not quite sure what to expect. It had been years.

"Thank you. Thank you for coming."

"No trouble," the dark man said, standing just inside the door. Beads of rainwater glistened in his gray hair. "I was due to deliver a load of salt up to Hobcaw Plantation. Lots of salt-making done around here these days."

It was not in Jacob's nature to force himself into a white man's establishment. Preston knew that, although there were other dark men in the bar, men with questionable business purposes.

Wilcox remembered his manners and cleared his throat. "A drink?" he asked Jacob. "Whiskey perhaps?"

Jacob looked at the men and recognized them for what they were. "No, sir. I think I'd like to walk outside," Jacob said. "I'd rather be in fresh, clean air, now that the rain's about over."

Without talking, the two men left the hotel and turned toward East Bay Street.

"Salt-making is big business, you say?"

"That's right, Cap'n. Salt collects on the marsh grass. People stay busy after spring tide removing the brine and boiling it down."

"Then your riverboat business is thriving."

"Yes, Cap'n. It is. A new factory's making wood buckets over at the old rice mill on Shem Creek, and I do all the delivering for them." Jacob's manner was business-like.

All along Market Street, women with baskets on their heads sold vegetables and flowers. Men with tool chests on their shoulders approached them offering their services as carpenters, masons, and artisans in wrought iron.

The harbor pulsed with life. Large frigates loaded with goods maneuvered past small fishing boats and all along the seawall freed slaves noisily hawked their morning catch of pink sea bass, fresh mullet, and large-eyed catfish.

"We call black fishermen in the small boats the mosquito fleet. All men are now free to make a living from the sea," Jacob said, smiling.

"So, business is good," Wilcox said, watching a wagon rumble by. When it splashed water, both men moved back from the street. Jacob pointed to a wrought iron bench and they sat.

Seeing the city busy rebuilding itself, Wilcox wanted to ask what was happening on the islands, but he drew a deep breath and said simply,

"Life seems to be getting back to normal."

"Yes, Cap'n, it is," Jacob said. "I kept my longboat in operation all during the bad times. But you are looking different. Like you had a hard time since I saw you last. You all right?"

"It's been a long time. A lot has happened."

"You married?"

"No," Wilcox said quickly.

"The child?"

"In Milford with her aunt."

"And you? What about you?"

"I went out West. Sold my business in Milford and started a new one out there," Wilcox said, hoping Jacob would mention Sarah, the island, maybe Edings Bay. The war was over but what was happening? He had to know. In the newspaper that morning he had counted fourteen columns of delinquent land tax sales. Land on the islands was being sacrificed on the auction block at an alarming rate. He knew, and Jacob must know, that plantation owners were suffering most.

"Your leg well?" Jacob asked, and Wilcox was quiet longer than he meant to be, remembering his sortie to cut the rail line and the night the Rebel sharpshooter found its mark.

"No doubt about it," Wilcox said. "You saved my life, Jacob. It was your knowledge and quick thinking that maneuvered us back to safety that night."

"Doing what had to be done, sir."

"And you and I were somehow spared," Wilcox said.

"That's right, Captain Wilcox, we were spared." Jacob's brow suddenly furrowed. "But things don't look so good out on the islands now. Sad feelings rest upon the minds of our people since the war. They're poor. They're homeless. They're begging, but the government turns them away, not giving them a chance. They tell us the law one way, then they tell us another way. The new government pretends to good feelings, but the people are losing faith."

"What about you, Jacob?"

"I'm taking my chances on the water. Business is growing and Sully and the children are down on St. Helena doing contracting work for wages."

Wilcox looked at Jacob. He had to know about Sarah. "What about the others?" He hesitated to speak her name.

Jacob did not take the cue. "Toby's already saved enough to buy his own land."

"Can they do that? Freedmen buy land, I mean?"

"With enough money, anybody can buy land."

"I see."

"Affey, she's coming to Avery Normal this fall to start her schooling. She's been with Miss Towne at the Penn School all this time."

Wilcox nodded and tugged absentmindedly at his clean-shaven chin. "Tell me about Miss Edings." He breathed deeply and spoke slowly. "What's happening at the bay? How is the teacher? I learned that she came back after the war." He stopped speaking and ran his finger around the arm of the wrought iron bench where they sat.

"Fair to middling." Jacob's answer was flat and uninflected, giving no more information than the words alone carried. Wilcox waited. "Miss Sarah and her papa are stayin' in a cabin behind the Episcopal Church. She's trying to keep the school open, but the new government's making it hard. They paying teachers to come down from the North."

"I should have shipped more books down when I came back East. I. . ." He caught himself. There was no need to make excuses. He had wandered around Boston and New Haven for months until he decided to come to Charleston. The only thing holding him to Milford was the daughter who hardly knew him. "I brought slates down with me. I thought she might use slates."

"I got to tell you frankly," Jacob said, shaking his head. "Things are not looking good. She's got no way to pay the taxes on her place, and the old master, he's doing mighty poorly."

"You know me well, Jacob. We worked together during the war. You saved my life. I must be honest. I've come to do business with you. You have done well with your longboat service, but the war is over. You need to get ready for what's happening around you. Opportunities are here, and I want to help you. I hope you will think of expanding your riverboat service. I want to back your operation financially."

Jacob wiped a bead of sweat from his lip.

Wilcox leaned closer. "God forbid that you should ever feel any arrangement between us uncomfortable."

"No, Cap'n. I do believe the Lord has His ways."

"Let me make my position clear. I believe it's time you added a larger boat to your fleet. Profits can be made with a steamer that can ply the waters offshore as well as inside the islands. You know the routes. You know the waters. You can put your people to work. They will contract with you. "

Jacob moved uncomfortably. "I can't add a steamer, sir. I don't have the means."

"You will if I offer you guarantees. I can offer a substantial sum. I'm now in a position to do that, and I'm willing."

Wilcox held his breath. He had more to say. "In return, you will pay the taxes on the Edings land. I don't want Miss Edings to lose her land. It's too dear to her."

"It would be the death of her. The old master, too." On Jacob's face there was genuine concern.

"You know the situation as well as I do. The provisional government jacked up the taxes. They're all out for blood. In a few months the land will be fought over. The battle will be serious, like another war. Creditors will come out of the woodwork. I don't know that the government can stop the foreclosures. That's why I decided to approach you. With the land up for grabs, I have come to you with this business proposal but with strings attached."

Jacob didn't flinch.

"I'll be candid. We both know her father is ill. He is unable to help her make decisions, but he would want her to fight for the Edings land as he would fight to the bitter end. That was his style. It's her style too, and she might be able to keep the land if given time. We can give her the time she needs if we pay her taxes."

"Oh, Cap'n, she won't let me . . ."

"That's the string attached to our deal. You must find a way. If you talk her into it, whatever you have to do, the steamer is yours. I will add the steamer to your fleet, and we divide the profits. But there's one other condition. Miss Edings must know nothing about our deal. This is a business deal between us. Let's just say you and I are making a smart move and helping Miss Edings keep her land at the same time."

The men were speaking, not looking at each other, just nodding, staring at the water and watching the sun strike the side of a seagull in flight over the harbor.

Jacob's smile dissolved. "If other planters find out we helping her, they'll spew out hatred toward her. That's what she might not be able to take."

"She'll not be timid when it comes to saving her land." That's one of the things Preston remembered about Sarah, one of the qualities he admired.

CHAPTER

Twenty-One

Four boys held their stomachs and grimaced as if from some acute pain. They told Sarah they felt "sickly" and needed to leave school. The next day five girls stayed home and sent word they were "tending to babies." All day Sarah thought of the northern teachers who enticed students to school with containers of city clothes. What an underhanded thing to do. If her students were sick, that was one thing, but she had her suspicions. Well, she'd take Coosaw for a ride and drop by after school.

When parents admitted sheepishly that their children were attending the school where the northern ladies were teaching, Sarah sat on Coosaw without moving a muscle, but she could feel her face turning red. Who wouldn't be irritated that these teachers, these foreigners, would resort to such silliness? Where was their purpose, their goodness, their nobility? Where were the northern teachers when danger was all around? Where were they when gunboats and rifles turned the children's eyes hollow and their stomachs to stone? She fought the twitch in her jaw and straightened herself.

"It's them fancy clothes, Missy. We sorry."

Sarah yanked at the reins, turned Coosaw sharply, and rode him hard, resentment surging into her throat. Where the road forked to the right, she slowed Coosaw to an easy trot and sat erect in the saddle. But at the sight of the Crawford Plantation, a hand flew to her mouth. Rabbits and pigs ran loose in the yard of a house that was now so dilapidated it looked dangerous. Chickens scattered before Coosaw, madly running about as Sarah pulled at the reins.

On the porch stood two girls, wild-eyed and dazed. Sarah stared, seeing in their eyes such utter and complete bewilderment that her own anger faded. She felt instead a blurred mingling of pity and some sort of responsibility, for the teachers were only children themselves, she thought, who had no idea where they were. Why would someone put children in the ruins of a war among a devastated and angry people?

She dismounted quickly. "I teach at the school across the island. Behind the Episcopal Church." She nodded in the direction of church.

The girls stood comatose.

"Sarah Edings," she said over the cackling of the chickens and the grunting of the pigs. She held out her hand and one of the girls came haltingly down the steps.

"Mary Ames," the girl said, wiping her hands on her skirt.

Sarah noticed the dirt under her fingernails, smelled the stench of chicken droppings all around, and looked away.

Suddenly, the girl seemed eager to talk. "It's been a month and we still have no furniture," Mary Ames said, "only one steamer trunk. Nothing has arrived. But we do, at least, have the clothes."

This was a delicate moment. Sarah tried to breathe deeply. She had heard about the crates filled with taffeta skirts and top hats, but the teachers didn't know that she knew. Should she explain the ridiculousness of it in a way that did not reveal their ignorance? She put her hands on her hips.

"Clothes?" she asked with a note of sarcasm, but it was lost on the girls.

"Clothes," Mary Ames said. "We shipped clothes down here for the poor little things. The crates were here when we arrived, and the students do so enjoy dressing up at school. Oh, but where are my manners? I'm Mary and that's my friend, Emily. Emily Bliss. As you can see, Emily rather misses home."

Emily moved slowly down the steps, her eyes filling with tears, her nose turning red.

Sarah swallowed. "And where exactly is home?"

"I'm from Springfield, Massachusetts," Mary Ames explained. "Emily is from New Hampshire. We are employed by the Boston Ladies Aid Society."

"As teachers?"

"Yes, and missionaries to our black brothers and sisters. It is our mission to clothe, feed, and educate them, so that they may enjoy the blessings of a life due to them, the life Southern planters took away."

There was a pause but Sarah decided to say nothing. She bit her lip and looked coolly at the foreign teachers.

"Oh, but we are about to have tea. Will you join us?" Mary's invitation came out of the blue. "We would like that, wouldn't we, sweet, sweet Emily?"

For a fleeting moment Sarah remembered life before the war, a time when she, too, was innocent and thought all other human beings sweet. She considered the invitation, cleared her throat, and tried to think of an excuse, but before she could think of any reason to flee, Miss Bliss said, "And crackers. I think we can find a tin of crackers. We packed English tea in the trunk we brought with us. We've been hoarding it. We would so like to share with you."

The room where they lived was bare except for one steamer trunk and three wooden crates where the fancy clothes were stored. The rest of the rooms were closed off. It occurred to Sarah that when their furniture did arrive, if it ever did, it would somehow disappear.

"We are here because our brothers and sisters desperately need an education," Emily said after blowing her nose and wiping her eyes.

"Well, it will take time," Sarah said, her tone almost motherly.

Mary Ames nodded her head sparrow-like. "It surely will, for the wickedness of slavery has surely torn at their minds."

Sarah watched Mary Ames' head go up and down, up and down, heard the girl's self-righteous tone, and chalked it up to missionary zeal. She'd let it pass. "There is wickedness everywhere in the world," she said quietly. "War is wicked. Poverty is wicked."

"Truly, I do suppose you are right," Mary Ames said. "And now that we have wiped away the evil of slavery, I pray we can bring this godless place back into the fold."

Sarah looked at Mary, who was still nodding her head sparrow-like, and found herself speechless, not knowing what to make of the girls. Neither of them was more than sixteen and had probably never been farther than ten miles from home. Now they had come to live among the refugees, thinking they would be welcomed and beloved. She looked at their innocent smiles, their pale skin shining against their once stiff taffeta dresses, and blinked.

"Please sit while I make tea. We must cook for ourselves. As you can see, we have found firewood," Miss Ames told her, proudly.

Sarah sat on one of the wooden crates, knowing full well that was where they kept the hooped skirts and top hats and thinking the northern teachers truly believed they were coming on an African adventure, and now that they were here, they realized they had made a terrible, terrible mistake, but it was too late.

And here she was sitting with them. Something about the whole situation made Sarah visualize an African hut across thousands of miles of water, with the three of them having tea under the straw roof.

"Oh, please," Miss Ames said, turning quickly. "Tell us what to expect of our scholars. We have met our students only a few times. Tell us what to expect."

What could she say? Students these days were not the children of three years before, island children filled with hope and gratitude, the kind she'd taught when she and Affey started the first school in the old praise house beside Jacob's cabin. These students were products of unfulfilled promises and false dreams. The students were suspicious and angry and undisciplined.

And these girls would be called on to sew up knife cuts after a round of fights in the schoolyard. They would have to nurse and doctor the sick after a bout of smallpox or malaria. Just the week before, Sarah remembered, she had saved a little boy's life after he was bitten by a water moccasin. She had sucked the poison out of the child's arm. What these girls needed to know was that they must have strong wills and nerves of steel, but she didn't want to tell them that.

She drew in a deep breath. "It is important that you teach numbers quickly. They will be signing contracts soon and must be able to calculate wages, measure land, and keep accounts."

Sweet Emily poured tea daintily. "I plan to begin with Plato."

"They can't read." Sarah felt the need to remind the girls of this.

Mary Ames perched on a box. "As teachers we need to lay the groundwork for a new democratic leadership. What the South needs is leadership, Miss Edings. The owners of the land, their old masters, never gave them the chance."

Sweet Emily perked up. "And American poetry. Why, I will have them memorizing 'Hiawatha' and reciting it in no time at all."

Mary Ames nodded. "And mine will learn the words to the 'Battle Hymn of the Republic' and 'Rally Round the Flag.' But first we will recite the entire Emancipation Proclamation."

Sarah bit savagely into a cracker and when she did, it crumbled into her lap. When she looked up, both girls were bending forward, their eyes narrowing, and Mary Ames was asking. "Did you own slaves, Miss Edings?"

Sarah brushed crumbs from her lap, balanced her teacup precariously, and uncrossed her legs. "My family has lived in the South for almost two hundred years. My father was a landowner. And, yes, we owned slaves."

When her answer reverberated in the all-but-empty room, the girls seemed unable to think of a response. Good, Sarah thought and went on, "If left alone, I believe the South would have rid itself of slavery. War was not the way to settle the issue. There were other ways."

Miss Ames was not convinced. "Great men tried for years, Miss Edings."

Sarah looked past them to the destruction of the old house, the ruined gardens, and the wasted fields. "Men on both sides tried," she said. "But it's over now." She hoped that might be the end of it.

But it was a weird nightmarish sound outside that stopped the discussion. The girls jumped up and rushed to the window. "It's that woman," Sweet Emily cried out. "She's come again."

"What woman?" Sarah was sure she knew and smiled for the first time since she'd arrived. It was so sad to see the house like this, so dilapidated, so ruined. Her grandfather had known its first owner.

Mary Ames tried to smile as if to make light of her fear and trepidation. "It's just an old woman who keeps coming by and looking this way," Mary said. "Sometimes she throws rocks."

"Or she throws dishes." Emily sniffed.

"We try to tell her we have come to civilize the children. But when we approach her, she leaves us. It's as if she disappears into thin air."

Sarah pretended to be puzzled. "The old woman disappears?"

"She looks rather uncivilized herself," Mary Ames whispered, "with a red bandanna wrapped around her head."

"Tied into points. She showed us the points and muttered strange words, as if she was placing a curse on us," Emily said. "Could she be a witch?"

Sarah debated with herself for a fraction of a second then said seriously, "It could be so." She straightened her shoulders. "People here do believe in witchcraft."

"She carries dolls and a canvas bag filled with roots," Mary whispered confidentially, using the tone that said this was absolute proof that Sarah should keep this knowledge from sweet, sweet Emily.

"Oh, my," Sarah said, explaining that if the old woman carried dolls and muttered strange words and if she knew roots and potions and looked like a mad woman, maybe. . .well. . .maybe the woman really was a witch doctor or a voodoo priestess.

The northern girls swooned. When they recovered, Sarah told them they should, by all means, be careful. They should take precautions to avoid the woman who was obviously mad.

"Yes, indeed." Sarah placed her hand over her heart, as if to ease her own heart's palpitations. "It is believed here that voodoo priestesses can place curses even on the innocent." Sarah spoke her warning with a smile that was ever so slight.

Leaving, she spurred Coosaw into a gallop and called back, "Good luck, Miss Ames. Good luck, Miss Bliss."

She felt rejuvenated with the wind in her face and her hair flowing back. She'd have to speak to Mad Rhoda and tell her to leave the northern teachers alone. Of course, there would come a time when she would apologize to the girls for Rhoda's behavior. She'd explain to the girls. Rhoda was not mad and meant no harm.

Or would she?

CHAPTER

he tree, decorated now with red holly berries and mistletoe, came from the banks of a nearby creek. She had cut the cedar herself, dragged it into the cabin and decorated it with what she could find. The tea she sipped came from cassina bushes. In her other life, she had never made tea from cassina, but occupation troops were shipping the leaves to the North by rail. They thought cassina had medicinal value. Rhoda wouldn't touch it.

Her second Christmas here. Still she had no way to pay taxes. Where had the time gone?

Sarah glanced at the letter on the table, delivered yesterday by the new Federal Postal Service. In the envelope were twenty Federal dollars, hardly enough to buy cottonseed for spring planting, certainly not enough to pay her tax bill, but tears came to her eyes when she looked at the money and thought of the man who had scrimped and saved and sent the money to her. The Rev. Alexander Bettis was a former slave himself and a teacher who had joined her on Sunday afternoons and each night after dark to help teach the slave children in Edgefield. Sarah sighed audibly and read the letter again to her father who did not hear and did not know the man who encouraged her and sometimes sent money.

Edgefield, South Carolina

My dear Miss Sarah,

 Your sister is well and awaits the return of her husband from the war. We pray for his return soon, for conditions here are in a state of fierce conflict. Every day there are confrontations between the U.S. Colored Infantry, which the new government has sent to us and the white citizens of Edgefield. In fact, just two days ago, one soldier was shot down and a leading white citizen arrested on charges of complicity in the murder.

 Everywhere, dear ma'am, there are rumors and rumors of threats. Destitution is everywhere; therefore, this is all the money I can send. The former governor who lives at his plantation called Edgewood is not well, but he will not see me because I am Negro. They say he suffers in the heart as well as the soul. His wife has not been seen and I am told she had escaped all this and returned to her home in Texas.

 As for myself, I appeared before the Edgefield Baptist Association last week to ask for ordination but was refused. They said that the matter of conducting prayer meetings may be interesting to some Negroes but they–the white Baptists–could not afford to have me mess up the Gospel. They believe we colored cannot help doing that if we are empowered to preach. But I can thank our Heavenly Father that all white people do not agree since our friend the Rev. Walker stood up for me. Last Sunday Mt. Canaan Baptist Church ordained me as its minister. Praise the Lord.

 Unknown to those who think I mess up the Gospel, I am organizing three other churches and one school I will call Bettis Academy. I can see the need for many more churches but as we

learned as we taught the children at Rev. Walker's church, we
need to educate our children first.

Your servant in the Lord,
Alexander H. Bettis

How many times she read the letter she did not know, but when she
heard the knock at the door, she braced for another battle with planters
who disapproved because she had parceled out some of the Edings' land.
Jacob had come up from St. Helena in September to help her get things
started, bringing transportation, farm utensils, and cottonseed. He had
divided the corn meticulously among the men he brought with him, all
her father's former slaves, and demanded strict accounting. Jacob was
proving to be a good businessman, a "driver" her father had called him
because he was good at driving others to do their share.

So, when she heard someone at the door, she expected another scene
like last night's. At dusk she had not been surprised when two white men
appeared. She had recognized Maynard Jenkins and one of the Mikell
boys, a tall, lanky horseman who stayed on his horse and kept his hand
on his rifle while they talked.

Jenkins, who seemed to be in charge, dismounted and tipped his hat.
"Miss Sarah, we've come to talk, if you please."

"May I offer you coffee?" She had smiled to herself remembering the
day when she would have offered port wine or Madeira in the parlor or
on the piazza overlooking the creek, but the floor in her cabin behind the
church had been used for firewood the winter after evacuation when
Yankees roamed the island. She lived in a room that was once a dining
room, now her combination bedroom and parlor. She knew the men
would not enter, although she had asked.

"I have coffee and I might find sugar," she had said, putting them off
as long as she could, knowing very well they wanted to talk about "niggers" living on her land.

Surely the planters had not returned, she thought, here in the light of
day and first thing on Christmas morning; but before she could put her cup

down, the door opened. There was Jacob holding oranges in both hands.

She took one he offered her and turned it in her hand as if it were gold. "You remembered," she said, holding back an urge to embrace him.

"From trees beside the plantation house," he said. "Robber man must be in London, so I helped myself. The guard was asleep." Jacob was proud of his steal.

She was once the one giving oranges on Christmas morning. Her grandfather had brought the trees from the south of France the year he wintered there. The orchard had grown and flourished and become such a showplace that the Marquis de Lafayette asked to see it after he christened the Seabrook baby and named her Caroline Lafayette.

"Not many left," Jacob said. "Soldiers cut the trees down for firewood." He warmed his hands at the small fireplace, then walked over and spoke to her father as if his former master were normal, bowing slightly and nodding his head. "Good morning, sir." He turned back to Sarah. "I came to bring Rhoda some of Sully's good food. I keep offering to take Rhoda back to St. Helena with me, but she's satisfied living down the road. She's happy near you."

"It's a comfort to have her nearby," she said. "Rhoda and Father sit for hours. They have no need to talk about the past, I guess," she said, never quite knowing what to say to Jacob when he dropped by to check on the sharecroppers. She suspected he came mostly to check on her.

"Father doesn't recognize you," she explained.

"Maybe it's better not to know." Jacob glanced at the oranges then looked away.

She wondered if Jacob meant it was better for her father not to know his slave driver was free or better not to know his orange trees were being used for firewood. Her father could not remember that he had ever owned either. His health had become so bad it was impossible to talk to anyone about him, a man who made guttural sounds and looked at her, but whose eyes were vacant.

"I brought you the latest newspapers," Jacob said. "But first, this comes from Sully and the children." He handed her a basket, and when she stepped back, making a sign as if refusing to take it, he placed the basket on the table. "They're not gonna stand for no back talk. The youngest girl made the fig preserves herself. Sully divides her vegetable crop with the white lady who owns the plantation. Now she's sharing her portion with you."

"Thank you, Jacob, but I. . ." It was true, she thought, stung with guilt;

in her other life she had taken food to the quarters, only now she recognized it as a gesture of apology or a redress for some action taken by a foreman or maybe even her father.

"Sully won't take 'no' for an answer," Jacob said. "She even made her special Christmas minced meat pie and sent it along. Like I say, we divide our crop with the northern lady. I'm selling our share of the cotton outright, and if we thrifty, we will have the means to pay for the seed in the spring. Sully and the children are free to do their tasks when the time is right. They choose when to do their work. They can come home out of the rain. They come home at dinnertime. They work hard. Give my Zack a good plate of food and he can work longer than Toby."

By now Sarah had gotten herself in hand. "Zack should be in school," she said, recalling her young student's determination. What a waste if he were not in school. The newspapers were full of stories about the Philadelphia Aid Society and Laura Towne's new building. "What about the Penn School? What about your girls?"

"They're all learning. The boys, too, when they're not working. They go to school. Zack's enrolled for a new colored college in Atlanta when it opens." The expression on Jacob's face showed excitement. "We work hard and we got money to pay our debts. We've got the means to pay taxes and have some left over. Besides, I got my riverboat business going good. It's going so good. . ." He paused and she thought he seemed nervous, as if there was another reason he had brought oranges.

As the sun streamed in the open door, she felt the warmth and when she turned back, Jacob was pacing as if he would not go away without whatever it was he had come for.

"I came to lend you the money to pay your taxes," he said.

She said nothing. Time passed while she waited for Jacob to change the subject.

He faced her squarely. "I've got enough, Miss Sarah. I could lend you more. I could lend you enough to plant your spring crop."

She bit her lip. She had searched her father's papers, but the Confederate bonds were worthless. People's Bank of South Carolina declared a dividend of one dollar per share, and any stock William Edings had in the Savannah and Charleston Railroad was without value. In fact, the provisional state government had foreclosed on the line then sold it for a pittance, invalidating the original issue. All her father's assets were gone, lost. There might be cotton in a warehouse in Charleston to sell yet, but the account books were missing, taken to Liverpool by the factors when they learned Sherman was marching to Savannah.

"Prospect Hill sold out to a cousin from up North," Jacob said, finally deciding to change the subject as he peeled an orange.

"What's going on at Mr. Grimball's place?"

"They carving Point of Pines up, dividing it into small plots and selling it."

"To squatters?"

"Any freed slave who says he once lived on the place. Like they doing on St. Helena. Selling to anybody who's got the money."

Sarah knew Jacob was telling her all this on purpose. She knew Tally Westcoat had sailed to Brazil, along with six hundred other planters, all under the auspices of the Southern Colonization Society. Andrew Johnson had issued a proclamation extending amnesty to the planters and returning their property. . .if they took the oath. Lee Westcoat and his wheelers and dealers refused to pledge any allegiance to the new government and instead were busy making friends with carpetbaggers and Republicans. Saving themselves. Who would save her? Yes, she needed help, but she looked at Jacob angrily and dropped in a chair with a loud sigh.

"Like I said, I could lend you the money, if it would make things easier." He looked away, as if embarrassed to be saying this to his former boss, his former owner. "I don't mean to speak out of turn, but these tax men, they looking to buy the land. They looking out for nobody but themselves."

"By law they can't put me in debtor's prison." She rocked in the old chair and glared at the fire. She'd not panic yet, even if she were left alone to grow old, the only white lady on the island, over-powdered and wrinkled as a prune, with hair so thin people could see her gray skull. She smiled ruefully to think of herself as old and gray.

"No, Miss Sarah, they can't put you in prison. Not yet. They got laws. But they can change the laws anytime they want to, to suit their pocketbooks," Jacob said, walking to the door ready to leave, ready to give up. "But if I may say so, it would be to your advantage to recognize the facts. The truth is, they will put your place up for sale, all the land except the little bit the robber says he bought, and that's just ten acres around the plantation house. They could put all the rest on the auction block. These people are mean spirited, Miss Sarah. They not waiting for the Lord to mete out retribution. They out to make white planters pay one way or the other." Jacob walked back to the table and all but slammed the newspapers down. "You got to decide for yourself."

Jacob left without saying goodbye, and when the door closed, the warmth of the sun left with him. She let him go, hating to hear anger and disappointment in his voice. His offer had affected her more than she ever thought possible, and she needed time to think of some way to say no with kindness. But she could not take Jacob's money. He'd worked so hard. He and Sully, too. They had saved for a future they could only dream about four years ago. Now the future was theirs, and she would not take it away. She could only pray he'd understand.

The fireplace in the cabin was large enough to take the chill from the air; nevertheless, Sarah shivered as she sat beside her father. Later, when she picked up the newspaper Jacob had tossed on the table and looked at it, a sound escaped from her lips. There on the front page of the *Charleston Courier* was a piece of someone from her past. She looked at the picture of the landowner and gentleman residing at The Grove and spoke Trent's name aloud.

PERSONALS - *We were pleased to meet on the street yesterday a well-known citizen, Mr. Trenholm Lowndes, who has just returned to the city after an absence in Europe.*

Our friends will be interested to know that Mr. Lowndes is still connected with his uncle's shipping company. He brings with him a large stock of English goods and has arranged for the regular consignment and arrival of goods aboard one of his vessels. Mr. Lowndes will be more familiarly remembered as the principal before the war of the blockade runner the Caroline with offices at the corner of Bay and Market and after the great fire and shelling, at the corner of Bay and Calhoun.

He has recently accepted a position on the Special Committee and joins those who wish to intervene on behalf of Messrs. Jeff Davis, A. McGrath of this city and his uncle, George Trenholm. We congratulate our friend on his safe arrival, and in due season.

Trent's father had been buried. Trent's mother, the paper said, was living permanently on the Hudson. The Grove now belonged to Trent. She stared at the picture, ran her fingers across his face and down his broad chest, as if to invoke that old attraction. She pictured nights at the bay and long rides in his skiff. But when she thought of the way she had treated him in the carriage that day on the docks in Charleston, she leaned back against the chair. He'd deserved it. When she had last seen him, the rift between them was deep, but there were earlier, happier times. She could almost hear Trent saying, "You will need me after the war."

Just to think Trent was back made her breath quicken, and the thought struck her like a blow. Maybe, just maybe, there was a way to save her father's land. After all, Trent had made a fortune during the war.

But then she glanced at her worn nails, rubbed her callused hands together and wondered if Trent would want to see her like this. A year had passed since the war ended. She was penniless, more destitute than ever. And four years older. Her skin brown and leathery. She hated looking in the mirror because she disliked what she saw.

She sat dry-eyed and immobile, pulling her thoughts together. For a long time, she seemed to be floating somewhere between action and resignation. Suddenly when she heard the cry of gulls, she looked out to see the sky filled with a flock flying toward the Atlantic. Then the wind seemed to change, as if to swing around, and something within her stirred, an echo from the past, the feeling that the future was up to her. Her Edings ancestors lived and breathed in her. She could not let them down.

She'd go see Trent.

She straightened up the room and plumped up the pillows under her father's arms. She poured a glass of Madeira, opened the door, and sat on the steps. Trent would come to her aid. She knew how to make it happen. Plans had to be made. She'd pull herself together and rally. She was, after all, the last of the Edings left on the island, and her kind of people did not give up easily.

She went to the door and looked out at the blue sky above the trees as if it were a new day, thinking if she planned it right, she'd be back in a week with more than enough Federal dollars to pay her taxes.

CHAPTER

Twenty-Three

Within days she had made arrangements. Jacob would bring Zack from St. Helena. Zack would manage school while she was away. Rhoda would stay with her father while she traveled to Charleston with Jacob on his next riverboat run.

Feeling like a survivor at last, Sarah was grinning as she packed away the slates and made out lesson plans for Zack before she left. She could see her way out of debt.

Trent's life was filled with people she didn't know, but he'd remember her and honor their past. Would he recognize her now? That was her worry, but she refused to let that thought dampen her spirits. She wrote notes to the children, wiped dust from the tables, then closed the schoolhouse door.

"Sarah."

In a long silence Sarah was sure she was making the shape of another name with her lips but no sound came out. What she felt was warmth she had not felt since the old days, as if something lost had been found.

"Affey. Affey, you are here."

Affey did not answer. There was no need to explain. She only stood and smiled, then moved into Sarah's arms.

"Oh, Affey, let me look at you. A married lady, they tell me."

"Toby and I had a regular ceremony in a real church."

Affey was no longer the thin, newly freed slave girl Sarah'd left a lifetime ago. Affey's face, then strained from worry and constant fear, was now filled out. Happiness shone in eyes that were large and brown and flashing now with newfound freedom.

For a moment Sarah fought back a wave of fear. She stepped back. Why had Affey come?

"Toby?" Sarah spoke quickly. "How is he?"

"Oh, very well. And very busy."

Affey looked older. They were both older. Three years upstate, one year here waiting for something good to come along. That would make them twenty-one and far more mature than their years.

"And you, Sarah? What happened? How are you?"

There it was. The question. Four years to cover in an instant. How could she do it? For that matter, how could she explain things that were best forgotten? Sarah looked at her friend who was once a servant, once a slave, and thought it was a miracle. Had time collapsed? Years could disappear, she'd learned.

"Oh, I am teaching. I am older," Sarah admitted. "Perhaps wiser."

"And your health?" Affey leaned toward her.

The woods in front of Sarah grew black. What happened to the sun? She felt disoriented, as if blood was withering in her veins. For a moment she felt there was a sudden death in her body. It took a while to get her breath.

"I am quite well, thank you. Except I have the hands of a poor dirt farmer. And Rebecca?"

"Mama escaped during the evacuation. To Barbados. That was her home, you know."

No, Sarah didn't know that Affey's mother had come to the Carolinas from Barbados. She'd never thought about where Rebecca or Affey were from. Now that she thought about it, she blushed with shame.

"It is lonely without our mothers. I do have Father, but he doesn't know me. He recognizes no one. It is sad. Rhoda takes care of him while I'm at school."

"Yes, I know. I arrived as Rhoda was sitting with him this afternoon outside. There was a cool breeze. We sat together under the trees. He did not recognize me."

It was only a little after six, but already the sky was blue-black and smooth as glass. When they were young playmates, they had sat so many nights on the bottom step of the kitchen house looking up at a sky like this, wondering what made the stars shine, what kept them hanging in the sky.

Her father had often joined them. He'd show them the Big Dipper and teach them how to find the North Star. They'd try to count the stars. Affey learned her numbers by counting stars. Her father would smile proudly when Affey learned her numbers. He'd hugged them both. Sarah looked at Affey, thought of her father smiling proudly and realized it was her father who encouraged Affey to prepare for freedom. He knew all along she was teaching Affey to read.

Sarah's mind whirled with the question, why are you here, but she drew back, afraid to ask.

"Tell me about the Penn School. Are things going well with Miss Towne?"

"The Penn School is going very well, thank you. Jacob told me the new government is threatening to close your school. I am truly sorry."

"Don't be. We will find the money somehow."

She shuddered to admit the fantasy of that statement, yet here she sat pretending. The reality was that Reverend Walker had to depend on donations from his friends in Philadelphia to pay her wages. And as for herself, she was so poor that Jacob brought her food. Her land would soon be on the auction block.

Affey touched her arm. "I know how desperate things are. But I have saved money teaching at the Penn School. I can loan you enough to pay your taxes."

Birds flew in to roost in the live oaks, night sounds that once soothed her, but suddenly the weight of the situation hit her and the sounds made Sarah's blood run cold. She stood, crossed her arms, and walked into the yard, unable to admit her shame, her embarrassment. Sarah Edings, daughter of cotton planter William Edings, reduced to accepting handouts.

A new order was sweeping through. The old ways were being wiped away by war and freedom. The changed stations in her life made her feel naked.

Affey followed. "If you don't pay, if you don't agree to pay whatever they say you owe, they will take your land, divide it into parcels and sell it."

"You are too generous, Affey, too forgetful of yourself. You saved for your schooling. Avery Institute opens next fall. Besides, I don't owe that much."

"It doesn't matter what you owe. The taxes must be paid. You don't have to put up a front with me. I know you are afraid."

Afraid?

Sarah left it alone for a minute. All through the war, all those years, she had never felt this kind of terror. She was resentful, yes, angry, yes, but she had never felt terror until now. Without money, she had no hope, no future that she could imagine. Now she was about to lose the land, the last tangible evidence of anything that resembled her old life, the only life she had ever known.

Yes, she was afraid.

"Government agents are selling land to squatters. I know how much the place means to you. Toby and I can pay your taxes. We could buy it, but we've chosen to invest in the Fripp place over on Bohicket Creek. We just thought you might accept our help, but I see how stubborn you are. I guess I'm not surprised. We're too much alike, you and I."

Night herons screeched and beat their wings. Sarah looked at Affey long and hard, yearning to cry.

Don't say any more. I don't want to know.

Something held her back. She waited for Affey's words.

"Perhaps you will not accept my help, Sarah, but you must accept the truth. And the truth is this. My mother was more than a housekeeper."

Affey's voice sounded muffled, far away.

"Did you hear me? More than a housekeeper. She loved Father more than you will ever know. We are of the same blood, Sarah. He is my father, too. We are sisters."

Sarah gasped. What happened to the air? Maybe her lungs were bursting. Was all the night air gone? Out of the corner of her eye, Sarah glimpsed the herons flying off. She thought she was screaming, heard a sound and realized she had slapped Affey hard.

Affey stood rigid.

Sarah slapped again. "How dare you imply . . . .."

"I'm not implying," Affey said softly. "I am telling you the truth. My mother and your father loved each other like husband and wife. They loved each other. Please, Sarah, don't resent me. Let's don't doom what's left by being ashamed of the wrong thing. Don't be stubborn. You are my sister. Please take the money. I want you to have the land. Don't you believe me?"

In the stillness Sarah remembered her father's eyes, his pride when Affey learned to do her numbers. She looked at Affey's profile, saw herself and felt a flash of recognition she could not ignore, a bond she could not deny.

"Why wouldn't I believe you?" Sarah's voice was chilled.

Affey didn't answer, and Sarah didn't expect her to.

She left Affey standing in the yard. "I will not take your money. That's yours for Avery Normal. Don't worry about me." Her voice trailed off.

She walked into the cabin and kissed her father good night. In a few moments, Affey came inside, and she, too, kissed their father good night.

Affey left the room, went down the steps, and in a moment was lost in the night sounds and mist. Sarah sat sleepless all night and when daylight came, she was ready to do what she knew she had to do. But she would not take Affey's money.

CHAPTER

Twenty-Four

If the story Sarah pieced together from the newspaper was correct, Trent had returned a rich man. No doubt about it. After his blockade runner was captured, Trent was imprisoned in New York, but the Union courts had failed to make the case that blockade running was the same as pirvateering, and he was released. That's when he went to Liverpool, the cotton port of England and made a name for himself with his uncle, the Confederate shipping tycoon, George Trenholm.

She and Trent had been friends, she reasoned. More than friends. What was the harm in asking? At a shop on Queen Street, she bought a dress and had it delivered to the Mills House. The streets were quiet as she walked back to the hotel. A year after the war, the roving mobs and looters were gone. Buildings were being restored. New businesses were popping up everywhere. A new coffeehouse advertised French coffee. A commercial school next door to the icehouse offered writing lessons for a dollar an hour.

She made a mental note. If all else failed, teaching in Charleston was a real possibility. She turned toward King Street, automatically thinking of Mr. Russell's bookshop, but it was no longer there. His shop and all his leather bound books had burned in fires that raged during the final days of the siege.

In her room at the Mills House, she tried to read the *Charleston Courier* but had trouble concentrating. She worried that she had spent more than a month's wages as a teacher on one dress, but by nightfall she was standing in her new green taffeta that shimmered as it fell to the floor over its own hoop skirt. "New for 1866," the sales girl said, "made of steel spring," the girl insisted. "Always flexible and comfortable, a Duplex Elliptic Skirt keeps its shape twice as long," the brochure promised. She looked in the full-length mirror, satisfied with what she saw, and wondered how Trent would respond.

Downstairs in the lobby, she held the hoop as casually as she could, nervous as she was, and outside on Meeting stepped into her rented broughton with its own driver.

"The Grove." Sarah forced herself to give directions boldly and within seconds they were careening from Meeting onto Bay, stopping only for the colored policeman stationed at the old city gate when he put his white-gloved hand out.

"I must know who you are, ma'am, and where you are going." The policeman's voice was impatient, but he asked no other questions. She answered politely, then he waved her carriage through.

Rolling toward the Italian-styled villa Trent's father had built for his bride just outside the city, Sarah practiced what she would say when she saw Trent. It had been so long since she had seen him that day on the docks. How would she begin? Once or twice the thought crossed her mind that he might not want to see her, but she pushed it aside, convincing herself that he still cared for her. He would gladly lend her the money.

But what if he had married while he was in England? What if a wife stood beside him in the grand reception room? The carriage jolted and she jumped, but then she realized it was the driver cracking his whip. They were passing the hanging tree. Once, when she was a little girl, she had asked her father what happened at the hanging tree and her father demanded that she leave the table. She had gone all day and night without dinner.

It wasn't until years later that she learned about the lynching after the uprising Denmark Vesey planned so meticulously and came so close to executing. The uprising had terrified her family, frightened all white planters on the islands, as well as those in Charleston. Vesey's name was never spoken in her home, his story never told except in whispers.

Affey had been the one to tell her about Denmark Vesey and the hanging tree. "Things changed after that," Affey had whispered. "Our churches were closed. That's why we worship in your balconies."

"Oh, Affey, why? Why would slaves plan a bloody insurrection when they are loved and needed and taken care of? Why aren't they happy like you?"

Only now, a lifetime later, she remembered Affey never answered but turned and looked far, far away, as if all the way across the water.

Within minutes The Grove was in sight, well-lit and as impressive as Sarah remembered in the old days. Her broughton would not be the only conveyance there tonight. All around the circular driveway bejeweled women emerged from carriages, and for a moment Sarah lost her courage, unable to move as she watched the women, hardly innocent girls coming to shyly flirt with sons of wealthy white planters. No. These were worldly, elegantly dressed women wearing yards and yards of expensive gauze and imported silks, with necklines that sparkled as they alighted on the arms of dark-skinned footmen. Her heart sank as she watched the women glide effortlessly across the driveway and into the reception room.

Her courage lost, her hopes fading, she sat listening to water cascading down the granite sculpture in the center of the circular driveway.

"The Grove, ma'am," her driver was saying, holding the carriage door, his face expressionless, but suspecting that she, too, was a woman of the night coming to meet a wealthy carpetbagger from the North. The idea occurred to her that Trent had turned his home into a brothel like the one downtown on Broad Street.

"Do not leave," Sarah told the driver. "You are to wait for me. Do not leave."

Reminding herself that she must do what had to be done, she took off her bonnet and loosened the combs in her hair. Curls fell to her shoulders. She breathed deeply, adjusting the neckline of her silk taffeta bodice low, very low.

No jewels left. All sold for a lost cause, she thought with a shrug, and started for the steps.

Tinted glass bowls of gas jets cast shadows across the black and white marble entranceway. Inside the reception room, she found herself looking for the teacher who ran the school for free persons of color, the light-skinned mistress. The teacher had fled to Canada.

Strange dark faces moved around the room. Servants moved quickly and obsequiously among the guests, holding trays of silver goblets filled with champagne. Long tables, covered with fine white linen, were loaded with oysters on the half shell, turkey, ham, beef, and whole pigs, roasted and barbecued.

Some of the guests wore white cutaways with silk top hats; she recognized the cutaway, the new uniform for the fire companies, pictured recently in the *Charleston Courier*. Other men wore double-breasted blue frock coats with silver buttons, vests that matched, and gray pantaloons with velvet stripes; new uniforms for the new city policemen, the paper said.

She felt out of place. The realization that Trent had new friends and a life that was foreign to her only heightened her uncertainty and she wasn't at all sure she could do this. Could she be so bold? Coming to see Trent had not been a wise decision. She turned to leave, only to hear a familiar voice booming behind her.

She was trapped.

"Sarah." Trent's clothes spoke of money and the latest fashion. He wore a pearl gray short waistcoat, cut straight across the front, a dark green cutaway with the fashionable, extra wide lapels, and a white shirt with a crisply pleated frill; his cravat was pearl gray, too, and fastened with a silver stud.

She lifted her face and turned her cheek for a kiss. "I imagine you are surprised to see me."

"Not as surprised as you might think." Trent seemed pleased.

She looked around at the glittering chandelier and the glasses of champagne and blinked. "If you think this is easy, it is not."

He took her hand. "Your hands are cold."

Her heart pounded with the thought that she was here, penniless and willing to beg. She shivered, feeling unclothed, exposed.

"If you think this is amusing. . ."

"No. No. I don't. I do not think this moment amusing."

"May we go into the parlor?" she whispered. "It's all these people."

Trent closed the door and nodded back toward his guests. "This is not what you think. It is not a celebration. It is business," he said.

"Making business deals with your new friends?"

"Why, yes," Trent said blithely.

She remembered Lee Westcoat's political strategy and recognized Trent's friends for what they were. She made no attempt to hide her contempt. "Alliances. Daniel Chamberlain is here on business?"

"Of course. He's down from New Haven. You remember him. He came many times for Race Week before the war."

"I remember." She recalled Chamberlain's cool Ivy-league accent. She hadn't trusted him then.

"Political decisions, Sarah. The provisional government is soon to be replaced, and when it's time for elections, we need to be on the right side."

"And what side is that?"

"The side of business and finance. The time is now. You are, no doubt, making decisions yourself. I know you, Sarah. You decided to come here tonight because something is on your mind. What is it? Can I be of help?"

She glanced toward the door. "I don't know how to do this." She sat on the settee.

"Do what?" He sank to his knees beside her.

"Ask . . ." She felt her lips tighten.

"Ask for anything, Sarah. Yes. I will happily take you for my wife."

"Since you are in a position to make a loan, I came to ask for a note to pay taxes on my father's land. Father is incapacitated. I can't rely on Daniel whom I've heard from only once and says he doesn't plan to return. It's up to me now."

"I'm flattered that you chose to ask. Marry me, Sarah. It would be more logical if we were allies."

She pulled back. "Be serious."

"I am serious," Trent said, rising and moving away to the fireplace, resting his arms on the mantle. "Marry me. Together we can build an empire. There's nothing to prevent our return to prosperity, the kind our grandfathers enjoyed. Think of the opportunity. There's money to be made. Land to be secured. Here. Now. Marry me, Sarah."

Sarah adjusted her neckline. Trent was offering her security. A life that she once knew. A life that would be set in one true course. She could live like a little clockwork figure she'd seen once, wound up and displaying little gestures no matter what happened. She could marry Trent. She sighed, fighting the temptation. But what of her self-respect?

"I am not part of the bargain, Trent. Neither is my land."

"Why not?" Trent smiled as if this opportunity was too vast, too glorious, and too magnificent to reject. "We'd make a great pair," he said, "the two of us. You carry a name filled with Southern respectability. I carry my mother's impertinence, her Yankee know-how. And I know the right people."

She glanced toward the reception room. "Your people are parasites, carpetbaggers here for political gain. Contemptible."

"See the man in uniform?" He pointed to the drunkest man in the reception room, sitting on the lap of one of the light-skinned whores. "He's a shoo-in as the first Republican governor. I'm backing him. He's a doctor, you know."

"Charlestonians would die first. What makes you think they would vote for him?"

"They will when he talks about loyalty and service and the welfare of others. Southerners fall for that. And we have the colored vote because we have Robert Smalls in our pocket. The pilot of the Planter. Remember when he slipped through the harbor? Right under our nose. He's running for the legislature and sure to win. Louis Cardozo will win big. Look at him. Tall. Dark. Princely."

"These people will stand by you as long as they can use your name and your money. When they gain power, you will mean nothing to them."

"It means I know the right people, Sarah. It means I've got the avenue to make inside deals. That's the way we all must go now. We've got to be realistic if we want to survive. Don't you want in? Other planters want in."

She shot a glance toward Trent's new friends, feeling hot and resentful, her poise gone for the moment. "Who wants in?"

Trent's eyes glistened with his new role in history. "Lee Westcoat for one. Perhaps your brother. Others," he said. "Anybody who wants to be part of the new leadership. You can be part of it. Remember the old days? We can create new power, Sarah, a new system. I can save your property. Together we can save the islands. Marry me."

She wanted to lash out but held her anger. "I don't love you, Trent. Nothing has changed."

They stood face to face.

"I wouldn't expect you to love me." Trent reached out, pulled her to him and held her so close she felt the curves of his body next to hers. His mouth came down on hers, forcing her lips apart.

"I'm not one of your women."

She broke away, whirled around, and in the fury of the moment came face to face with a servant holding a tray of crystal and champagne. The tray and the glasses clattered to the floor, and she froze, the thought occurring to her that everything was shattered. Standards. Traditions. Nothing reigned here but chaos.

She crossed the reception room as a band struck up the cords of

192 | VOICES *Over Water*

"Columbia, the Gem of the Ocean."

Outside with the music still vibrating in her ears, she motioned to the driver to pull away, and at the Mills House she stepped out into a rain that was falling in torrents.

She felt so tired she thought she could not make it up the wide marble staircase, and in her room she sank into the feather bed mattress, hoping it would swallow her up.

But she could not sleep. Sometime during the night, the lamp sputtered and went out. She was still awake the next morning when Jacob came to meet her.

CHAPTER
Twenty-Five

Palm fronds rustled in the morning breeze. Sarah ate a biscuit from Rhoda's supper the night before then poured coffee and watched it curve in the cup. Knowing what she had to do, she smiled shamelessly. She had gone to Trent for help, found her answer in his hollow life, and resigned herself to the inevitable. Reclaiming her father's land was an unattainable goal.

But something else might not be unattainable.

While she was in Charleston, she had made a decision, the most important of her life. No one was forcing her. She was making it herself. On this day she would make something happen that she could not keep from happening.

She pulled her watch from her pocket. Only a few hours left.

The trip to see Trent had roused a host of memories—some good, some bad—and she had stayed awake all that night reliving scenes of Edings family celebrations. She'd remembered birthday parties and dance recitals. She'd thought of her mother seated at the keyboard of the piano in the upstairs music room, her hands rippling through the notes in "Yankee Doodle Dandy."

She had thought of Christmas Eve and imagined her father galloping up the driveway dressed in his green cutaway and silk cravat, his cape thrown over his shoulders. William Edings was strong and dashing back then. He rode straight to the front steps at the plantation house where all the children and house servants stood waiting. When he dismounted, his arms were filled with gaily-wrapped packages. His wagons were loaded with loaves of brown sugar and hard candy, store-bought wooden pails and flannel cloth.

She had recalled the long debates around the dining room table, heated discussions about issues that now seemed pointless, as if spoken in foreign tongues. And Daniel. She could see her brother Daniel, hotheaded and emotional, storming out to be the first to volunteer.

Her heart bled for her brother who had come back disillusioned and filled with hatred, refusing to take the oath and, instead, settling in with a cousin on the mainland. His one letter to her resounded with bitterness. She had found the letter this morning, unfolded it, and read it once again.

Edingsville, South Carolina

My dear sister,

I suppose you think somebody from Washington will tell the squatters to get off the Edings land and everything will be all right. You think you will be safe. You think you will have your school and the struggle will be over. But that's not true. I trust you are prepared to stay and teach and take care of the people for a long time because another kind of war is just beginning. It is my decision to stay on the mainland, a crossroads, really, that I call Edingsville. This is one Edings who is not willing to take the oath, neither am I willing to work out terms with the squatters.

Daniel

Now she looked out across the island where the freedmen fretted and fumed because the government gave them land then turned around a month later and took it back, where white planters planned and plotted against the government, and she had to admit that Daniel was right. She looked across the barren fields and had to admit her prospects for holding on to Edings land were slim indeed. Her options were dwindling and time was running out. The war might be over for businessmen and politicians, but the misery it was causing others ran deep, the wounds long-lasting.

She pushed back thoughts of Preston Wilcox and that warm day in February when she sat beside him on the old plantation cart. Her dreams had bloomed with the flowers he handed her, and she thought the war would end soon. Order would return. Preston Wilcox would come calling. He'd find her.

But the years had taught her to trust only herself. The sad truth was, the Union captain had not come calling in Edgefield. He had made no effort to find her. She had not so much as received a letter from him.

She stood at the door to the cabin behind Trinity Episcopal trying to put the past in perspective. What a strange thing war is, she thought, the way it brought Preston into her life. If it weren't for the chaos, the destruction, and the tumult, she would never have met him, would never have felt his lips, his tender touch, the warmth and safety of her arms.

As the sun peeked over the cabin next door, the one she used for her school, she thought of the innocence in the eyes of the children. Watching them grow was like watching children open a package at Christmas. There were times when she worried they'd unwrap a box and find only the hard stones of hatred. Anger was out there in the real world-revenge, suspicion, bitterness-and she couldn't help wondering what would happen when her innocent children met whites filled with hatred, those who needed more time to heal, those who might never heal.

When Affey arrived, she stood in the doorway looking uneasy, fidgeting with her reticule and the handkerchief she held in her hand.

"Father seems well enough, physically," Affey said.

"You rode by the bay to see him?"

Affey nodded.

Self-consciously they stood apart.

Sarah closed her eyes then opened them again. "The sun does him good. Rhoda takes him there when weather permits."

Affey drew in a deep breath. "There's nothing wrong with Father, is there? More than . . ."

"No, our father's physical health is fine."

Affey sensed her discomfort and changed the subject. "I brought a photograph of Miss Towne's new school. The Penn School."

Absently, Sarah took the photograph, which showed unfamiliar men and women posing in front of a frame building surrounded by a cluster of live oaks. She stared at the brown-tinted image, thinking how unjust. All that Philadelphia Society money was given to a school on St. Helena, when her school needed it so. Jealousy crept over her. She grabbed a shawl from a chair.

"Let's walk for a while," she said.

They circled the narrow brick path along the cemetery and when she looked sideways at Affey, she recognized a striking familiarity.

"Does . . .did . . .Father know the truth?"

"Of course," Affey said with a sigh. "He was always kind and generous. He loved your mother, Sarah, but he loved mine, too. Please believe that. He never wanted to hurt you."

"Did my mother know?" Sarah heard the fear in her own voice.

"Yes," Affey said, walking more slowly now. "That's why she did not feel well that summer and traveled to Hendersonville for her health."

Sarah wondered how her mother could not know the truth. "The summer you and I stayed at the summerhouse with Rebecca?"

"Yes, and Father remained with us. Your mother had learned. Maybe she always knew." Affey's eyes filled. "My mother was afraid she would be sent away, cast out, banished. Her heart was broken. I remember how she cried. But when your mother returned, she did none of those things. She was kind. That fall she started calling me into her sitting room and giving me lessons in elocution and speech. She encouraged me to play the piano. Remember? She said I should learn everything. She wanted me to be like you."

Sarah blinked and looked down at the brick path thinking that in all those years there had been no hostility between her parents that she remembered, no vindictiveness. She'd never heard harsh words. She remembered their songs, their laughter. Her mother had found something deep within that gave her the power to forgive.

The women stopped walking and sat on the schoolhouse steps. "I brought papers for the transaction," Sarah said. "It's quite legal. Father has been declared incapacitated. I sought counsel while I was in Charleston. When you pay the taxes, the land is yours. The papers simply say you promise to divide the property into parcels and sell the land in small lots. But it is my desire that you sell first to any former slave who promises to work it."

Affey seemed unsure. "What about Daniel?"

"Daniel refuses to take the oath," Sarah answered. "He has no plans to return. He prefers to begin a new life on the mainland."

"Are you sure about this?"

Sarah couldn't help smiling. "I'm not sure about anything, Affey. So much has happened, but yes, I am as sure as I can be that I want to disperse the land in this way."

Once she had pictured herself returning after the war triumphant. While she was upstate in Edgefield, she could see herself coming back when the war ended; she'd come back as a heroine, the schoolteacher returning down the avenue of oaks with a whiff of jasmine in the air. The fields would be green with newly planted cotton. The people in the fields would be working, singing, welcoming her home.

Today, she was handing over the deed to the Edings holdings to a newly freed slave woman, actually her sister and as much her father's child as she. It was a transaction sure to be fraught with controversy, and a new sense of freedom came over her. How strange. But she felt relieved.

They walked back to the trees where Affey's horse was tied, the same two girls, Sarah thought, who held hands as they slipped away from the summerhouse. The same two innocent girls who followed along the narrow path to Mad Rhoda's, running this way and that to avoid a palmetto bush here and a clump of sandspurs there. The memory was so clear in Sarah's mind that she could see the marsh grasses along the path swaying, luring her to Rhoda's house and the unknown.

Affey mounted, grasped the reins, and turned to face Sarah. "Rhoda and Father are waiting for you at the summerhouse. You must go. You must go quickly. Someone else is there. Someone is waiting to see you. It's the captain. Preston Wilcox is waiting for you at the summerhouse."

Affey said this as lightly as if she were saying, "Rhoda has found your mother's portrait. She has it hanging in the living room over the mantle. It's there at the summerhouse waiting for you."

Sarah stared at Affey in bewilderment.

"He. . .? She was reluctant to even speak his name.

"Preston Wilcox," Affey said. "The captain is waiting. He has come to see you. He says it's important."

Sarah knew her face was blank. She felt numb. Very nearly stammering, she asked, "What do you mean?"

"He wants to speak to you in private," Affey said. "It's been a long time."

Sarah trembled. Affey stared.

"Do you still love him?"

Affey's question exploded in the air. Sarah felt her knees weaken. The ground seemed to shake. It took a moment to recover. "It was so long ago. The time was short."

Affey spoke quickly. "The time was short, but in the dead of winter you always remember what summer was like, Sarah. How could you forget what it feels like to love someone? When you see him, you will know."

"I'm not sure . . ." Sarah heard the doubt in her voice. She ought not to see him, ought not to want to see him.

"I must head back to the landing," Affey said. "Jacob's expecting me." She held the deed and papers for the legal transaction close to her bosom. "I know how hard all this is on you. Believe me, I do. I wish I could make it easier for you. I promise to return after I face the government tax men."

Alone in the cabin, Sarah wandered about in a daze. Would she recognize Preston? Why was he here? She felt a sudden urge to flee in the opposite direction, run, not to the bay but to the mainland and beyond. The shock of his coming back, even hearing Preston Wilcox's name, left her breathless, jittery, astounded.

Why had he never written? She looked in the mirror and took the combs from her hair. Her hair fell to her shoulders. In her reflection she saw a woman not at all like the girl the captain had known. She was not the girl who flirted as they watched the young foxes play.

The invaders were gone. The war was over, but she felt maimed. She was not the girl who relayed messages to Adams Run and thought in her naiveté that she could help end the war. How blind she had been. How utterly blind.

Should she rush to the summerhouse? Once, long ago, she had rushed to field headquarters to see him, thinking the captain would welcome her and take her for a walk in the woods. She had pictured the moment for weeks, looked forward to the afternoon with great bliss. She'd been intoxicated with the expectation. The reality was that the captain was not at field headquarters.

The memory of that afternoon had driven into her soul like a wound.

No, she would not go to the summerhouse. He would not be waiting. The house would be empty. She needed time to think.

She tied her horse in the same place she had tied the cart and old mare so long ago. She crossed Frampton Creek, holding up her skirt like riding britches. A sea bird flew over, casting its shadow in the water, as if watching her. Stepping from rock to rock, she wondered what she would do when she saw him. Would she run to him? Make a fool of herself? God forbid. She'd keep her self-control, she decided, stepping slowly to the opposite bank.

The sea bird caught an air current and flew out to sea. The thought flashed through her mind that it was an omen. She should fly away, too, refuse to see him and return to the cabin.

Perhaps the captain was not alone. Maybe he'd brought a wife, another demure, porcelain-skinned wife like the one in the miniature she'd found in his haversack. Perhaps he'd brought with him a misguided northern teacher and a box of party clothes for her poverty-stricken school children.

The surf pounded. When the sun struck at the sand, it shimmered in the afternoon light. She shaded her eyes as she looked in the distance, and there among the trees was the summerhouse, a shell now, weather-beaten and wrecked by soldiers and squatters. On those steps she had first seen Preston Wilcox, holding his revolver, already weary of war.

Something in her said she should not go closer. She should choose the bittersweet memory of that day so long ago and just let it go.

A sudden sound behind her made her jump. She was not prepared to see Preston. There were questions to ask. So many questions, but where would she begin? The sound came close and when Sarah whirled, she came face to face with Rhoda.

"Where is Father?" Sarah spoke quickly. "Is he all right?"

"He out on the beach," Rhoda said, smiling.

"Out on the beach?"

"Ridin' like he use to. But he don't have his gun today. He ridin' so slow and calm-like wid the cap'n beside him. It do look like the evil spirits been wiped away, Miss Sarah."

"The captain is riding with Father?"

"He be waitin' when we got here."

"How long has he been back? The captain. Here, I mean."

"Lord chile, how would I know? Rhoda work magic, but she cain't read a gentleman's mind. She not ask private questions."

When Sarah saw the riders out by the surf, she was not surprised that her father was dressed in his white linen suit and riding calmly, rising and sinking, rising and sinking in the saddle, as if guarding the water's edge and content to be there.

When the second rider appeared, taller than her father, the second horse falling into cadence with her father's, she put her hands to her lips. Preston Wilcox was in civilian clothes but wore his wide-brimmed Union hat. Its shiny silver medallion glistened in the sun.

"That be the captain, Miss Sarah. It's gittin' late so I gonna take your papa back to the cabin before the sunlight leaves us in the dark. The captain, he come back just to see you. You go on down to the water's edge and talk."

This must be done on a gracious level, she thought. He had called her a Southern belle once, and she had acted the part then. Now she stopped walking almost without breathing.

He dismounted when he saw her, walked toward her and stood as if looking through her. So much had happened, yet he stood as erect in civilian clothes as she remembered him in uniform. She felt a strong urge to run to him, to wrap her arms around his neck, but she did not move.

"Sarah?"

Her eyes burned.

"Sarah?" He called her name again and she blinked. When she looked again, he stood so close she could touch him.

"Is it really you?"

He looked so serious, so solemn, she was suddenly afraid, and when he put out his hand to help her over the dunes, she stepped back.

He reached for her arm. "Are you well?"

"Yes, of course. Why would you ask?" She crossed over the dunes and faced him.

"No reason," he said, "except that I thought of you and the school children so often while I was away. Now that I'm back, I had to know."

"You're back," she said. The truth was she had envisioned this scene on many a lonely night and said this to convince herself of the reality.

"I'm back," he said, extending both his hands, expecting to clasp both hers, but she touched his arm lightly and moved away, pretending to be taken by the sun-drenched surf behind him.

How could they possibly take up where they left off? She couldn't bear remembering the day she begged for his permission to stay here at the summerhouse and his determination to follow orders and evacuate the island. He followed her down to the surf.

They stood looking back at the house.

"I seem to remember stumbling up those steps and falling into your arms. Did that really happen?"

She cut her eyes his way. He was smiling.

They discarded their shoes and walked apart, keeping their distance. She'd dreamed once they'd be walking like this along the water's edge. In her dream they had embraced, cried, gone up to the piazza and talked, when suddenly a porcelain-skinned woman appeared. She did not like the dream and had stayed awake the rest of that night to keep from dreaming again.

Preston stopped walking and faced her. "I'm glad you were not here when . . ." He paused. "I'm glad you got away before the shelling and the deserters and the starvation."

He spoke as if he had been planning this speech a long time. "I dreamed that you and the children were on the rail line. I dreamed you were in the line of fire. It's a nightmare I've had every night since I left you. I dream it still. I wake up and I see you and the children in the explosion. I call your name, but you will not move away and the sparks rain down and I . . . it was my duty. Please forgive me."

"I'm safe," she said. "I returned after the war. I teach for the Episcopal church. I plan to start another school, a free school for all the children. I will call it Seaside School."

"Brave Sarah." There was a long silence during which they both realized this was not the time for a sweet, inviting kiss.

She told him about the government processors and the indignity of taking the oath. There would be time enough to reveal her decision to sell the Edings land to former slaves and the truth about Affey.

The shock of his sudden and unannounced appearance began to sink in, and she stood staring at him. What she needed to know was why had he not written. A letter would have meant something to her. She needed to know why certain promises were kept. Others forgotten. Why had he not found her?

"I have questions, Preston." She raised her voice. Time and tide had taken a toll and there they stood, like strangers.

"Pressing questions." She said the words again.

Out in the bay the water was taking on a dark luminous hue, reflecting the sun as it turned orange and dropped into the marsh behind them.

Before she could interrogate him, he explained he'd spent the winter of '63 in the hospital on Hilton Head. He'd given a letter to Jacob, but in all the confusion he supposed it was never posted. Once he went out West, Preston said, the war in the East seemed unreal.

Four lost years.

"You left your daughter in Milford all this time?" She meant this to come out with light irony; instead it sounded petty and accusing. She knew this was not going well and fought for self-control.

"My daughter is well-loved and happy," Preston said, "But she needs a mother."

They stood several feet apart, their arms dangling at their sides, forgetting to look at the sunset or intentionally not looking. She remembered other sunsets in his arms and suddenly wanted to touch him, hold his hand, but that would make this more complicated and the next parting too painful.

She braced herself. "You did not marry? In all this time you have not. . ."

When he said "no," she sensed there was more to be said. What did he mean? Perhaps she should not delve too deeply. People on both sides had suffered.

"I've been waiting for you all this time," he said.

She looked out beyond the breakers. The sand on which she stood shifted. It occurred to her they were on dangerous ground. Water lapped at her feet. "How could you possibly think I would wait for you all this time?"

She felt herself sinking.

"I did not expect you to wait," he said softly, attempting to clear his throat.

"You did not ask me to wait." She heard the tightness in her voice. So much for Southern gentility, she thought. But then, the Edings were not Southerners, not even English, but Scottish. Fighters, she thought, brave and independent.

"I wanted to ask you," he said, "but I couldn't."

She tossed her head. "I had to go on with my life. I found a way."

"I worried about you."

"I taught white children by day and slave children by night. And when I looked into the eyes of all those innocent children, I had no choice but to survive. They depended on me."

At last he spoke. "Are you saying there is no room for anyone else in your life now? No room for family? For love?"

"What I did I did because of love," she said. "I survived because I found the children. I found love. The children needed me."

"I need you," Preston said. "I will always need you. I came back to ask you to marry me."

"And leave this place?"

Then, as if she answered her own question, she knew she could. She'd been waiting for Preston Wilcox since he appeared at the schoolhouse door holding his wide-brimmed hat behind him.

The sand shifted and she sensed the pull of gravity. Was the entire earth tilting away from the island? She opened her eyes to the sky and breathed deeply to give Preston the answer he was straining to hear.

He was waiting, giving no sign, standing still.

A warm feeling spread over her whole body as she moved toward him. There was, of course, much left unanswered and much that was best forgotten. They would get to that later. She closed her eyes and stood at the edge of the surf, knowing full well that after tonight her world would never be the same.

HISTORICAL NOTES

Queen of the Confederacy

Lucy Holcombe Pickens was uncommonly beautiful and the only woman to have her portrait on two Confederate bills. At the age of twenty, she was already a published writer, having written under the pen name, "H. M. Hardimann"; she was also independent, ambitious, and politically savvy. Born in Tennessee, Lucy grew up in Marshall, Texas, and attended a girl's boarding school in Pennsylvania. When she married the prominent politician, Francis W. Pickens of South Carolina, it's a safe bet she married him for his social and political stature. In a letter he wrote to Lucy in 1857, he proposed with a promise to take her "through scenes abroad that will deeply interest you and make you one of the brightest of this earth." In Chapter Thirteen, Trent uses Pickens' words to bargain with Sarah in the carriage ride through White Point Gardens.

Lucy and Francis Pickens were married the next April and immediately after the wedding ceremony, they sailed for Russia, where Francis served as ambassador and Lucy quickly became a favorite of Tsar Alexander II. In 1859, she gave birth to her only child at the Imperial Palace. But when times grew troubled in South Carolina, Francis Pickens returned home. He was elected governor; and Lucy, in her best Paris gowns, her jewels, and Russian sables, became known as "Lady Lucy," and sometimes as "Madame Governor." Is it any wonder Carolina women were jealous? Mary Chestnut vacillated between scorn and admiration for

Lucy and wrote in her famous diary: "We flatter each other as far as that sort of thing can be done. She is young, lovely, clever, and old Pick's third wife."

Whether it was her wit, charm, or beauty, Lucy Holcombe Pickens was the governor's best political asset in those troubled political times, but even Lucy could not save her adopted state from the aftermath of secession.

Gift from the Queen

Readers of *Voices* may question Lucy Picken's gift of precious jewels to the Confederacy, but war fever was so inflamed that women all across the South were passionate about doing their part. Some sewed shirts and trousers. Others rolled bandages and knitted woolens. Mothers followed their sons to the war front to launder, cook, and nurse. And, yes, some women, like Sarah, became involved in espionage. Women's Aid Associations sprang up to raise funds for purchasing supplies and clothing. And in her inimitable way Lucy did her part by donating jewels she had accepted from suitors before and during her marriage.

Tsar Alexander II was so enamored with Lucy and her baby born in the palace that he gave one large diamond a month for the child. It is believed, however, that those diamonds were not contributed to the Cause. Those jewels Lucy saved and quietly sold to hold off creditors after her husband left office. Through the gradual sale of jewelry and valuables, she saved her husband's plantation house called Edgewood. The house has been moved to the campus of the University of South Carolina at Aiken and placed on the National Registry of Historic Places.

In Chapter One Sarah secretly delivers Lucy's jewels to the Holcombe Legion. However, in real life Lucy made her donation with great fanfare, appearing before the Holcombe Legion in Adams Run with bands playing, flags waving and she mounted sidesaddle watching the Holcombe Legion pass in review.

Francis W. Pickens (1807-1869)

Francis W. Pickens never received a pardon for his part in the Civil War. It is ironic that he died a man without a country since he came from a family that had been steeped in patriotism and politics since the Revolutionary War. His grandfather was General Andrew Pickens who led the partisans against the British at the Battle of Cowpens, a battle that marked the beginning of the end for Tarlton and his Redcoats. General Pickens was eventually elected to the U.S. Congress and named Commissioner of Indian Affairs. The general's son, Andrew, (Francis' father), served in the state legislature and was the first man from upstate South Carolina to be elected governor.

Francis Pickens grew up in a family that expected its children to succeed and bring honor to the family. He recognized his duty and, after completing his education at South Carolina College, answered the call to public service. But the Pickens' dynasty ended with Francis. His fire-eater brand of oratory and his unwillingness to recognize slavery for what it was, the antithesis of everything basic to human rights, led him down the path to his own political destruction.

After the end of the Civil War, Pickens took the oath of allegiance to the United States but never received the pardon required of those of high rank in the Confederacy. As the War Governor, he was despised by the Rabid Republicans in Washington and considered a traitor. Andrew Johnson could not afford an issue within the party and argued, "the traitor has ceased to be a citizen and treason must be made odious and traitors must be punished and impoverished."

Rev. Alexander Bettis (1836-1895)

Born the son of slaves, Alexander Bettis was so convinced that religion and education was his people's hope for the future, that he founded forty Baptist churches and organized a school that was the only one accessible in the Edgefield area during Reconstruction. The curriculum fostered literacy, mechanical and agricultural arts, and home economics.

Like his fellow South Carolinian, Septima Clarke of the Twentieth Century, he concentrated on citizenship and relating education to the problems people face in everyday life. Unlike Clarke, however, he was not an activist. He stayed out of the politics of Reconstruction and sought to avoid confrontation with the white population in an era filled with explosive divisions and violence.

Through three administrations, the school maintained Rev. Bettis' philosophy of accommodation and when the struggle for civil rights was at its height, Bettis Academy, the school that bore its founder's name, found itself out of step with the times. It closed in 1954. Today, the site is an African-American Heritage Museum and Cultural Center and listed on the National Register of Historical Places.

Laura Towne (1825-1901)

Other Northern teachers came to St. Helena Island but soon gave up and left because of the hardships. Emily Bliss and Mary Ames came to Edisto Island after the war but stayed only eighteen months.

Like Sarah, Laura Towne came soon after the fall of Port Royal. She stayed throughout the war then through epidemics, crop failure, and the sale of the plantations for unpaid taxes. And when the Pennsylvania Freedmen's Association shipped a school building in sections, she saw that it was assembled opposite the Brick Baptist Church, which had been the school. Laura Towne christened the new school the "Penn School" for its benefactors and stayed on St. Helena forty years, teaching the children she came to love.

With her friend Ellen Murray, she bought a small house on the Sea Island and adopted several African-American children.

The Penn Center was founded in 1962 to work on community-based projects, such as farmers' co-operatives, better housing, and health care. Dr. Martin Luther King held annual meetings there; and in 1974 it was named a National Historical Landmark. It continues as a conference center and is being studied for possible inclusion in the National Park Service.

Soldier of the Cross

Col. P.F. Stevens was wounded at the Battle of Sharpsburg while commanding the Holcombe Legion in Virginia. After the Civil War he joined the ministry and served at Black Oak Church in St. John's Parish, an area now under water, flooded to form Santee Cooper Lakes, a 1930's electrification project.

At Black Oak, Rev. Stevens worked tirelessly with a large Negro population. He became professor of mathematics at Claflin College, the first college for black students in the state, and he was named a bishop in the Reformed Episcopal Church.

Edisto Island

Vacationers did not start coming to Edisto Island until the 1810's when William Edings built a summerhouse on the north end of the beach. He called it Edingsville. Sarah knows it as Edings Bay. Today, Edingsville is inaccessible to the public, blocked off by an upscale-gated community.

Most present-day vacationers know only an area called Edisto Beach, but the island is nine miles long and nine miles wide and is still home to family descendants: Caucasians who live in antebellum plantation houses and African-Americans who live on the same land their ancestors claimed after emancipation.

Residents still drive down country lanes canopied by live oak trees and surrounded by vistas of marshes, water and open horizons. They still cast nets into saltwater marshes and tidal creeks for an evening's meal of crab and shrimp. Unlike resorts like Kiawah and Seabrook, Edisto seems content to keep its low-key ways.

Plough Mud

Plough mud, sometimes spelled "pluff," is marsh sediment, a mixture of decomposed plant life and dead marsh animals that lines the bottom of creeks, feels gooey, and oozes between the toes. The dark sediment smells like rotten eggs to some visitors but like heaven to most locals.

Home Remedies and Root Doctors

Lowcountry women~black and white~relied on home remedies during the nineteenth century. With plantation houses built in mosquito-infested areas and slave cabins only slightly above the water level, illnesses and emergencies led to quick thinking and a thorough knowledge of plants. Home remedies, however, are not to be confused with the practices of a "root doctor," who used artificial powders, charms, broken glass and sticks to put on and take off a hex.

Sarah calls Mad Rhoda a "root doctor," but Rhoda was more; she was also well-versed in home remedies. Like others of her time, she knew how to mix tonics to relax the nerves; bring down high blood pressure; stimulate the appetite; cure breathing disorders, sore throats, and diarrhea; and abort unwanted babies.

Natural medicines, such as life everlasting (Gnaphalium uliginosum), a highly prized weed, may be found in the Charleston Market today. Attempts to produce cassina or yaupon (Aquifoliacia) commercially were made as late as the 1930's when a plantation known as Jouette Cassina Tea Plantation failed in Mount Pleasant.

RHODA'S RECEIPT FOR CASSINA TEA

Take 1 small handful of fresh leaves.
Boil for 5 to 8 minutes. The more bitter
the better. Take as a cold remedy.
In case of fever use to bathe patient.

Immigration to Brazil

Readers may find it hard to believe, as Sarah did, that secessionists sailed for South America after the Civil War. But Tally Westcoat would have been among at least one thousand to immigrate from the Confederacy to Brazil between 1865 and 1869. Most came from South Carolina, Alabama, and Texas and settled in the Sao Paulo State, where today exists a town called Americana.

Descendents of these immigrants gather in Americana each summer for an annual party, complete with Southern fried chicken, corn bread, and square dancing. An organization called "Fraternidade Descendencia Americana" maintains an Immigration Museum that houses memorabilia from their Confederate ancestors.